1

Acknowledgements:

I would like to make mention of some important people who have made this book you are about to read possible. First and foremost Lulu.com for giving me the opportunity to share my work with the world. Thank you. Karen Sorenson and Lauren Simpson, thank you both. Your encouragement and guidance helped me get to where I needed to be in my writing and without it this book would not have been. My family and friends for your love and support. Your encouragement made me brave enough to take that giant leap and have faith in my ideas. Thank you Joseph Campbell for your life and work. Your studies have influenced me and helped me in so many aspects of my life that I can't even measure it. You continue to amaze me and I only wish I had some way to let you know how much you've helped me to follow my bliss. George Lucas. Your world has inspired me time and again and without it my introduction to mythology may have come at a much later age. Your vision has been the subject of my daydreams for years and will continue to fascinate me. Thank you to Michael Cerullo for his help in designing the cover art and his wonderful foreword. To Danielle Tortorici, Veronica Swain, and Sally Seng for their help in editing. To anyone I have left out I apologize. Hopefully someday I will be hearing about The Boon of Orsidire on television or in the newspaper. If all goes as I hope, then I'll be making a film version. Thanks goes out to all of you and I just want you all to know what you mean to me and how you've helped me to achieve a dream.

This book is dedicated to those who dare to dream big. This book is for you. Do not fear the adventure. Live it.

FOREWORD

In the fall of 1999, during the production of my first film, a dark sketch-comedy called Nation of Degeneration I met and began to work with someone who would eventually become a confidant, a close friend, and a respected colleague. When Nathan first came on board, he was an extra, just along to watch us make fools of ourselves... it wasn't long before he was making a fool of himself right beside us. With Nathan's desire to entertain and create it was only natural that he carved himself a place with us, and it wasn't until he became part of our group that we knew we were finally complete. No matter what the project was, it didn't feel like the family was there if Nathan wasn't part of it. What I knew then about him was that we were both huge Star Wars fans and had a passion for sick, twisted and random comedy.

What I didn't know was that we also shared a love of storytelling, and the wonder that is creation and imagination. It's amazing when we talk about our childhood's as if they were a place long ago and far away, a time when imagination was as vital to our existence as having air to breathe. Some people daydream to escape reality. We daydream to create our own. The greatest part about dreaming is fighting with every fiber of your soul to see those dreams become your reality; something Nathan and I have done and will continue to do.

The journey into your imagination does not begin with a step it begins with a thought. A question. An idea. The Boon of Orsidire begins in this same fashion, which proves the saying "you write about what you know". The journey it's author has taken to turn his dream into reality was as amazing as the story he is about to take you on. For me, it has been an honor to be part of this journey, and I anxiously wait to see what the future will hold. With creation and imagination, it's never about what is done. It's about what is next. The road ahead in life, and in this book will sometimes be long and hard, filled with heartache and tears, but in the end, when it's all said and done... damn if it doesn't make a great story to tell...

Enjoy this tale, it was written for you.

Michael Joseph Cerullo
-Story Teller

"The adventure of the hero represents the moment of his life when he achieved illumination- the nuclear moment when, while still alive, he found and opened the road to the light beyond the dark walls of our living death."

Joseph Campbell   -The Hero with a Thousand Faces

"It is only by considering the impossible, that you can get to it."

George Lucas

"The privilege of a lifetime is being who you are."

Joseph Campbell

The Boon

of

Orsidire

A Myth

Written by:

Nathan L. Andrews

PROLOGUE

"Who am I?" The voice rung out and echoed off of the walls of his mind, the words resonating in their wake. It called out the question again, and the young man stirred once more. He seemed to recognize the voice, although he knew that in waking life that very voice would have been foreign to his own ears. He tried to focus on the tone, but to no avail; the words faded out of hearing and in a moment the young man was awake.

"What is it?" Came another voice from across the room, although this one was familiar to him. The young man could make out the shadow of his brother in the moonlight that shone through their shared bedroom window. "You were dreaming."

"I know." Came the young man's answer. His mouth was dry and he reached out to clasp the cup of water that he had set on the stand next to his bed only hours before. The water ran down his throat and soothed his parched mouth. The faint hint of a breeze crept through the partially opened window, cooling the room with its gentle fingers.

"What were you dreaming about?" His brother asked, his brown eyes slightly reflective in the light of the moon.

"A voice in the darkness. I knew it somehow, although I wouldn't have known it in any other place than my dreams."

His brother nodded. His gaze searched the hardwood floor of their hut and then they settled back on the young man. "Very strange." Was all he managed to say.

The young man nodded back to him, feeling the light through the window on his face.

"We had better get some sleep." His brother said. "We have to make sure that we can follow Mother and Father without them noticing us."

The young man smiled, momentarily forgetting the voice that had spoken to him in the quiet of his mind. Perhaps the dream meant something. Perhaps it was just his subconscious dealing with unaddressed issues raised in his waking life. Either way, all he knew was that he and his brother had a mission in the early hours of the morning.

As he lay back down, he smiled knowing that he was about to see the one thing that would inspire him to travel the world.

He could feel the shift in the air as his brother settled back down in his bed, and before long he could hear his soft steady breathing. He turned his head slightly to face the semi-open window and peered curiously at the moon shining through the glass. He breathed deeply and sighed. The light seemed to fill him with wonder. He dreamt of seeing far off places and doing things that no one before him had done, grand things. Things that no one else could do. He could not recount how many nights he lay in bed, restless, his mind filled with dreams of promise and excitement. Something was missing. He could feel it in the deepest part of his being.

The life of a hunter's son was an honorable one, but not the life for him. He had always imagined that he could have done so much more. And that was why he needed to depart the next morning. He couldn't wait any longer. As far as he was concerned, he had waited long enough. He knew that if he didn't see this one thing that he would never leave, and the thought made him quiver with heartache. The young man closed his eyes and tried to envision himself at their destination, his heart leaping with excitement. In a matter of hours, he would lay his own two eyes on the dragon sword.

Something stirred in the quiet, and the young man awoke. He had fallen asleep again and he turned to see his brother was no longer in bed, but was sitting on the cold floor, silently lacing his boots.

"Wake up Aris." His brother whispered. "Get dressed, they're about to leave."

CHAPTER 1

"We better not get caught. They'd kill us if they knew we went," Kallevick said brushing some dirt off his dark brown pants. "You really want to do this, be an explorer, don't you?" He adjusted his black tunic, unbuttoning the collar a bit to let in some of the breeze. He stood a few inches taller than his brother, and had a head of thick black hair that was closely cropped and stood up in short spikes. He ran his callused hands through it as they walked down the heavily trodden dirt path.

"More than anything in the world." Aris said, his face lighting up with excitement. His high cheekbones seemed to stretch even higher as he smiled. He brushed away his long brown hair to get it out of his eyes. "No one really knows all that much about what's out there in the world, and I want to be the one to come back and tell everyone what it's like."

"Yeah, I suppose coming here would be the perfect place to start."

"Finish telling your story. You where about to name the elemental gods."

"Oh yes, the elemental gods. There was Altos of Water, Talos of Fire, Norg of Wind, Cedris of Earth, and the fifth, Mistal, the goddess of Spirit. The sword was forged in a sacred place, here in the realm of men, a sword that could stop the evil god Dinemid. But before it was completed, Dinemid attacked and the god Cedris didn't have a chance to put his blessing into the sword to make it whole. In desperation the gods then captured Dinemid, and bound him to a rock with magic chains, until they could find Cedris who had disappeared. But no one has been able to find the dragon, and the sword sits in the square of Nari Island waiting, for it is said in prophecy that the sword cannot be blessed without Cedris being found."

"See, I told you that you tell it better than I do," Aris said. "You'll make a great bard someday Kalle."

Kallevick's thin beard shifted as he smiled. "We're almost there," he said, looking up. Aris followed Kallevick's gaze and he began to quicken his pace as they approached a clearing. He started moving forward faster, and he found himself half-jogging towards the open space ahead. His legs couldn't seem to catch up to his eyes and he couldn't stand the excitement. They were really here. Exactly where the gods once walked.

The Nari Island annual trade bazaar was bustling with people. Aris looked into the cloudless blue sky, shading his eyes. Gauging from the position of the sun, it was late afternoon, he thought. The air was warm, and the sun felt even warmer on his back. Voices were bouncing up and down the edges of the square and as Aris squinted he peered through the expanse between himself and the crowd. Adults were slowly browsing the booths and children ran excitedly around, weaving through peoples' legs as the booth holders shouted their vocal advertisements to the open air. Various cart-pushing vendors mulled through the crowds, shouting offers for cool drinks and numerous types of food.

Aris stood on the edge of the square, staring in amazement at the commotion while Kallevick caught up to him from a short distance down the path. Kallevick stood next to him and looked at his younger brother with a slight grin on his face, a sly light glinting in his brown eyes.

"Well, is it what you expected?" the young man asked.

"More," answered Aris, still staring fixedly on the crowd before them. "Let's see more."

Kallevick turned his gaze from his brother back to the crowd in front of them. "Keep an open eye for Mother and Father's booth."

"I know," Aris said, his stare finally peeling away from the scene before him. His intense blue-gray eyes were alight with curiosity, and a smile crossed his face.

Kallevick nodded, and the two young men began to move into the square along the western edge, peering at some of the booths as they walked by. Some were filled with exotic overripe fruits ready to burst with natural juice, while others were overstuffed with handmade toys. A group of excited children swarmed up behind them to gawk at the colorful trinkets when the two brothers passed. They kept a modest pace, despite Aris' desire to move along quicker, as they carefully mixed into the crowd as best they could. His heart thumped eagerly in his chest and Aris wanted to keep moving, knowing that something in the nearby booths was likely to catch his interest. The smell of roasted meats and firewood greeted them as the walked, and a crowd of colorfully dressed performers passed in front of them, some juggling, others on stilts. The sky was a blaze of colors with the banners of each booth holder flying high.

He was so busy looking at the blues, bold reds, and bright greens of the banners that the elbow of Aris' olive colored tunic brushed a man walking by with a pitcher of water. The water sloshed up and over the side of the clay pitcher and wet the left shoulder of Aris' tunic.

"Hey! Watch it kid!" the man said in a raspy, unfriendly voice.

"Sorry," Aris said with a slight grin.

The man passed by with nothing more in response than a slight shake of his hatted head.

"Are you trying to get us caught? Watch where you're walking will you?" Kallevick asked as they continued on through the booths. Kallevick looked down at his tunic momentarily wondering if their clothes would stand out too much in contrast to the other people mulling about. He looked at two pretty girls a few years younger than him who were admiring some finely woven garments hanging on a wooden rack at a booth some thirty feet from them.

"Sorry. I didn't see him." answered Aris, eyeing a table a few rows down from where they stood.

"Just watch your step. I know that you've never been here before, but try to keep your wits about you, all right?" Kallevick said sternly, not turning away from the girls.

"Sure," the younger man said facing him. "I just want to take a look at those knives at that table over there. Mine's too dull. It barely holds an edge anymore."

Kallevick faced his brother, his quarry suddenly forgotten. "You aren't actually going to buy one of them, are you?" Kallevick asked, his face pulled back in disbelief.

"Yeah, why not? What are you so worried about?" Aris responded without turning to face his brother, his pace quickening.

"And just how do you think that you are going to explain that one to Father when he sees it on our next hunt?" Kallevick asked.

"I'll just tell him I traded with Tenen when I saw him last," Aris said, confident that his ruse would fool anyone. "And that *is* if he sees it in the first place."

17

"Tenen couldn't afford something this nice. You know that," Kallevick said as they reached the table. "Come to think of it, how can you afford it?"

"I've been saving some money and doing some trading on my own," Aris replied smiling as he picked up a long wide hunting knife. It was thick on one edge and sharpened with steely precision on the other. The blade reflected a perfect mirror image of Aris' face on both sides as he turned it over in his hand. "Nice finish," he said as he went to touch it.

"Don't mar up the blade," the booth holder said his eyes widening. "Everyone knows that you can hold Darigo's knives but you ain't allowed to touch the finish. It's not good business selling steel with fingerprints all over it. The polished blade is his trademark, you see. Strong tempered steel too, won't dull for quite some time."

The man eyed the boys curiously through bushy brows, and Kallevick cleared his throat, trying to act natural.

"You two aren't from around here are you?" the vendor said, sizing them up.

Kallevick knocked Aris in the shoulder, and he looked nervously around. Aris elbowed him back.

"Sorry," Aris said lowering his hand. "How much do you want for it?"

"Uh, that one is, let me see that," the scruffy man said reaching for it. He regarded the two for another moment as he took the knife from Aris, who held out the tool to him handle first. The vendor then turned and took it to another larger man near the back of the tent that made up that section of the booth and started talking quietly to him. Neither Kallevick, nor Aris could make out what was being said, but they assumed that they were haggling over the price. Kallevick looked at his brother and knocked him in the shoulder again.

"Ow!" Aris said, looking back at him. "What was that for?"

"For bringing too much attention to ourselves. I said that it would be all right to look but we should keep moving." Kallevick began pulling Aris' arm, but Aris kept his stance as best he could.

"Stop it." Aris hissed.

"Let's go." Kallevick said through gritted teeth.

18

"If you keep doing that then he might suspect something, and he might assume that we are trying to steal something while his back is turned. Then we *will* get caught by Mother and Father."

Kallevick dropped Aris' arm. "Just hurry up, will you?" He said, barely moving his mouth as he spoke.

Just then the smaller man waddled back over to the table scratching his brow.

"Darigo says he'll do fifty," he said cocking his head back over in the direction of the larger man. "Not a bad price. It's an older style, but still a good solid piece. You interested?" The man asked.

"Yeah, I'll take it." Aris said. The man began to wrap it up as Aris rummaged through his pouch for the right amount of coins. Aris paid the man, and stuffed the package inside his boot for safekeeping before moving on.

Kallevick's mind couldn't seem to shake sense that the vendor was watching them as they walked on into the throng of people. It didn't help when he looked over his shoulder to see the salesman peering through the crowd at them. He shifted bluntly, and nudged Aris further. The two young men kept circling the western edge of booths when all of a sudden Aris stopped dead in his tracks. "There it is."

"What?" said Kallevick looking around for any sign of their parents. "You see them anywhere?"

"No," Aris said lightly jabbing Kallevick. "That," he said pointing to a spot in the square where the crowd had cleared. Aris stood, staring.

Kallevick turned, his expression shifting with his stance. Next to a round stone well stood a short pedestal about three feet tall. Floating a foot up above it in a bluish white haze was a sword. Its' blade was long and it was polished to a brilliant shine. The most curious thing about it was the round pommel. Engraved deeply into it was a wheel pattern; it was a perfect circle with five arms spiraling clock-wise out of it at even intervals, one short pronged hook at the end of each arm.

Aris walked over to it, never peeling his eyes away. He looked hard at the sword and watched as the blue haze that surrounded it shifted in the air and vanished. He looked around to see if anyone else had seen this change, but no one took any notice. Kallevick seemed to be looking around nervously and Aris thought it best not to disturb him. *This might also buy me some time to examine this sword,* Aris thought.

Kallevick walked a few paces away, trying to peer through the dense crowd.

Aris reached out to touch the sword, but before he could he saw that the wheel design on the pommel began to glow with a white light. Aris pulled his hand back instinctively, and as he did he heard a voice.

"I am Orsidire, the keeper of the Wheel of Midgail, the key to the realm of the immortal gods of Galebraith."

Aris halted his approach, and he blinked, shaking his head.

"Through me you will restore the gods' immortality." The voice said again.

"Wha..." Aris stammered, and turned to look around to see no one paying him or the sword any attention. He turned back to look, and the sword appeared to glow.

"You Aris, can save the gods."

"How?" Aris asked, his amazement turning to puzzlement. "Dinemid was bound and left for dead. How can he destroy the gods? They're immortal."

"Mankind is an extension of the gods. If mankind stops believing that the gods exist, then they will lose their immortality. It has already begun. The hearts of men doubt already, bringing about the world's decay. If the gods die, then the universe will be no more."

"Well if man knows this then why don't they believe? Are you saying we are equal to the gods?" Aris asked, surprised at his own bold thought.

"A man is a man, and a god is a god. The gods are the only ones who can maintain the universe, but you Aris, are the only one who knows that man has the power to give immortality. The gods and man cannot live without each other. Just as Dinemid was cast out of Galebraith, so he seeks to be freed and finish what he failed to do. Dinemid broke the harmony of the cosmos and with that same power he means to destroy us."

"But how do I restore the gods immortality? Where can I find Cedris? How do I destroy a god?" Aris' head reeled with hundreds of questions, so many that his thoughts overran one another, smashing into nonsense. The sword's glow began to fade, and as it did, it spoke again to the young man. The voice slowed and warbled, trembling as it began to trail off.

"Do not fail, for if you do, a dark age will swallow us all, and we will be no more."

Aris' head buzzed and he closed his eyes for a moment to clear his mind. His eyes shot back open and he focused on Orsidire, and saw that it sat on its pedestal, floating, unmoving as it had been when they arrived at the fair. The shimmering white glow had faded and dissolved.

Realizing that they were vulnerable to discovery, Kallevick scanned the crowd. In an open spot he caught sight of a blue robed man. The man was old, as if time had worn his features into a cracked desert of deep brown skin. He had long hair that was mostly gray with streaks of white. The man looked up from where he stood and stared directly at Kallevick. Something about the man's stare seemed to pierce through him as if he saw something that the boys didn't. Kallevick felt uneasy and broke his own gaze and pushed Aris.

"C'mon. We've got to keep moving," he said pulling his dazed brother away from the sword. They began to walk quickly.

Aris stumbled and his awareness flooded back to him. "What's going on? Did you spot Mother or Father?" He said.

"No, there was this man, wait…" Kallevick cut himself off as they rushed past an ale vendor.

"You are so paranoid Kalle. No one's following. Oh." Aris was cut short. A flash of movement caught his eye over Kallevick's shoulder, and he spotted the blue robed man walking towards them. "Oh boy." Aris snapped. "C'mon."

The boys started walking away quickly and as they did Kallevick motioned to Aris.

"Look, over there," Kallevick said pointing off away into the distance behind the man to a booth covered in the familiar furs and yellow leather banners of their parents. "Well Mother is watching the booth, maybe Father just went for something to eat."

"Yeah, I don't think they saw us, but I can't be sure," Aris said.

Kallevick shook his head. "I wasn't the one standing in the middle of the crowd staring at that thing."

"You didn't see that?! That was unbelievable! You didn't see the blue mist disappear? Or hear it talk?" he said looking back over his shoulder at the weapon.

"No, I didn't see anything. I just see a sword floating in the air, no mist, no voices, no nothing." Kallevick hissed at him.

Aris turned to respond to his brother and seeing the old man was catching up to them, they quickened their pace. The old man was almost running and the boys zigzagged around a crowd of people to lose him before ducking behind some barrels. The man walked past them, looking down the path the boys came down to enter into the Fair. He scanned the area for a moment before turning back to examine the rest of the crowd.

"Whew, that was close. You know that everyone that lives here must have seen that sword a thousand times so it wouldn't be a big deal to them." Kallevick said easing his way around the barrels. He headed for a quick exit while Aris followed.

"Yeah but, hey where are you going? Aren't we staying?"

"No. I don't think it's safe to push our luck any further. It may have only been a quick glance but you got to see the Fair."

"All right Kalle." Aris said, turning back one last time to see the sword as they walked to the edge of the Bazaar. "Orsidire. Father never mentioned the sword's name when he told us the stories of the gods, did he?" he murmured.

"No, now come on!" Kallevick said turning to grab Aris by the forearm. "It was bad enough that we were almost caught, and if we are, I sure don't want to deal with Father's wrath. And that old man didn't look too friendly either."

"Yeah," Aris said half-aware of his brother's urgent tug on his arm. Aris looked away and turned around to follow Kallevick toward the woods and the Great Bridge linking Nari Island to the mainland.

CHAPTER 2

*T*he well-worn hut of the Desarta family was warm, Tenen thought to himself as he rubbed his hands together. A welcoming fire blazed in the hearth, but the young man knew it was more than the fire that had him at ease. The humble dwelling radiated a time worn comfort that was due in part to the fact that Aris and Kallevick's father had built it with his own hands.

The sun had set and Aris, Kallevick and their old friend Tenen sat in the small parlor that was their dining area. A hand crafted, light colored wooden table sat neatly on four simple rounded legs that were marked with dents and scuff marks from age old encounters with two rough housing youths. The walk from the Island to the mainland had taken up most of their afternoon, and Aris was glad to be home, even though his mind was still fixed on the sights and sounds of the Fair.

"That was quite a risk you two took, going to the Trade Bazaar like that," Tenen said, shoveling a spoonful of stew into his mouth. "I wish I could've gone with you. I've never been before." he said, swirling the hot food around in his mouth long enough to chew it. His hair was a brash red, and his pale skin reflected a bit of light from the hearth.

Tenen could blend easily into a crowd and his smile could charm anyone, and that would have been a great asset to them earlier today, Kallevick thought to himself. He guessed that had Tenen accompanied them that the vendor at Darigo's booth probably would have paid them little attention, even when Aris bought that knife. Perhaps they should have invited him to come with them that morning.

"Well, I've told Aris about the place for so long now, I had to show him what it was all about." Kallevick's arms were crossed along the edge of the table and his own bowl sat empty in front of him.

"Yeah, but Kalle wasn't all too generous with time when we where there." Aris said chuckling.

"Well," Kallevick said defensively, "I would have been interested to see the sword too, but we were in a hurry." Kallevick's expression shifted to one of unease. "That old man was starting to follow us too, and I didn't like the way he looked. It's like he was staring right through us." He grimaced sourly and adjusted in his seat.

"Wait, you were chased?" Tenen said. "You should have had me come along. I don't stand out as much as you two."

"What's that supposed to mean?" Aris said, his lip curled up in mock confusion.

"It means that no one would have bothered you two if *I* walked into the Fair. I mean, would you be looking at anything else if you saw this face walk into a crowd?" Tenen said, smiling wide and exposing a chipped tooth.

"I guess not." Aris said laughing. "Kalle was so nervous."

"Well Aris had a conversation with the dragon sword," Kallevick interrupted, attempting to bring the attention away from him. "What did you say it called itself Aris?" he asked, slightly grinning.

Aris became serious and his expression had Tenen worried for a moment.

"I swear to you, it spoke to me. It called itself Orsidire, the keeper of the Wheel of Midgail." Aris said, his mouth curled down in frustration. He leaned his chair back a bit, and as it rested momentarily on the stone wall behind him, another voice burst out from around the corner before Tenen had a chance to respond.

"Well I could have told you if he was telling the truth Tenen, but Aris wouldn't let me go with him and Kalle!" A young woman's voice said.

"Mafre, you aren't even allowed to go on hunts, what makes you think that we would be able to have you tag along with us?" Aris said, his voice changing from frustration to annoyance. His chair tipped down, the front two legs hitting the smooth wooden floor with a clunk.

The slim figured young woman came around the corner, her hands covered in soap, holding a dish and rag. A look of shock crossed her round face, and her brown and copper eyes flashed Aris a mean look. An apron was about her narrow waist, with small spots of bubbling soap popping as she stepped forward. She looked hard at her brother.

"I could have gone with you and Kalle, I'm not that much of a burden, am I?" she said, her shoulder length hair beginning to fall out of a loose braid.

"You would have gotten lost in the crowd, staring at dresses," Aris said coldly. Tenen, who sat with his back to Mafre, cringed as he looked at Aris. "And you probably wouldn't shut up either." Aris managed to mumble under his breath.

Kallevick shot Aris a mean glance. "Oh and you didn't keep us held up when you bought that knife at all?" Kallevick said, his voice razor sharp with sarcasm. A look of annoyance crossed his face.

"Dresses, huh? You just think I'm some little girl, don't you?" Mafre said, throwing a towel at him.

Aris didn't answer.

"Well, I'm not a little girl." she said, instantly tipping Tenen's chair back and kissing him.

Kallevick and Aris' chairs screeched back in shock at the suddenness of it all, and when Mafre let go of Tenen, she looked at Aris snidely, obviously proud of herself. Tenen's shock was even more exaggerated, and as Mafre released his chair it hit the floor hard along with the baffled young man. Without even looking at his fallen friend, Aris stood.

"You weren't even a part of this conversation when it started, so why don't you finish washing those dishes like you were before and mind your own business!" Aris said.

"Fine!" Mafre yelled back. "I'll just have to tell Mother and Father where you both went when they get home." She started to round the corner where the large wash basin sat, holding a few dirty utensils.

"Oh no you won't," Kallevick interrupted, standing up to help Tenen to his feet. "Mafre, just ignore Aris and go to your room."

"But Kalle, he started it! He thinks I'm some kind of kid!" She whined, stepping from around the corner and bumping the wash basin as she passed.

"You could have fooled me because right now you're acting just like one. Now go to your room before Mother and Father get here." Kallevick said, his voice kind, but stern.

Mafre moved to argue with her older brother, but thought better of it and turned back to Aris who stood there silently smoldering as she stuck out her tongue. She threw the apron at him and when Aris moved to get around the table, Tenen, who had witnessed the whole thing from the floor, moved in his way. Mafre, seemingly satisfied, turned and went into her room, appropriately slamming the door as she went.

"I would swear that you were her age sometimes Aris!" Kallevick said, turning to face him. Kallevick walked over to Tenen to help him up, and then sat back down at the table.

"She was just being obnoxious…"Aris began. He picked up the apron and hung it on the hook next to the wash basin.

"And you weren't?"

Aris didn't respond.

"Now, if we are all done arguing, can we please sit and talk like civil people? Besides, Tenen here may never come back after all of this." Kallevick said, smiling to ease the tension.

After a long pause, Tenen finally spoke. "So, was the Fair as exciting as this?" Tenen asked, as he scratched the back of his head and sat back down at the table. There was no immediate response, but slowly Aris smiled, and Kallevick was glad to see his anger waning. "What was that all about anyway?" Tenen asked, an embarrassed grin on his freckled face.

"She's been in love with you for years," Aris said, his smile softening even further. "I could just kill her sometimes." He sat down.

"Tell me more about the Fair." Tenen said, eager to change the subject.

"It was nothing like I've ever seen before. There were people every where, and the booths were over flowing with things to buy. They had all these brightly colored banners flying high in the air." Aris said, his eyes alight with excitement.

"They had tables set up all over the place too, and look at this." He said, excitedly pulling out the knife he bought. "I found this at one of the tables."

"Kalle mentioned that before, and I was going to ask you if…" Tenen's voice trailed off. "Wow, that's a Darigo blade, let me see." He said reaching his hand out.

"It sounds like you've seen one before," he said, passing the knife over to Tenen.

"Yeah, my Father has one. He uses it all the time, and he must have had the thing for years and I've never seen him sharpen it. You're pretty lucky, it must've cost a fortune." He turned the blade over in his hand.

"I've been saving for a while now, doing a little trading on my own." Aris said.

"That explains the extra hours you've been spending when we go on a hunt with Father." Kallevick said as he leaned into the back of his wooden chair.

"Extra hours? That's Aris alright. When he wants something he goes for it," Tenen said, handing the blade back over to Aris. "That thing will never dull you know, sharper than a dragon's tongue."

"Yeah, I've been going to some other places in the woods that we don't usually head to," Aris said looking back at Tenen. "I found some deer that had been grazing there every so often," he added sheathing the knife in his boot. "I must have chased them for a mile or so off our usual path before I could get a clear shot of them with my bow."

"So much for being an adept hunter." Kallevick laughed.

Tenen chuckled to himself, eating the last of his stew and shoving his empty bowl away from him.

"I didn't mean chase, I just meant that they weren't where we usually look, that's all." Aris said, his voice lowering.

"Right," Tenen said laughing softly, his voice lightly hinting sarcasm. "You said something about the sword telling you its name?"

"We're home." A voice said from the doorway as it opened.

"Orsidire." Aris whispered to himself.

Martaban stood on the doorstep and wiped her feet with Cabral only a step behind her. They entered the room, and Cabral shut the door behind him.

"Oh, hello Tenen. How are you?" Martaban said, moving to give the young man a hug. Tenen complied, and then took Cabral's hand and gave the man a firm handshake.

"I'm well. Our garden is almost overgrown with vegetables thanks to those seeds you sent my family. Thanks again." Tenen said.

"Hello firebrand!" Cabral said teasingly as he messed up Tenen's hair. "How are you? Always good to see you." He let go of Tenen's hand, letting the pack slung over his shoulder slide off and hit the floor. He gave it a nudge with his foot, and it lay still next to the half-closed door. He smiled warmly at his sons' friend.

"Good to see you too sir," Tenen replied while getting his hair out of his face. "I just stopped by to visit. Haven't seen Aris or Kalle for a while. Mafre is getting so big, how old is she now?"

Kallevick stifled a burst of sudden laughter. Cabral didn't seem to perceive the movement, but Kallevick still needed to cover his face momentarily to ensure that no one noticed. He looked at Aris, and his brother had a smile at the very corners of his mouth, though Aris did not seem to regard him.

"She'll be fourteen in a few months," Cabral said. He yawned and stretched his arms out wide.

"Yeah, it is getting dark out," Tenen said, looking past Martaban through the window, and turned to face his friends. Without a word, Tenen knew that he had best not overstay his welcome, and even though no one had asked him to go, he had the feeling that he shouldn't stay any longer, especially if Aris and Kallevick got reprimanded for going to the fair. He silently hoped that they had gotten away with it. "I have to get going. I'll see you both soon, all right?."

"Glad you stopped by Tenen, come back soon," Kallevick said as he wiped down the table and waved to the young man.

Aris walked over to his friend and shook his hand. "Take care. I'll stop by in a few days if I can."

Tenen nodded, his reddish orange hair shining slightly in the hearth's light. He walked around Cabral and Martaban to the door. Aris waved.

"Good luck." Tenen silently mouthed back, and closed the door behind him.

"Well, that was nice, I haven't seen him in quite a while," Martaban said, seating herself on a chair near the hearth. "Where's Mafre?"

"In her room." Kallevick said calmly.

"Kalle, is there any of that stew left?" Cabral said.

"Here." Kallevick said, handing a clean bowl over to his father's open hand.

"Thanks." He scooped a few large spoonfuls into it from the pot hanging over the fire and seated himself down at the table.

Aris sat in the other chair across from his mother.

"Did she finish the dishes like I asked her?" Martaban asked.

"Yes, she did," Kallevick said quietly. "Aris and I finished clearing out the mess from that small brush fire we had the other day too."

Martaban nodded her approval, and sat back with her eyes closed, rocking slightly in her chair. Her features were worn with age, but still held a strength and beauty that never seemed to fade.

Cabral held no expression, but sat quietly eating his dinner. Some time passed before he spoke again, and Aris felt it best to not disturb the silence.

"So," Cabral began, "Did you boys have a good day?" He said as he pushed his empty bowl off to the side, resting his right hand on the table. His left hand hung loose at his side.

"It was pretty uneventful." Kallevick said with ease.

Aris looked at his brother, trying not to let the fear inside him grow.

"What did you two do today?" Cabral asked.

"Not much really," Aris said looking at his mother who sat silent, her brown eyes staring at the fire. "Why?" He asked, not turning to look at his father. Suddenly he knew why Kallevick was so nervous that morning, and he wished that he could hide his own anxiety as well as his brother was.

"Oh, I don't know," Cabral said, adjusting his belt. "You two didn't happen to go anywhere today did you?" He shifted in his seat, opening the collar of his tunic to let some air in.

Aris could feel his father's eyes upon him. "No." Aris said staring at the floor, hoping that he could just bury himself then and there.

"I saw you Aris," Cabral said quietly, his voice sinking down to the level of the crackling fire. "I saw you both."

"What do you mean?" Kallevick said unmoving.

"I saw you boys at the Fair today," he said without turning. "Don't tell me otherwise either, and if I hadn't seen you there, I know a Darigo blade when I see one." he said pointing to the knife in Aris' boot. His gaze would not leave Aris and the young man began to reposition his seating.

Aris turned away, afraid to look at his father, and tucked the knife in deeper.

Kallevick stood behind Cabral, not sure if he should sit.

"I told you kids that you were not to go to the Fair. Your mother and I have business there, and you know how important our sales are this time of year. You both know better." Cabral said, his voice rising slightly. "I understand that it is where the dragon sword is. Believe me, the gods have sanctioned Nari, and I can understand your curiosity, but your mother and I have asked you to do something and we expect you to comply with our wishes."

"But why?" Aris asked, finally facing Cabral, knowing full well he was now unable to avoid this talk. "What's so wrong about going to see Nari?"

"Aris, you must understand that we are some of the few believers left out in the world, and your mother and I don't want you going out on some mission. You could be hurt, or even worse."

"I just want to be in the place where the gods once were. Besides there's more to this than I think you're telling me. I saw something there, something that you and Mother never told me about."

Cabral's brow furrowed.

"Father, the sword, it spoke to me! It told me that its name was Orsidire, the Keeper of the Wheel of Midgail."

Cabral's face went white.

"What, what's going on, what does that mean?"

Mafre exited her room. "I was going to tell you that Aris and Kalle went to Nari." she said, her face smothered with satisfaction.

"Shut up Mafre!" Aris bit back.

"Mafre, go to bed." Cabral shouted.

"But Father, I just…" Mafre began.

Cabral turned to face her and she stepped back, noiselessly complying.

"I just hadn't been before and you and Mother go there every year to trade, and I wanted to see what it was all about. I don't see what the big deal is. It's not like we were going to steal something." Aris said. "I don't understand. What's going on?"

Cabral gathered himself. "We took Kallevick once when he was young. I'm surprised that he even remembers the place. But that never happened again ever since…" Cabral's face visibly tightened, the color returning to his skin. His expression conveyed a momentary sense of vulnerability, as if he had revealed too much. "I have my reasons Aris, and you just have to obey me."

"Why?! It's just the Fair! Kalle and I weren't going to get into any trouble. You do realize that I am going to be an explorer some day, and I'm going to travel all over the world whether you like it or not. How can I even do that when I haven't even seen the island? How could I leave without seeing that?"

"I want you to forget what you saw, and go to bed. You, Kallevick and I have a long hunt ahead of us. I want you two to get some sleep, and tomorrow meet me at our camp in the woods, I have an errand to run before I meet you boys there."

"Forget what I saw? How can I forget? Father, please tell me, what's going on?" Aris said, his eyes pleading.

"You need to listen to me when I tell you to do something!" Cabral said. "I don't tell you these things for my own benefit, I'm looking out for you. Trust me. Now go to bed."

"I'm not a child anymore. I need to know what I saw! Why won't you tell me?" Aris shouted, as he leapt from his chair.

"I will not have my own son talk to me like that!" Cabral yelled in answer, also rising from his seat. The firelight shone red on his whitening beard.

Kallevick backed up a few steps, bumping into the washbasin, water spilling on his pants.

Martaban sat with a worried look on her face. She looked at Aris, her eyes pleading, but Aris' gaze would not turn from his father.

"Now I want an apology young man, one for disobeying me, and two for raising your voice to me!" Cabral shouted.

Aris did not answer.

"Well?" Cabral said, his voice still tense with anger. "Will you not do this?"

"No. I will not apologize. I want to know what's going on!" Aris yelled.

"Aris!" Martaban shouted. "You've already defied your father and I twice, don't you dare take that tone with us!"

Aris looked at his mother, who looked at him with stern but forgiving eyes. He then turned back to his father who stood with clenched fists.

"Will you not do this?" He repeated.

"No, I will not." Aris said.

Kallevick moved around Cabral and crept towards the hearth, hoping the fire was cooler than his father's anger.

"Aris, I… I can't tell you, but trust me when I say that I'm looking out for you." Cabral said his eyes smoldering with fear.

To Aris, the fire seemed dull compared to the look in those eyes. "Well they're my dreams and I'm going to fulfill them whether you like it or not. I don't care if you support me or not, I'm not your servant."

"Aris, please," Cabral shouted in desperation. There were tears beginning to well up in his blue eyes.

"Whatever it is Father, I know I can handle it." Aris said.

"That's what you don't understand son. You can't handle this, not yet."

Kallevick stood silently off to the side trying to decide what to do next. His back was pressed against the wall next to the hearth.

"This has nothing to do with going to the fair does it? Something is happening, something you're not saying, and I mean to find out what it is."

With that said, Aris turned away and stormed towards the bedroom he shared with his brother. Then Kallevick followed and shut the door behind him, thinking that it would be best if he could calm him down.

As the door clicked shut Cabral sat back into the seat at the table, his head falling into his hands, tears running down his cheek.

"Cabral," Martaban said in a soft voice. "I know how you feel right now, but you are right, he disobeyed us, and he needs to understand that." She put her hand on his shoulder and began to rub it gently.

His hand met hers and patted it. He turned to look up at her, the tears from his eyes glowing red in the dying firelight.

Martaban shook her head knowingly.

"It's too dark to leave tonight," Cabral said softly. "I need to see Ellchant in the morning."

CHAPTER 3

Cabral sat uneasy in his saddle, and his loyal horse, Jandrilla seemed to pick up on his tension. The horse whinnied, shaking his head slightly. "It's alright Jan." He said, patting the horse's neck. They passed under a low tree branch, and were at a quick pace towards Nari Island, while Cabral replayed that morning's events over and over again in his mind. Aris and Kallevick had already been awake when he had risen. Kallevick was eating breakfast and Aris was sitting in the same chair he was the night before, looking out of the round window at the small vegetable garden they had outside. Mafre and Martaban were outside tending to it.

"Are you boys ready?" He had said.

"Yeah." Kallevick said, rising from his seat, putting his bowl of grain into the washbasin. Aris said nothing.

"Now you two know where to meet me, at the third camp out towards the west, right?" Cabral looked outside and watched his wife for a moment. She was so beautiful to him, as if he hadn't seen her in many years. Yet there was some sort of sadness to her face as she worked. Perhaps he was exaggerating. The sun had not risen and the quiet blue of predawn was probably giving her that appearance.

"Yes. We'll see you there later. How long do you think you'll be?" Kallevick asked.

"Not too long." He broke his gaze from the window.

"Why are you going to Nari? And who is Ellchant?" Aris finally piped in quietly.

"How did you know I was going to Nari?"

"I heard you and Mother talking last night. Who is Ellchant?" Aris pressed.

"A customer. I have to deliver a leather piece I made for him."

"How come we've never met him?" Aris said, his face turning from the window and looking at his father.

"Aris, he's very old. I won't be long alright, just go with Kallevick and meet me where I told you to, ok?"

"Why won't you tell me what's going on? Does Kalle know?" Aris asked, looking at Kallevick.

"You got me." Kallevick said shrugging his shoulders.

"Aris, just go with your brother, please. I'm not trying to be mean, you just have to trust me. This is for your benefit."

"All I did was ask you some questions, and you won't tell me anything. It's not like I'm an idiot Father!" Aris said rising from his seat and standing stiffly in front of the hearth.

"I never said you were. Aris, I'm sorry I yelled at you last night, but you and Kallevick disobeyed your mother and I."

"Oh, and why haven't you yelled at Kallevick yet, if he is just as much at fault as I am? Why are you singling me out!" Aris' voice began to rise in anger and he stepped closer to his brother.

"Your brother came to me and apologized last night after you went to bed. Besides which, he got a lecture from me too."

"Well you aren't going to get an apology out of me."

"Fine, then just meet me at the camp ground, I will be back as soon as I can. I'm already running late. I don't have time to argue about this Aris. We'll finish this later."

"There's nothing to be said. All I want are some answers to some pretty simple questions."

"They are more complicated than you realize."

"Well, if you would open your mouth and tell me, I might actually believe that you care about what I'm asking you."

"I do, but like I said before, I have to go."

"Fine, go then, I never want to see you again."

The image of Aris' face was burned into Cabral's mind. It just wouldn't go away. The look in his eyes, the lack of emotion; it seemed to burn right through him. Aris had stood there, unmoving, and Cabral had turned and walked out of the hut. He walked over to Mafre and kissed her forehead. She looked up at him and a wide smile spread like sunshine across her face. She hugged him. He smiled, but the tears could not be held back. He then walked over to Martaban, and grabbed her by the waist and held her for a long moment, not wanting to let go. Once he did he looked her in the eyes, the same eyes that Kallevick and Mafre had, and he leaned in and kissed her. His lips melted with hers and she leaned into him, kissing back passionately.

He slowly let her go, their eyes locked once more, and she smiled. He smiled back and wiped a few stray tears that had gathered in the crow's feet on his face. He looked back into the open door of the hut, and Kallevick smiled and waved. He looked at Aris who had moved to the door to watch him leave. The look on his boy's face lingered, and there was a coldness there that Cabral had never witnessed before, and to say that it frightened him would be an understatement. His little boy said those words, had actually said that he never wanted to see him again, ever, and he couldn't shake the feeling that Aris meant them.

He looked around the village as he mounted his horse and set off at a brisk pace. By sunrise the hills and clearings that made up the village of Mulroy would be flooded with light and the villagers would be out and about, tending their fields or doing farm work. The village was the most beautiful in the morning, with the fields of wild flowers blooming, the friendly faces of other villagers, and the colors of the forest.

But the image of Aris' face, and his words sunk back into Cabral's mind, the collar of his tunic seemed to tighten, and he quickened Jandrilla's pace with two short squeezes of his legs to the horse's side.

*   *   *   *   *   *   *   *   *   *

When Cabral stopped his horse in front of Ellchant's small hut, he knew that the old man was around back. The scent of ripe firewood greeted him as he tied Jandrilla's reins to a nearby tree and rounded the back of the hut. Ellchant was tending the fire, sitting while quietly stirring a wooden spoon in a boiling pot. He looked up as Cabral approached.

"Hello old friend." Ellchant said, in a deep pronounced voice. The statement seemed ironic to Cabral, and despite the lingering thoughts in his mind, he had to smile slightly. In all the years that he knew Ellchant, he could only guess at his age, but he seemed, in a way, ageless. He had pale gray eyes, with deep-set lines running in spirals from the pupil out. His smile was warm, like the sun in the deep of winter.

"Hello Ellchant, how have you been?"

"Oh, well, the same story as always. Just enjoying the weather, and the wildlife. I saw you had a bigger booth at the Fair this year, very impressive. Sorry I didn't have a chance to stop and say hello. I was busy chasing your sons away." Ellchant chuckled lightly to himself, and looked back at his pot, continuing to stir. "Actually I wanted to talk to them."

Cabral's expression deepened drastically, and Ellchant seemed to want to ease some of the tension by offering a bowl to his friend. Cabral took it without looking, his weathered hands running along the sides of it, his mind in deep thought. Ellchant sat back down next to him, tucking his graying hair behind his ears. He crossed his legs, using his one free hand to tuck one leg under the other, being careful not to spill the contents of his bowl. His leather sandals were worn and the straps that held them on were wrapped around a thick off white material covering his shins to the knee.

Cabral sat motionless for a moment and then came to and spooned himself a bowl of the stew. He looked back at the old man.

"You're beginning to get white streaks in your hair." Cabral said, his face softening a bit.

"Yes, and I've let it grow too. I can tie it back now." the old man said setting his empty bowl down on the ground in front of him. "Enough about me, aside from the package I requested, what brings you here? What's troubling you?"

"You know, you have a way of reading me sometimes. I know we've known each other for a long time, but there are those times, when you just seem to know things."

"I knew that you were an adventurous spirit even the day I met you. When I pulled you out of that pit in the woods all those years ago, I had a feeling about you. You know your son Aris gives me that same feeling. I've known you for quite some time now, and I haven't had that same feeling until you had Aris. That's what brings you, isn't it?"

"What, Aris? Yes actually it is. Ellchant, he saw the sword. He said it talked to him, told him its name. I... I hate to say it, but I'm afraid."

"For your village?"

"Yes that too, but my family. They are in danger. I have a bad feeling that won't leave me. Aris and I got into a big fight last night and right before I came here he told me he never wanted to see me again."

"Children, especially one's his age, can be like that sometimes. He was just mad, I'm sure he didn't mean it. He'll calm down with some time."

"But you should have seen the look in his eyes. They were so cold, and it..."

"I know." Ellchant said, putting his hand on Cabral's shoulder. His mouth turned downward, his voice became grave. "The prophecy, I fear, is coming true, that should he hear the sword speak, he will enter great peril. A dark power is rising in the west. You must go and gather your children, and Martaban. Take them far away, for I fear something wicked is coming."

"Ellchant. Will you do something for me?"

"Anything my friend."

"Promise me that you will watch over my kids. Especially Aris. Something is wrong, and if Martaban and I are taken from them, I need to know that they are in safe keeping."

"I promise. I will know if they need me, and I will come. Now go, take them as far away as you can."

"Here." Cabral said handing over a neatly wrapped package. Ellchant opened it to reveal a chest plate made of sheets of thin metal work, and thick leather.

"Thank you. I just hope I never have to use it."

"Me too," Cabral said heading back toward his horse. "Did I do the right thing, by not telling Aris what's happening?" he stopped walking and turned slightly. "I felt so guilty, all he wanted were some answers."

"Cabral, I told you that he would ask you questions, but you were not to answer. You did the right thing. Trust me. It will be revealed to him in time. The gods have a way of revealing the answers when they are necessary. Besides, Aris can't run off by himself. He needs guidance. Remember that is why you, Martaban, and I all agreed that we would not let him know of this until we could gather a plan of action."

Cabral turned and walked back over to his friend. "I can't escape this feeling, and I fear I may never see you again." He embraced Ellchant tightly. He jogged back to his horse, and climbed right into the saddle.

"The gods are with you, and I promise, your children are in good hands."
Ellchant waved as the man on horseback rode off at top speed.

*   *   *   *   *   *   *   *   *   *

Cabral rode as fast as he could through the dense forest, the thick green trees whipping past as he rode further toward the shoreline. The tree line faded out some as he got closer and the dirt began to get lighter in color as it receded into the water. Cabral looked out to see the water, which looked black and ominous at first glance. He blinked and looked again, as though his eyes had fooled him and it was a rich blue as it always had been.

When he reached the Great Bridge he passed swiftly by taking no notice of the onlookers heading onto the Island. The rumble and clacking of Jandrilla's hooves on the wooden planks of the bridge dissuaded anyone from getting in their way. The sun was at about noon. *Had that much time passed already?* He thought. He couldn't seem to ride fast enough, as though he was in a nightmare and his dark thoughts were robbing him of speed. He rode on and as he came to the village he heard screaming. He hoped to the gods that he was having a nightmare, and when he rounded the last bend of the trail, his heart sank into his boots. This was no nightmare. This was real.

CHAPTER 4

Aris kept pacing the campground with uneasy footsteps while Kallevick sat leaning against a tree stump. Nearby a small version of their hut back in the village stood, though the woodwork was cruder and it was in slight disrepair. Kallevick glanced at the structure momentarily and a passing memory of his father building the hunting home flashed through his mind. His gaze focused back in front of him at the unlit campfire. An open patch in the treetops aligned perfectly with the fire pit to allow the smoke to rise into the sky like a natural chimney.

"Will you relax Aris? What's with you?" Kallevick said, a bit of annoyance creeping into his voice. "You said some pretty mean things to him you know." The tree stump felt smooth under his back and he recounted many nights sitting in that very same spot talking with his father and Aris while the campfire roared. The other stumps that circled the pit were empty and Aris paced around them, his footsteps filled with a tense energy. Kallevick shook his head and ran his knife across the branch. He hadn't whittled a walking stick in ages, he thought.

"I know." Aris straightened, his pacing slowing for a moment. "Father just gets me so angry sometimes!" He said kicking a fallen tree branch.

"Yeah, he can be kind of stubborn like that," Kallevick said. "Kind of like you."

Aris looked up at his brother. "Thanks a lot."

Kallevick smiled, sliding the blade across the wood once more.

Just then, a thundering sound came from the east and the boys both looked over in the same direction.

"What the hell was that?" Aris said, the tone of his voice shifting from frustration to fear.

"It didn't sound so good, whatever it was." Kallevick said dropping the branch, his project all but forgotten.

They walked a little way from the camp and everything seemed as it should. The sky was slightly overcast with small specks of pale blue that fought their way through the clouds. The trees swayed in the wind and with the breeze came the faint scent of a fire. Aris walked a little further into the woods, crushing some heavy foliage under his dark red leather boots and peered deeper into the dense mass of trees.

"Kalle, do you see what I see?"

"I see something moving but it's too far away to tell what it is. I smell something burning, don't you?" Kallevick said sniffing the air.

"Yeah I smell it too."

At Aris' last words the approaching something came into clear view. A mass of deer, birds, squirrels, grazer beasts, and other wildlife were running towards them at top speed. The noise of the creatures was deafening, as a fusion of hooves and paws crashed through the thick undergrowth and tore from the soil, snapping roots and scraping rocks as they too were ripped out of the ground.

"They're headed right for us. They'll stampede us!" Kallevick shouted over the growing rumble. "Aris, come here!"

Aris ran over and placed his foot into Kallevick's laced hands, hoisting himself onto a high tree branch. Aris looked across the way and saw that the animals were now only twenty feet from where they stood. He looked back down and saw Kallevick staring at them.

"Kalle!" Aris yelled, his voice barely audible. He held his hand down to him. Kallevick grabbed on and climbed up the tree. They managed to scramble up a little higher just as the horde reached the base of the tree and ran past at an incredible rate. The boys watched as hundreds of animals rushed past them, paying them no heed, trampling over one another in a mad dash. The branches of the tree jarred causing ripe green leaves to fall off in giant clumps.

"What are they running from?" Kallevick shouted, shielding his eyes from falling pieces of bark.

"I don't know, I'm going to the top to see!" Aris shouted back. He began to scramble up the tree when a grazer beast hit the base and shook Aris free of the branch he clung to. He fell for a moment but grabbed another branch, stabilizing himself.

"Wait until they're gone!" Kallevick shouted up to him. He looked down, watching the stunned grazer shake its woolly head and stumble off with the rest of the pack. The boys waited another minute until the screaming horde of animals was gone.

Aris then scrambled up to the top of the tree, and as branches hit him in the face he climbed as fast as he could.

When he reached a sturdy branch he propped himself up and looked out over the deep green tree line. Off in the distance he spotted a line of thick black smoke and the unmistakable scent that accompanied it. He stared for a moment in shock and then began scrambling down the tree.

"I've never seen anything run so fast." Kallevick called up to Aris.

"Well, there's definitely a fire, and it's coming from the village." Aris called down to him. He rushed down the tree, nearly falling off as he reached his brother. "We've got to head home, something's wrong."

"Right." Kallevick said, his face getting stiff.

     *   *   *   *   *   *   *   *   *   *   *

The boys ran as fast as they could through the forest, their leather boots leaving deep footprints in the moss as they trampled through the undergrowth. Aris was in the lead when Kallevick fell behind, stopping to catch his breath.

"Aris," Kallevick managed to shout. "You've got to…slow down…I …I can't keep up." He gulped huge breaths of air like it was water and Aris backtracked over to him.

"Sorry," he said. "We've got to keep moving though." His voice was haggard, and it cracked as he spoke. They waited a few minutes to regain some energy, and then began again, only a bit slower this time. The trees rushed past them as they ran and they jumped over rocks and streams along the way. They didn't see or hear a single animal along the way, although they would have likely scared any off with the sound of their harsh breathing as they ran.

Most of the day had passed as the boys reached the edge of the village and it was only an hour or so before sunset. They had run most of the way, but towards the last few legs of the journey their lack of strength forced them to practically crawl, weary and fatigued through the last mile. They exited the forest and walked about the clearing, collapsing on the spot in exhaustion.

"We made it." Kallevick said in a hoarse voice.

"Yeah." Aris said, his own voice nothing more than a dry crackle. He lay on the ground facing the sky, breathing deeply. The two rested for a few minutes, no sound around them but their labored breathing. "Come on, let's see what's going on."

They got up and walked around the hut nearest them and headed for the village. As they passed the hut Kallevick noticed that the roof had caved in and that most of it was charred and blackened. He moved to point it out to Aris but when he looked ahead of him his brother was a far ways off. Kallevick started to run after him. Daylight was failing. He wondered if Aris had noticed the damage done to the hut. He looked over his shoulder, back towards the ruined home as he ran. Kallevick realized that he must have seen it because when he turned around to see where he was going, his brother was already out of sight. Aris was way ahead of him, and was running faster than the animals that almost stampeded them earlier that day.

CHAPTER 5

Aris pushed himself further into the village. His chest began to ache with exhaustion but he tried his best to ignore it. Something was wrong and he had a feeling that the ruined hut on the edge of the forest was the least of the damage. Something far worse awaited him and Kallevick at the center of Mulroy. He knew it. Every few feet Aris noticed more and more destruction. Huts were not only burned but some were completely demolished, as if a giant had taken an enormous hammer to them. Horses and cattle were scattered everywhere, innards ripped, stretched, and thrown onto the ground.

Kallevick, though he saw the damage as well, couldn't keep up with Aris and he did his best to ignore the pain in his own chest and legs. Aris was well ahead of him but Kallevick could not push himself any further. He dropped to his knees. The shadows began to creep in and set a gloomy dimness to the village.

"Hello!!!" He yelled. "Is anyone here?!!!!!" *Where is everyone? What happened?*

Aris heard Kallevick from behind him and began calling for someone, anyone to answer. Not a sound came back to greet him but his brother's own unanswered cries. His muscles were running on pure adrenaline now and he rounded another disintegrated hut before running headlong for his home, which lay before him.

"Kalle, hurry!!!"

Kallevick rose, feeling an instant surge of adrenaline upon hearing Aris' desperate call and kept yelling as he caught up with his brother. The two stopped in front of the remains of their hut. It was set ablaze and as the fire plumed like a great whip lashing its way across the night sky, the boys began yelling frantically.

"Mother! Father! Mafre! Where are you?" Aris shouted, his voice cracking.

"Mafre, Father!" Kallevick chimed in.

They ran around the neighboring huts looking around every corner for any sign of their family, any sign that anyone was in the village. There was no life here in the darkness, no sound but the cracking of fire and the shouts of the young men. Not a thing stirred. Save for the huts that blazed with an unnatural ferocity. The wind picked up and rustled through the trees, brushing Aris' long hair into his face. He ran further, heading for the well in the center of their village. Water buckets were shattered and the further he got into the heart of the area, he started seeing the bodies. By now the sun had set and was casting grisly pall on the faces of the dead. Their eyes were open wide in shock and horror.

Kallevick caught up with Aris and the two ran into the next cluster of clearings that made up the center of their village. They ran around a series of trees that divided one clearing from another and Aris ran ahead when Kallevick quickly grabbed his brother's arm to keep him back. Kallevick wasn't sure if he could believe his eyes.

"MOTHER!!!! MAFRE!!!! FATHER!!!!" Aris yelled, his voice screaming in agony, tears pouring from his eyes.

Kallevick tightened his grip on Aris' arm, looking at what lay before them, his own eyes flooded.

About thirty feet before them lay the entire village. Bodies piled up on top of one another in a gruesome sort of stack. A huge bon fire lay behind them, blazing yellow and orange in the dawn of the evening. Limbs were hanging in all directions and they almost looked as if they were toys unceremoniously dumped into a heap. In the center three poles were erected, each with the remains of Cabral, Martaban, and Mafre tied and stretched onto them. Kallevick tried to pull Aris away, but the younger man broke free and ran to the feet of his father, crying out. Kallevick could not believe what he saw, and the illusionary quality of it all kept feeding his head with dark thoughts. He must be having a nightmare, this couldn't be the truth, he thought.

The adrenaline that had carried him through the woods all that day finally failed him and Kallevick collapsed to the ground. His vision blurred and the last thing he remembered before the darkness took him, was the sight of his dead mother, her eyes opened wide in terror.

*   *   *   *   *   *   *   *   *   *

It must have been hours since he had passed out, but he still felt the soreness of his body as he opened his eyes. Kallevick looked around nervously, not remembering where he was at first, hoping that all he had seen was just a devilish dream. But he turned his head to the left and saw Aris next to him, his head clutched in his hands. Aris looked up at him, his eyes red and his face swollen with grief.

"Why? Why did we listen to him? Why didn't we stay in the village with them?" Aris said, his voice no more than a whisper.

Kallevick knew that the tone was more from shock at their discovery, than from all the running they did. "I know Aris." He sat up, reached his arms out and embraced his little brother and they sat there for a long moment holding each other. "You're not allowed to leave me brother, you got that?" He said, choking back the lump in his throat.

Aris said nothing but cried quietly into his brother's shoulder.

Kallevick let go of him and slowly got up on unsteady feet. "C'mon. We have to clean this up."

The two walked over to where the mass of people lay and reverently approached it. The fire had dimmed considerably and the noise it made was no more than a hush in the solitude. They lingered there for a moment, their raw eyes brushing across the faces in the pile. This was not a horde of ravaging pillagers, Aris thought, this was a sacrifice. Aris' eyes slid along the ground in shock, and then settled them on his father. He stepped forward and gently closed the deceased's eyes.

They closed the eyes of their mother and sister and took them all down as respectfully as possible. They scrounged around for a shovel and dug a series of holes and buried them, placing some nearby stones as markers at the heads of the graves. Kallevick began to sing and Aris slowly joined in. It was a song that Cabral had used to lull the animals out of hiding. It was an old song, a song passed on from one generation of hunters to the next, taught to them by Cabral, a song that his father taught him. But the boys knew that the chance of any animals being anywhere near this place was very slim.

> *When the bird and the beast come to the wood.*
> *When the sun hides behind the cloud*
> *Then man will come and take one down*
> *Where the bird and the beast once stood.*
>
> *For the gods are gracious enough to give*
> *The bird and the beast that lay down their life*

45

They give us warmth, and feed our wives
They die that we might live

Where the bird and the beast come to the wood
And now we pray that the gods may grant
The peace that once was, another chance
Where the bird and the beast once stood

"I can't believe this is happening," Aris said hoarsely.

The boys stood there sniffing and quietly crying, their hoarse voices breaking the silence of the night. After some time they began to bury the bodies of the remaining dead. When they finished they sat next to the graves of their family. Kallevick curled up into a ball and wiped fresh tears from the corners of his eyes and Aris joined him. It wasn't long before they were fast asleep.

    *   *   *   *   *   *   *   *   *   *

"Aris, Kallevick, wake up boys," a voice said softly.

The two wearily opened their eyes and looked in front of them to see that it was still very dark out. They looked all around and did not see where or from whom the voice came. The trees seemed to loom over them.

"Who's there?" Kallevick called out into the darkness.

"A friend." came the answer.

"Where are you?" Aris asked, rubbing his eyes.

"Right behind you." he responded.

They were startled and turned around. Standing in front of them was the blue robed man.

CHAPTER 6

"Who are you?" Aris asked, a slight curiosity creeping into his voice. Ellchant knelt down next to the boys and ran his fingers through his beard. He carried a pack and it slid down to his side as he knelt. He smiled slightly. "My name is Ellchant Pendergast. I don't presume you know of me. But I am a friend of your father's and knew your mother well."

"Why are you here?" Kallevick asked moving closer to Aris in a protective manner.

"Your father came to me when I saw him last and he asked me to watch over you two and your sister should something happen to him and your mother. I'm sorry that I couldn't get here sooner. I came by way of Nari Island. Boys I'm so sorry." Ellchant wiped his face before the tears fell. The deep lines under his eyes appeared to sink even further.

"How do we know you are who you claim to be? And why should we trust you?" Kallevick asked.

"Because your father delivered this to me this morning," Ellchant said as he turned and pulled the leather armor from his pack. "I was the reason your father was late to getting to you both this morning."

"How do we know that you didn't kill them? You sent him back to the village!" Aris said.

"Aris, I know you are upset right now, but I didn't do this. You know I couldn't have." Ellchant said calmly. He knew how the boy must feel and his tone hinted that he understood this. He inhaled slowly and released the breath knowing full well that now was the time for Aris' questions to be answered. "Rundagg raiders are responsible for this."

"Goblins?" Kallevick and Aris asked simultaneously.

"Yes. A band of them swept through the edges of the forest and crossed the Great Bridge trying to ransack Nari. They were pushed off the island before they could do any real damage, back over the bridge and from there they fled."

"But what are Rundagg doing over here? Why come all the way here in the east?" Kallevick asked.

"They were looking for something, or should I say someone." Ellchant said looking to Aris. "I think that they also had another motivation to come to Nari."

"Someone?" Kallevick asked, almost afraid to hear the answer. He felt the hair on his arms stand on end and he looked at his brother who sat silently. He noticed too that the thin peach fuzz side burns on Aris' face also began to rise.

"Aris, they were looking for you. They were sent to kill you. That is the reason your village was destroyed. Unless they use a prisoner for sacrifice, Rundagg never leave survivors."

"Then it is my fault." Aris' said as his face sunk down in shame.

"No Aris," Ellchant said gripping the young man's forearm, his spiral gray eyes searching deep into the boy's face. "This was not your fault. None of this was your doing. You were in the right place and you now live, be thankful for that."

"But if I was here, I could have...."

"Died. These raiders are not human and you wouldn't have lasted a single breath were you here. You would have been killed and the Goblins would have succeeded in their task. Aris, this is not your fault. I promise you."

"Something even worse has happened than this. The sword that was in the Nari Square is now gone, taken by the same band of Raiders. I would have gotten to it sooner, but after having to fight some of them off myself, I ran home to get some supplies and then to retrieve the sword, but when I got there it was gone."

"Wait, back up a moment, you said you were going to take the sword? And do what with it, besides how could you take it? No one can." Kallevick stared at the old man.

"The sword is encased in a blue haze that is invisible to the naked eye. It acts as a barrier against thieves. I was planning on taking it so it wouldn't fall into the wrong hands."

"Take it with you where?" Kallevick asked.

"Wait, you said a blue haze? When I saw the sword in the Square that day, it told me that its name was Orsidire, the keeper of the Wheel of Midgail, and then the blue haze that was surrounding it disappeared."

48

Ellchant's eyes went wide and his face seemed to physically process this information just as his mind turned the thoughts over in his head. "That's how the sword was stolen. The haze deteriorated when it spoke to you Aris. That's how the goblins were able to take it."

"Ellchant, you said that you were going to take the sword somewhere. Where were you going to take it?" Kallevick insisted.

"To find and destroy Dinemid."

"Dinemid!!!" Aris shouted. "Were you going to do this all by yourself? Are you crazy?"

"No, when you were old enough, I was to take you to find and destroy the evil god. Only you can do this Aris. But things have gone awry and I now come to you in a desperate hour. We must find the sword, for I fear that the goblins will try to bargain with Dinemid, and if he gets the sword, he will find a way into Galebraith and kill the gods."

"The sword told me that the immortality of the gods comes from the human race's faith in their existence alone. What does that mean?"

"The world no longer believes in the gods and should Dinemid destroy the Lords of Galebriath, then the universe will die. When I saw you boys at the Fair, I wasn't trying to chase you off, I was trying to bring you to your father, and have him join us so we could take the sword and start the journey. Mulroy being destroyed was a fulfillment of the prophecy. When the sword spoke to you Aris, Dinemid was awakened. His time for revenge has come. He must be stopped."

"Why wouldn't my father tell me any of this earlier, I kept asking him and he would never tell me."

"I told him to wait because your father and I planned to do this when you were older and stronger. Not to mention the fact that Cabral had always been worried that if he told you too soon that you might run off alone and unprepared. I instructed him to wait until he talked with me before he let you know about any of this. You weren't ready for this, but now things have escalated to the point where you will now have to be ready, because we have to get Orsidire back."

"But what of the dragon Cedris? Will we have to find him now too? Doesn't he have to complete the sword before it can destroy Dinemid?" Kallevick asked, his stories of the Lords of Galebraith becoming even more vivid in his mind. Didn't Aris realize what this meant? That he was among one of the prophecies that had been unknown to their whole family? Kallevick looked in surprise at his little brother.

Aris' attention was fixed on Ellchant, and Kallevick couldn't be sure that this was all registering with the young man.

Ellchant passed Kallevick a knowing glance. "Yes, but that is another matter entirely. Our main concern now is to get the sword back before Dinemid has a chance to acquire it from the Rundagg. Get some sleep now boys, tomorrow we leave."

CHAPTER 7

Aris woke to the sound of birds chirping and with his eyes closed he thought he might still be dreaming. He sat up, rubbed his face and yawned. He took a deep breath and scratching the back of his neck he opened his eyes. Nothing had changed and his awareness slowly came to him. *No this is not a dream. Mother, Father, and Mafre really are gone,* he thought. *Kalle and I are all alone. Or are we?* Suddenly Aris remembered the old man, the old man from his dream. *Was he a dream?*

He looked down at Kallevick who lay on the cold ground next to him sleeping. He had a dark brown cloak wrapped over him and Aris looked down at himself to find a pale green cloak laying over him. He shook Kallevick.

"Kalle, wake up."

"What?" He asked groggily. He rubbed his eyes, and sat up letting the cloak fall at his waist. "What is it?"

"The old man, is he here?"

"Who, Ellchant? Yeah I think so."

Aris looked around and saw that there was a fire that was placed near them, and the last embers of it were now dying down, leaving behind thin wisps of smoke.

"We better go find him." Aris said standing, letting the cloak fall off of him. He grabbed it and put it on, wrapping the fabric snug to his body. "Boy it's cold out here."

"Yeah it is." Kallevick responded and in turn put his cloak on.

They walked along the edges of the center clearing looking around for any sign of the old man and saw nothing. It looked as though Ellchant had been busy that night and most of the chaos that they had witnessed the night before had been cleared away. The boys began wondering if the old man had made them dream strange things. The sun was on the rise, casting away the dark shadows of the horrible night that lay behind them.

"Let's check the other clearings, he couldn't have gone off too far." Kallevick said moving to the eastern clearing.

"Right." Aris said heading in the opposite direction. He looked around and called out, but with no response. The birds seemed to be awake and ready for the day, but Aris was feeling the weight of the previous night. Although he wished to find the old man to ask him more questions, he was rather frightened to begin this journey. He always intended to become an explorer, but not under these circumstances. Not like this. He began calling louder for their remaining friend.

Then when his thoughts seemed to get the better of him, he heard Kallevick call out. His voice was shrill in the cold morning air and Aris bolted off in the direction of the call. *Don't you go anywhere on me Kalle!*

"Kalle!" Aris yelled as he neared the eastern clearing. He stopped to find Kallevick standing calmly in the morning light, staring at the sunrise. "You all right?"

"Oh I'm fine. I found Ellchant," he said without turning, "Look." He pointed straight ahead of them at a hilltop off in the distance.

There on the hill, with the sun rising slowly but surely behind him, was Ellchant. His silhouette stood out, blotting out a portion of the blazing yellow-orange sun. The old man was moving. Not with the slow gait of one whom is aged, but with one who has the speed and grace of a skilled fighter, for in his hands was a sword. Surrounding him were what appeared to be posts of some kind. Ellchant swung the sword, wielding it like a white flame slashing with blinding speed at the encircling posts, taking them all down to half of their height in a matter of seconds. He paused for a moment, seeming to regard the figures of the two boys, then raised the sword and felled the last of one of the posts in a single lightning fast swipe.

Aris and Kallevick stood watching in utter shock as the man began walking over to them and as he got within range they saw he had a grin on his face.

"That was, I don't know what to say…" Kallevick began.

"How did you do that?" Aris asked, his face drawn with excitement.

"With this, I can do almost anything." Ellchant said holding up the sword. It shone bright in the morning. The sword was completely white, from the pommel to the tip of the blade. "This Aris," he said wiping some dirt off of the shining blade, "This is for you. You will need a weapon on this journey."

Aris hesitatingly took the sword from Ellchant's hands. He held it firm in his grasp and swung it experimentally. It was lighter than anything he had ever held and he was almost sure that it was lighter than his Darigo knife. It felt good in his hand, though he didn't know what to say to the old man for the gift. "I don't know if I can take this Ellchant. This is a fine weapon. Besides, I don't know how to fight."

He tried to hand it back to Ellchant but the elderly man pushed Aris' hand back. "I insist. Besides, as I said before, you will need it. And I will show you and Kallevick how to use these weapons."

"Weapons?" Kallevick asked as Ellchant walked a few feet away to a pile of supplies that the boys hadn't noticed. Among them stood another sword. This one was simpler in design and was mostly silver with a black, leather wrapped hilt. Ellchant walked back over to them, handed the sword to Kallevick and the young man hefted it to feel its balance. It felt nice in his hand, and he suddenly recognized it.

"This was my father's sword."

"Yes. I found it among the wreckage. Your father must have put up one courageous fight because I had quite a time pulling it out of a Goblin carcass. I cleaned it and oiled it for you. Keep these blades close at hand and wield them well boys, for they will save your lives."

"Thank you." they both replied. The boys nodded and Ellchant led them over to the pile of supplies. Aris took off his cloak as the sun began to rise higher in the sky, and Kallevick followed suit. "Ellchant, here's your cloak." Aris said handing it back to the man.

"No my boy, those cloaks are yours and your brother's, they will keep you warm."

Again the boys thanked him. They each took a pack and took one last look around at their village.

"I suppose this will be the last time we'll see this place." Kallevick sighed.

"All this time here that I dreamt that I was away from home, exploring, and now here we are ready to go, and I don't want to leave." Aris said, the tears starting to well in his eyes.

"There is nothing left here for you boys. But destiny lies ahead of you, never behind. This was once your home and some day you may return, but now Orsidire calls, and we must be off." Ellchant said, his voice a low rumble on the morning breeze.

"Good-bye, Mother. Father. Mafre." Aris said blowing a kiss in the wind toward the graves of his family. He couldn't hold the tears back anymore and his face fell into his hands once again. The tears dripped from between his fingers as Ellchant, and Kallevick each placed a hand on Aris' shoulder. Kallevick's face was just as wet. With one final good-bye they turned and began walking down the path towards the western edge of the woods.

CHAPTER 8

T he day was rising steadily as they reached the path to the edge of the woods. They had headed southwest so as to avoid having to waste time crossing over the southern tip of the Kmorath mountain range. The hike was long and monotonous, yielding little in the way of new scenery. The woods were thick and green and the undergrowth flourished in the rich soil, much the same as it was in their village of Mulroy. Ellchant was in the lead followed by Aris and Kallevick walking side by side. Aris stopped as his brother walked a few steps ahead and then Kallevick followed the gesture by halting his pace.

"Where are we going Ellchant?" Aris asked, his throat now less sore and his voice clearing with each new breath of air.

"Well," Ellchant said, backtracking a few meters to sit down next to the boys. "We are headed southwest and we should be heading for a small stretch of plains. From there it should fade out into desert."

"Is that Lania desert?" Kallevick asked, adjusting his pack.

"Yes, it is." the old man replied. "Your father told you of it I presume."

"Yeah, he told us about it. He said that it reaches far to the west with silver tinted sand dunes as far as the eye can see." Aris stated.

"We'll camp near the edge of the woods tonight. Once we reach the end of the plains we can rest there for a night and then we'll head straight for the Desert City."

"Desert City? You mean people live out there? How do they stand the heat?" Aris asked, his eyes lighting slightly.

"Oh, people live all over this great big planet. Mulroy is not the only inhabited place in the world."

"I know. It's just new that's all. It's just hard to imagine sometimes, especially when you grow up in a place that's so small."

Ellchant nodded, his whitening beard wagging in the breeze.

"We ought to keep moving. It will be afternoon before you know it and then darkness will come fast. C'mon." he said standing up and stretching his legs.

The boys stood up and followed him as he walked onward towards the sun. They walked all afternoon, stopping only once for something to eat. Ellchant had packed some bread and dried meats that he had scavenged from the remains of the village and though it was not fresh, they all welcomed the nourishment. They drank occasionally, sipping briefly from their water satchels. Thinking ahead to the Desert City that lay before them they filled the extra pouches that had been wrapped in their packs from a nearby stream.

Ellchant walked fast and at times the boys had a hard time keeping up. It seemed as if an unseen force was driving the old man and though the boys hiked often, they were amazed at his endurance. They continued on throughout the afternoon and by sunset they had reached their estimated destination. The end of the path was a mere twenty feet or so from them and they decided it best to camp under the cover of trees. Not a cloud had been in the sky all that day but it was best to be prepared according to Ellchant.

They struck a small camp and lit a fire, eating some more of the food they carried. The sky was a deep blue and through the branches of the trees the stars shone bright like pinpricks seeping through the netted canopy. The moon was half full and it shone silver in the velvet sky. The three sat around the fire, quietly thinking. Ellchant sat on a fallen tree and shifted the burning coals with a stick, sending off tiny sparks flying into the air that mimicked orange fireflies. Kallevick sat motionless with his legs crossed, peeling the bark from the same fallen tree on which the old man sat. Aris sat across from them and lay on the ground staring up into the sky, his cloak wrapped tightly about him.

"So," Ellchant began, attempting to break the looming silence. "How are you two doing?" He felt somewhat foolish and uncomfortable, a feeling he didn't too often get, as he waited for a response. What could he say to comfort them? They lost their family and he had lost one of his closest friends. No words seemed to fit right. But the quiet demanded that they speak. Perhaps a talk would help and just as Ellchant's mind began to overlap in repetition, Kallevick spoke.

"Ellchant, I know that we are after the sword, but where exactly are we headed?"

"Well," the old man said, welcoming the interruption from his thoughts. "If my guess is correct, then the Rundagg horde should be headed back towards Chadurian in the west. Hopefully we can intercept the sword before they get there."

"What is the Wheel of Midgail?" Aris asked, still staring up towards the stars.

"Hmmm," Ellchant tucked his hair behind his ear and began stroking his beard. "Midgail, how do I explain it? Well you already know of the two realms, Galebraith, and our planet, the realm of men, Andellius."

"Yes, of course."

"Midgail is a link between those two realms. Mid- meaning in between, and Gail being the first part of the name of Galebraith, which means realm of the immortals, in dragon tongue. Exactly what it is, is unknown to me. It could be a celestial body, a bridge, I honestly don't know."

"So if Dinemid gets the sword he will pass over, or travel through Midgail, and get back into the realm of the gods, right?" Aris asked, turning on his side to face Ellchant.

"Yes, but more importantly, he will regain his immortality. If he accomplishes this, he will become invincible. That is why we must find him after recovering Orsidire, and destroy him."

"But if he regains his immortality couldn't we just stop believing in him and end him that way too?"

"No because his evil will has kept him alive. When he was cast out of Galebraith the gods thought he was as good as dead, yet he lived. A most unnatural creature was Dinemid. Whatever kept him alive in our realm will surely allow him to survive in Galebraith. If he becomes immortal again, it cannot be undone. He will never die."

"But didn't the gods foresee all of this? Didn't they sense him plotting to overthrow them? Couldn't they have prevented the whole thing?" Kallevick questioned.

"Ah, that is where Foresight comes in."

"That's the second time you've mentioned it, what do you mean when you say that?" Kallevick said, his curiosity peaked.

Ellchant smiled lightly, looking at the two young men, happy that he was able to get their minds off of the last few days.

"Well, there is something that the believers of old called Ostendore. That is the dragon word for law or rule. You see the gods created the universe on three principles, laws that keep the world from spinning out of control. The first is the gods' ability to see the future. Once they see it they cannot undo it or alter it, but the Lords of Galebraith know what will happen, when and why. The second is the ability of the gods' to control time and space, and our surroundings. This also allows them to control the situations around us."

The young men peered at him curiously.

"Well namely, the environment and such." He paused momentarily. "But for all their power and all their might, mankind and all the other intelligent races of this world, have in their hearts the third law and that is Freewill. The gods may know where you end up at the end of your life and they may influence you and guide you, but it is ultimately up to you where you choose to go."

"But if the gods know where you end up, then is it not just a matter of following a predetermined path? Does that not undo the whole concept of choice?" Aris questioned. "If the future is already written then are we not doomed to follow what has been laid before us?"

Ellchant smiled.

"That you see, is the mystery of the relationship of the gods to mankind. Besides, their Foresight does not by any means invalidate or degrade the importance or emotion that is evoked in your life. They are still your decisions. The gods aren't making them. You are. They just happen to know what path you'll choose."

Aris seemed to consider this for a moment and looked at the old man with an expression of pure fascination.

"It is up to you to determine the magnitude of your fate." His expression shifted as his mind turned back to their mission. "If Dinemid becomes immortal he will destroy Ostendore and will attempt to control the universe, and in turn will destroy it. His thirst for power has made him so blind that he does not see that he will even destroy himself."

"But why did we not know of these laws? All our father ever told us were the stories of the gods and the history of our world. He told us all about Dinemid trying to seize the throne and being cast out of Galebraith. But he never mentioned anything about Ostendore." Kallevick said. He wrapped his cloak around himself, and pulled the hood up over his head, yawning simultaneously.

Ellchant shifted his position on the fallen tree. Aris sat up and rubbed his hands together, placing them over the fire to warm them.

"You have always known Ostendore. The very act of living has engrained that knowledge into the very imprint of your soul. You yourself just said that you know the story of the gods. By knowing that you know the first principle. Without it, prophecy would not be possible. You two are some of the few left who believe in the gods. Cabral raised you well. I am honored that he has left me to watch over you both, though I only wish that the circumstances were different."

"You know," Aris piped in. "Father mentioned that they used to take Kallevick to the Nari Fair when he was little."

"Your parents used to bring him to the fair, yes " Ellchant said looking at Kallevick. Ellchant turned back to face Aris, who got up and walked around the fire to sit down in front of the old man.

"Tell me more." Aris said, his voice trailing off into the cool night.

"You, Aris, are the man born of faith." The old man paused, seeing how this information would sink in. Aris seemed to be more intrigued than surprised and so Ellchant continued. "You see your parents were fairly young and they had already had your brother." The two looked over to Kallevick who had suddenly dozed off. "They wished for another child and they prayed to the gods in desperation when they had trouble conceiving. They were blessed when you were born and then they were rewarded for their faith with your sister. Have you ever heard the poem?"

"You mean the origins of Andellius? Fragments of it. Father knew that we only had sections of it and that much of that knowledge had been lost to the passage of time. Why?"

"Then I assume that you don't know this." The old man cleared his throat and began to recite from memory.

> *A man would come, one born of faith*
> *The messenger of Galebraith*
> *He would cause evil to fail*
> *And through his plight all good prevail*

But the seeds of doubt were deeply sown
And mankind's doubt had only grown
So now the gods sought out that man
A man who could finish what they began

He would take the sword made by the gods
And with its blade on evil trod
But should this man fail to defend
All life will cease, and time shall end

The last words were barely out of Ellchant's mouth when the faint rustle of leaves came from a nearby bush. The two turned suddenly and Kallevick's eye's popped open in full consciousness.

"What was that?" He whispered.

Ellchant stood quickly, but noiselessly and crept nearer as it got louder. From his robe he pulled a small dagger and took a final step, standing a meter or two from the noisy foliage.

"Who's there?" Ellchant demanded in a deep pronounced voice. "Come out and show yourself."

At these words Aris and Kallevick stood, both drawing their weapons, brandishing them unsteadily. Their hands shook fiercely, more from fear of what lay near them and the old man than for their lack of fighting experience.

Ellchant cautiously stepped closer and on a mental count of three he leapt at the rusty colored bush and poked with his hand wildly. He felt the branches snap in his palm and when his hand felt something akin to clothing he grabbed ferociously and pulled with all of his might.

Aris and Kallevick stepped backward and Kallevick almost tripped backwards over the fallen tree. Aris' face melted from fear into a wide smile that had his brother shooting him a mean look. Kallevick looked back at Ellchant who stood, a hand full of a rough-hewn vest of sorts in his grasp. Standing in front of the three companions stood a peculiar looking creature. He was dressed in a fur vest and long dark brown leather pants. A very confused look came over the creature's face and Aris could not stop smiling. Ellchant's gripped loosened and his hand fell to his side, his face gone wide in utter shock.

"An Ellion." He whispered, and concealed his dagger back into his cloak.

"Hello." The creature said, waving his hand stiffly.

"I'll be a grazer beast!" Aris began to laugh. "It's an elf!"

CHAPTER 9

The three humans and elf stood unmoving for a few minutes staring at each other, quite unsure of what to do next. Finally Ellchant turned to face the young men and waved his hands downward, motioning for them to put away their weapons. Aris did not move for a moment and then without breaking his stare he sheathed his sword. Kallevick hesitated and stood, unmercifully gripping the hilt of his sword in both hands.

"It's alright Kallevick. You can put your sword down now. It's safe." Ellchant said turning back to look at the elf.

Kallevick stood as though he did not hear Ellchant's words and adjusted his footing. The group held their positions for another moment and finally Ellchant turned to face the armed young man when no one moved.

"Kallevick!" Ellchant yelled, his voice commanding and deep.

The young man finally broke his gaze from the elf and looked at the old man.

"Put your sword away, it's alright. He will not harm us. Relax." His voice was calmer now, like the breeze that swept calmly between them.

Kallevick complied and sheathed his weapon. But though his body visibly loosened, the tension in his hands was still firm. For a silent moment he wished he were still armed. Aris looked at his brother and felt the compulsion to comfort him, for something in Kallevick's eyes seemed wrong. He was remembering something dark. Something back in Mulroy.

"I'm cold, is it alright if I sit by your fire?" The elf asked, his brows raising. He was a unique looking being, Aris thought. But the longer he watched him he found a chaotic beauty to his features. He had thick long hair, about shoulder length and it was cream colored with thin streaks of very pale lime green throughout. He had delicate long ears that pointed up to the stars and a regal looking face with pale but firm skin. Around his eyes was the same pale green that was in his hair and the eyes themselves were copper colored.

Ellchant inhaled deeply and after regaining his calm demeanor, took the elf by the arm and led him to the fire pit. After the events of the last few days it was hard to imagine that the trio would so easily accept the company of a stranger but Ellchant knew that had it been anyone but an elf they would be more cautious, if not threatening.

Kallevick backed up a bit not sure what to think of the whole thing. A sort of fear, but then again fear was not the right word to describe what he felt. Kallevick felt uneasy, yes that is what it was uneasy, for something about the creature made Kallevick cringe internally. It wasn't his appearance and it wasn't the look on the elf's face that bothered him but something about him seemed familiar. Kallevick sat back down on the tree stump, trying to hide any hint of fear from his face. It was an old hunting skill that came almost instinctually to him and Aris.

The elf sat down at the fire rubbing his hands together and then over his arms which were exposed to the cool air. Aris noticed that he had no hair on his thin and wiry arms, yet they were very muscular. His boyish curiosity overtook him and he felt compelled to ask a million questions but looked over at Ellchant who sat quietly looking at the elf as if he had just found a long lost family member. Aris looked back at the elf who seemed too concerned with warming up to really pay any of them really close attention. The thought seemed to weigh heavily on Aris' mind and he felt all the more obligated to start asking all kinds of questions. He couldn't resist the temptation and just as he opened his mouth to start, Ellchant spoke.

"What is an elf doing here in the woods a day from the villages?"

The elf looked at Ellchant and smiled and Aris was transfixed by it. The last few days had robbed him of any reminder of happiness and this exchange between man and Ellion fascinated him. Here they all were, talking with a real elf. This was really happening, Aris thought to himself.

"What is your name?" Ellchant asked a little more boldly this time.

"Oh forgive me for not introducing myself. My name is Braeburn. Braeburn Dahlgren. Who sir, may you be? And the names of your companions, if I may ask?"

"I am Ellchant Pendergast. This is Kallevick Desarta and Aris Desarta." Ellchant answered.

"Brothers?" Braeburn pointed at the two young men. He shook his head in understanding. "Pleased to meet you," He said standing up and walking around the fire to shake hands with them all. Ellchant stood and shook firmly back, a sobering look still on his face. The creature walked past the old man to where Aris sat.

Aris stood and eagerly shook Braeburn's hand and added, "Pleased to meet you. I've never met an elf before."

Braeburn smiled back in response. His expression likened to a renowned historian whose admirers unabashed enthusiasm upon meeting him would always be met with a smirk that conveyed a speck of the impersonal. He took another step and Kallevick slowly stood, hesitatingly taking the elf's hand.

"Hello." He managed to say.

"Hello, Kallevick." The elf said, slightly surprised at his reaction, although not all that unpleased.

Braeburn continued around the fire and sat back down in the seat he had originally occupied.

"Well I have been wandering if you must know," the elf said, as if he was continuing an involved conversation that had been interrupted by formal introductions. "I was in the woods and it was dark and I lost my Igris sticks so I couldn't start a fire to keep warm. Then, as if that wasn't fun enough I lost my fur cloak so I didn't even have that."

"How did you lose it?" Aris asked, enthralled by the creature.

Braeburn's face went still, the smile melting through the flames of the fire as he looked through them at Aris. His tone dropped an octave. "Rundagg."

The young man went silent.

"What about them?" Ellchant asked.

"I was wandering as I said and I heard something crunching through the trees and I began to run. I didn't have a light or any weapons and in case whatever it was was not friendly, I decided it was best to not be seen. My cloak got caught in a thicket as I ran past and it tore free. The noise got louder and I heard the hoarse laughter of goblin voices. I hid in a hollowed out tree and they passed by me. I kept hoping they didn't see me or hear me."

"When did all of this happen?" Ellchant asked, trying to gauge the time frame of the events.

"Maybe a night or two ago. It's kind of hard to recall how long it was. I stayed in the tree for a while. It sounded like there was a whole group of them and I didn't want to get caught."

Ellchant nodded.

"I saw your fire and I was cold. I tried to creep closer to warm up so as not disturb you all. I'm sorry if I frightened you. I almost hate to ask, seeing as how you are kind enough to let me join you but do you have a scrap of food that you could spare. I was in too much of a hurry to stop and eat after that encounter with the Rundagg."

Kallevick got up from his seat and sat on the ground, leaning his back on the fallen tree. Aris rummaged through his pack and pulled out a hunk of dried meat, handing it to Braeburn. The elf stood and took it, bowing low, a gesture that Aris mused was an elven form of thanks. It struck Aris with amusement at how the elf ate with a voracious appetite and consumed the meat in a matter of seconds. He must have been hiding in that tree for a while, he thought.

Then Braeburn turned and pulled out a small leather canteen that was strapped to his belt and drunk heavily from it. If any tensioned remained among the group it lie mostly with Kallevick but even he had a hard time of holding in his laughter as the seemingly polite and courteous elf emitted a thunderous belch.

As the mild laughter died Ellchant looked to the two smiling young men and he felt their inner warmth. It was so good to see them smile, even if only for a moment. He had only known them for a day or so but he felt bound to them in spirit, as if his promise to Cabral had been fully realized. These were now his boys, almost like his own sons. He smiled to himself at the thought. That was something he never had, children of his own. Ellchant only wished that it wasn't at such a terrible price that he was able to have the honor of watching over such kind young men. They were his children now and he vowed to himself that very moment that he would do his best to keep them from harm.

Braeburn sat quietly staring at the fire, rubbing his eyes and settled some into his seat. Before long his lids became drawn with sleepiness and he lay down on the grass and quickly dozed off. Ellchant stood, pulled an extra blanket from his pack and laid it over the sleeping elf. He then went back to his own seat and lay down with his own blanket. He nodded to the boys, but they where too involved in their own conversation to notice his gesture so he rolled over and closed his eyes. The memory of the boys smiling kept showing over and over in his mind and the jovial thought put him right to sleep.

"Kalle, why didn't you put your sword away. Ellchant said that everything would be fine. We are safe here. Braeburn is a friend."

"I remembered something from back in the village. When we were young, Mother used to tell us stories of the Ellion. Do you remember?"

"Yes. She used to tell us those kinds of stories all the time."

"I just remember her telling us those stories and the next day she looked at me after having apparently retold the story and she said that I could tell a story just as good as any Ellion could."

"I've told you that many times. So has Tenen and everyone else. You're a great storyteller. What does that have to do with Braeburn though?"

"I just remember that Mother had such a sad look on her face. She must have been thinking about us leaving. Do you remember what she did after that."

"I remember now, we were very young. She started crying and she grabbed us both and hugged us for what seemed like forever. I remember thinking to myself, why? Why is she so upset?"

"Seeing Braeburn just made me remember that and I got scared. I just have this image of Mother's face in my mind. The last look on her face. I...I just panicked that's all." he began to tear up. "I can't lose you Aris. I can barely stand that Mom and Dad and Mafre aren't here, but if you go, if you go I...I wouldn't be able to take it."

Aris leaned forward and hugged his brother and he felt a little strange. Usually Kallevick was bolder. He had never seen his brother so vulnerable and even though Kallevick was the strong one, there were times when they were growing up that Aris now saw in a different light. Usually Kallevick had been the voice of reason and the disciplinarian when it came to a fight between Aris and Mafre, or Tenen for that matter. Being the oldest of them, no one really questioned his judgement as it was usually sound. Now Aris had to be strong and comfort his brother. He began to tear up as well.

"I miss them more than they will ever know." Kallevick finally said pulling away from his brother.

"I know. Me too." Aris said, wiping his face.

"Your face is wet." Kallevick said, smiling.

"Shut up." Aris said, shoving Kallevick. "We'd better get some sleep. Ellchant's already out and Braeburn is snoring."

They lay down, side by side, covered up in their own blankets and soon they were out cold.

*   *   *   *   *   *   *   *   *   *   *

Ellchant walked further into the crowd and peered through a gap that had suddenly opened. There Kallevick stood, looking straight back at him with an uneasy stare. Behind him Aris stood in front of the pedestal with the sword floating above it. Kallevick turned to grab his brother's arm, and Aris stumbled. They began to walk away quickly. Ellchant walked the distance between them but the young men kept getting farther and farther away. He saw Aris turn and look over Kallevick's shoulder right at him. They kept moving faster and faster.

Ellchant ran to catch up with them and a swarm of laughing drunks passed in front of him. Their voices were harsh and loud. He kept walking but he saw no sign of the boys. He looked around for another moment, taking note of the packed dirt of the earthen path that lead from the Great Bridge to the Island and guessed that they must have run off and onto the mainland. It was only a few feet away. But maybe they hadn't. Maybe they were hiding. He looked down the path once more and then turned to scan the rest of the crowd. Then he heard a voice. Though it had not been spoken aloud, he heard the words loud and clear in his head. It was his voice. The voice of his own mind. And it asked him one question. Who am I?

Then suddenly Ellchant was looking down the path again. It was as if he hadn't even stopped looking down it. Only something felt different. The sun, the sun was higher in the sky. It was earlier in the day. And he was further away from the path, much further. He was standing still and a mass of bodies swirled around him. Their voices and movements were blurs and only the landscape seemed to be in focus. He looked at the path again. The mass of animated bodies kept walking in front of him.

Suddenly through the throng of people he spotted two distinct figures coming out from the end of the path and stop. It was Aris and Kallevick. Aris was staring at the whole commotion of the Fair while his brother looked on. Suddenly Ellchant felt a wave of elation as if he was floating. It was as if he had never seen Aris before and yet he knew him. He knew him well. He began to run towards him.

Ellchant sat up, inhaling as he did so. It was dark and it took a moment for him to gather his bearings. It was still night and the fire had sunken down dramatically. Braeburn lay on the ground near him snoring softly. Ellchant looked from across the dim firelight and saw the boys sleeping soundly. He sighed and stretched his legs. What a strange dream he thought to himself. A strange dream, but a good one. He gathered that it was a hopeful sign from the gods. Though what it meant was still a mystery. He rolled over and soon enough he was asleep.

CHAPTER 10

Ellchant was unnerved as he awoke. The sounds that caused his awareness were not those of the morning birds singing at the edge of the woods, but those of his companions.

"It's about time you got up." Aris said looking down at him.

The old man grumbled and got to his feet. "What time is it?"

"It will be noon in a few short hours." Came Kallevick's response.

Ellchant groaned. His dream from the night before had caused him to oversleep. He was eager to find the sword and after Braeburn's account of the Rundagg passing through he was even more anxious.

"Let's get going." Said the elf.

They had exited the edge of Obadia Wood and the landscape blended into a stretch of long rolling hills of green grass. They panned out for miles and beyond them lay their destination, the Desert City.

Braeburn and Ellchant led the group with Kallevick and Aris following close behind. The sun was high in the sky and the warmth caused the two young men to shed their cloaks. Aris responded to the increasing temperature by rolling his tunic sleeves up and Kallevick unbuttoned his collar. Kallevick felt more relaxed now and after he apologized to Braeburn that morning he felt the weight of his burdening thoughts lessen.

"I have been traveling for many years." Braeburn said as they walked along. "I am, as you all know, an Ellion. I have been searching for my fellow brethren, the Elves and fellow sisters, the Faeries. As you can see I have not had much luck. I fear that I may be the last of my kind."

"What happened to all of the Ellion?" Aris asked.

The two in the lead slowed their pace and the four companions walked side by side. Braeburn adjusted his walking stick then pushed back the rolled blanket that Ellchant had given to him out of his arm's way. He tightened the leather strap that held the bundle over his shoulder.

"Dinemid caused them to disappear. No one knows where they went. Ellchant told me of Orsidire and how it spoke to you. Perhaps the answer as to where my race

71

has gone will be revealed if I follow you. You see Aris, Dinemid made mankind doubt the gods existence because he made the Ellion disappear."

"I don't understand."

"The Ellion were created by the gods to tell the history of the Lords of Galebraith to mankind. Without the Ellion mankind began to doubt and forget the gods thus weakening them. I must find what has become of my people. Perhaps together we can restore the faith of men."

Aris nodded and looked deeply into the elf's golden eyes. They were filled with a deep concern and a reverence that made Aris sink within his own thoughts for a time. The foursome kept walking along, glad to have the green hills ahead of them and Aris was eager to be on to the city. Off in the distance they saw a herd of wild horses grazing. They were of many different colors with long silky manes flowing from the nape of their necks to the crowns of their heads.

The land sloped downward into a shallow valley and as the noontime sun reached its apex they stopped to gather some water from a nearby lake. It lay in a wide area of rock and shrubs and the water wavered in small ripples as the last of the mountain springs of the Kmorath dribbled into the lake. They rested for a while, eating and talking very little so as not to disturb the tranquility of the beautiful surroundings. The sky was blue and cloudless and the weather seemed to be favoring them as they journeyed.

The horses were nearer to them now and seemed to regard them with little concern. Looking to the edge of the plain where they sat Aris seemed to notice for the first time how deep green the trees of Obadia were. They were quite a contrast to the bright hues of the grassland.

"Kalle, look." Aris pointed over towards where they entered the plains. "Look how dark the trees look, strange isn't it?"

"You know, I never noticed that before but I see it now. That is strange. Everything here seems brightly colored."

"The sun lies closer to the land and especially towards Lania, that's why it's so hot there. Mulroy and Nari are a bit further north and the mass of the trees block a lot more sun than you'd think." Ellchant said, breaking off a hunk of grain bread that he had pulled from his pack and handed it to Kallevick. He handed a piece of the bread to

Braeburn who consumed it in seconds and leaned back, taking in the view. "Perhaps we can tame some of the horses and ride them into the city. It would save us quite a bit of walking." Ellchant said.

He broke off another piece from the loaf and made a peculiar noise towards a nearby horse. It was white with a few black spots on its hindquarters and had deep black eyes. The creature looked at the old man as if trying to guess at his intentions and slowly trotted over to him. It bowed low and Ellchant held the piece of bread out to it. It took the bread and ate it as Ellchant softly patted its nose.

Aris stared in amazement at the whole transaction and Kallevick sat quietly thinking as he watched. The horse whinnied and trotted off back to where it was grazing. Ellchant turned and smiled at Aris who sat staring at him with a dumbfounded look.

"Amazing creatures aren't they?" He said smiling.

"How did you do that?"

He smiled again and broke off another piece of bread, handed it to Aris and then gave himself a share. Aris looked at the old man for a minute and then turned his attention away to Braeburn who sat with his legs crossed and his back leaning against a rock. His eyes were closed and Aris wondered if he had dozed off.

"Braeburn, are you asleep?"

"No, " came the response. "I'm just taking in the fresh air. I'm not used to the forest and the breeze of the open plain is refreshing."

Ellchant breathed deeply and exhaled slowly. He closed his eyes momentarily and then they shot back open. "Do you hear that?" He asked.

Aris began to get nervous when he looked at the old man.

"What is that awful smell?" Kallevick said. He looked suspiciously at Braeburn.

"Something is here. Someone is here. Do you hear that?" The old man stood and dropped his food onto his pack. "Braeburn, get up! Boys, get up. Someone is coming."

"What's going on?" Braeburn asked wearily and for a moment Aris smiled for he knew that the elf had started to fall asleep. Braeburn stood.

Kallevick stood and tightened his bootlaces. "Should we hide, Ellchant? What should we do?" He turned and noticed that the horses perceived what the old man heard. They had stopped grazing and some were beginning to wander off away from the direction of the woods.

"Shh." Ellchant waved towards Kallevick and kept staring off at the tree line near the edge of the plain. "None of you hear that?" he asked in a hushed tone.

"Hear what?" Aris asked.

The wind rode heavy on them as they stood and through the trees came a crashing and stomping that Kallevick and Aris thought was another stampede of animals. But it was far worse. With lumbering steps a creature thundered through the trees, smashing and knocking all manner of plant over as it moved. This was no animal, Aris thought. Animals didn't hit trees and send them flying. He grabbed the hilt of his sword and Kallevick did the same.

"What is that?" Aris shouted to Ellchant as the noise grew deafening. He raised his blade in combat readiness.

"A Giant." Ellchant turned to face the group and he motioned for them to follow him. Braeburn grabbed a few large stones from the lake and Ellchant pulled an object wrapped in a cloth from his seemingly magic pack. It always seemed to have everything they needed, Aris thought. The thought did not stay with him long and the trio ran after Ellchant who sped towards the center of the valley. The horses began to scatter as the four companions neared.

"Did you say Giant?" Kallevick shouted, his eyes wide open in fear.

Ellchant nodded an affirmative. The horses neighed and bolted across the plains only adding to the growing clamor. They rushed past the friends with their bold muscles flexing and rotating in graceful motion. Ellchant stopped and turned abruptly to face the rumbling woods and his companions did the same. As the old man looked onward he was unaware that his three companions exchanged uneasy glances at each other as if to silently acknowledge that Ellchant had gone insane. The elf and two young men began to back away when Ellchant turned to see them. His eyes pierced through each of them, moving down to the ground and then back up at them as if to ask where they where going. They hesitatingly moved closer to him to make a tight battle formation.

The noise got louder and with incredible speed the Giant came crashing through the trees, ripping them out of the ground and snapping others in half like twigs. The creature stood about the size of three grown men and bellowed with an inhuman scream.

"Get off of my land!" It shouted as it ran towards the group. His arms were as thick as two men's heads placed side by side, his torso as round as a pillar of a great building, and his curly yellow hair was sticking up in all directions as if it was trying to flee its owner's head. Aris was certain that it was male because the deep voice booming through the air kept ringing through his ears. His face was terrible and distorted, mutilated to a hideous lump of flesh that sat squat on his broad shoulders.

He ran with a tremendous gait and stomped over the grass leaving impressions in the land. He was like a grazer beast gone mad, Kallevick thought. Not like the stampede where the fear in the eyes of the animals was apparent. This giant meant to kill them. He raised his sword to arm himself.

Braeburn turned to Ellchant who stood motionless. "What do we do?"

The old man said nothing and smiled at the elf, unflinching.

Just as Ellchant turned to face the growing clamour, the giant leapt straight through the air and landed just where the group had stood a moment earlier. Had they not run out of the way the creature would have squashed them all into a mass of body parts imbedded in the turf. Ellchant stood off to the side and Aris had not leapt far enough away and the giant swung his club like fist at the young man. Aris ducked in time to miss the deadly blow and swung his sword with all of his might at the giant's hand. His strike missed and the creatures' second arm found its mark, sending Aris flying ten feet from the crater that the Giant left from his leap. Though the earth seemed to yield to the giant, judging from the imprints left by his boots in the grass, Aris was not so lucky and hit the ground with an uncompromising thud.

Kallevick yelled and ran towards the creature with a bravery he didn't know he had and swung his sword. The Giant moved to avoid the blow but could not move fast enough and caught some of the blade, leaving a gash in his left leg. The Giant cried out in anger and tried to stomp Kallevick with his clumsy foot but was hit in the head with a large stone. The creature pivoted, his head rearing like a wild animal and saw Braeburn standing a way's off, tossing another stone up and down in his hand. He ran for the elf and when he moved out of the way Kallevick ran to Aris who was standing up with great difficulty.

"Aris, are you all right?" Kallevick said grabbing his brother's arm and helping him to his feet.

"Just got my breath taken from me." Aris inhaled deeply and grimaced as he did. "I'll have a bruise."

Braeburn ran around in a circle as if playing with the monster and teased it as it swung down to crush him with its hammer like hands. The giant kept missing and for every miss the elf made a nasty face, which further angered the beast. Again the giant bellowed.

"Gridel's plain, Gridel's horses! Mine! Mine! Mine!" He swung over and over but could not strike the elf. Another stone hit Gridel in the face and he beat the air wildly with his boulder like fist hitting Braeburn square in the chest, knocking him off his feet. The elf grunted with the impact of the giant's fist and he hit the ground.

Ellchant ran with a warrior's fury and jumped onto the back of the beast raising the cloth high in the air with his hand. He moved swiftly and wrapped the giant's eyes and attempted to tie the blindfold. Gridel brought his log like arms around his back trying to knock the spry old man from his shoulders but his arms were not that flexible. Just as one of his thick fingers caught hold of Ellchant's robe it hooked onto the fabric and he pulled with fierce strength.

Ellchant was spun around to face him, the attempt at the blindfold falling off of the giant's face. Gridel raised his hand to smash the old man between his hands like a soft fruit when he felt a sharp pain shooting in his lower back. The creature squealed in horror. Ellchant seized the opportunity and freed himself from the monster's grasp. He rolled sideways out of Gridel's fingers brandishing a long chain whip with a steel skull at the tip. He adjusted his grip on the studded wooden handle.

Aris yelled, pulling his sword free from the giant's flesh and Gridel hurtled around to face Aris. The young man swung again to smite his enemy but pulled his strike when Ellchant yelled.

"Gridel!" Ellchant shouted to the giant.

Aris ran off as Gridel turned. Braeburn, Kallevick, and Aris stood behind the monster and ran in a half circle to stand nearer to Ellchant.

"Now you all die! You come through my pass to take my horses and rob me! But you fail and so now you all DIE!!!!!" Gridel beat the ground wildly trying to crush the old man but Ellchant was faster and whipped his weapon around and sent it cracking. His first swipe missed the giant but flashed a lightning like cracking sound through the air. Gridel swung again and barely missed the old man. Again Ellchant cracked his whip and hit Gridel in the hand causing the giant to cry out in pain.

"Gridel!"

With one final swing Ellchant delivered the deathblow, sending the skull and chain through the air with a sizzling snap. The skull sunk right between the giant's eyes, killing him instantly.

They all stood and watched as Gridel collapsed onto the green earth beneath him, sending the turf up and along with it a rumble that they felt through their boots. The foursome stood quietly for a moment and looked one to another.

Braeburn was the first to speak.

"Just like a giant to come in and ruin lunch."

Aris, though he felt weak from the strike to his side let out a hearty laugh. Kallevick was too concerned in helping his brother to even crack a smile.

"I'm fine Kalle. Really. I just need to sit down for a moment." He sat on the ground and was grateful for the earth being softer than it had felt in recent moments.

"Why did you try to blindfold him?" Kallevick asked.

Braeburn looked at Ellchant as if he too was internally asking the same question.

"I feel bad that I had to kill him. I was trying to be merciful and not let him see his own death. Giants are normally peaceful horse herders. I don't know what his problem was."

Though his comment was unintentionally funny they all laughed.

"They wander the land overseeing the horses and gathering them up if a storm moves in and find safe havens for them. This is proof of the state of the world." He said his palm outstretched towards the mass of flesh.

"Ellchant did you notice this before or is it just me?" Braeburn piped in.

"Notice what?"

"Gridel, as I am assuming that is our late friend's name here, has only twenty or so horses. Don't the nomads usually herd them in packs of fifty?" Braeburn looked back at the hill that was Gridel's body.

"Let's have a look, shall we then?" Ellchant said, wrapping his chain whip back into the cloth as he neared the felled giant. He leaned down and searched the body for a moment while the others leaned in and watched in curiosity. He rummaged through Gridel's pockets and found a few scraps of meat, an unusual thing to find on the person of a giant. "Nomads don't eat meat." He mumbled to himself. He sniffed the half-rotten flesh and grimaced. "Here's your bad smell Kallevick," he said tossing the meat aside. He sniffed cautiously at his fingers. "Looks like this giant has been eating some of his own horses."

Aris' eyebrows raised and his face curled back in disgust.

"That's strange," Ellchant said, his voice slightly muffled through the thick hulk of the body.

"What is it?" Aris asked.

"Well," Ellchant said, moving to the left and lifting the arm of the dead beast. He unlatched a pouch on Gridel's belt and removed a few more items. "Not only is our friend a carnivore he is carrying something more unusual than that."

"You know seeing as how they travel so much why would he become so territorial?" Braeburn asked, looking around at the green hills. "That in itself is odd."

"What was he carrying?" Kallevick asked after considering Braeburn's comment.

"This." Ellchant rose, his hand placed on his knee for support and stood up straight, his other hand held out. In his palm were a dozen or so small shards of badly rusted iron ore. "Goblin gold. Relatively worthless, at least in most parts of the world. But what is a Giant doing dealing with Rundagg?"

CHAPTER 11

The horse quietly grazed, barely lifting its head to grind the wild flowers in its full mouth. It stooped down again to bite more from the patch that sprung from the ground in a little burst of purple petals. A noise caused it to raise its head, this time looking out onto the surrounding plain and it commenced to ground the flowers with silent satisfaction. It spotted the four bipeds coming towards it yet made no attempt to move as it didn't perceive them to be of any threat.

Ellchant was in the lead and he took slow calculated steps toward the creature so he would not frighten the peaceful horse. Braeburn walked with a more casual stride and came right up to it. Without so much as a friendly pat to show the horse he meant no harm he leapt right onto its bare back and it took off out from under him. The elf flew as he was thrown from the beast and landed firmly on the grass. The tan creature blew a lung full of air from its nose, appearing to convey its displeasure with the insolence of the Ellion.

Kallevick laughed and Aris smiled as he took his arm from off around his brother's shoulder.

"I'll be fine Kalle." He said giving his sibling a reassuring glance.

Kallevick nodded and looked back at Braeburn who sat on the ground still looking dazed. He moved over to him and offered a hand to help the elf to his feet.

"Stop trying to show off. That isn't a unicorn you know." Kallevick reminded him.

"I'm usually very good with horses." The elf responded. The pride in his voice had audibly weakened.

"Sure you are." Kallevick said smiling.

Ellchant had neared another beast and saved the animal the trouble of having to bend down by picking the wild flowers from the ground and he fed them to the horse from his hand. He rubbed right between its eyes and scratched behind its ears to which the quadruped closed its eyes and gave a happy snort. It stood tall and proud, it's black mane wistful in the wind.

"He's good with horses," Aris commented to Braeburn as he walked over to the old man. "Subtlety my friend."

"Shut up."

Aris chuckled. "If we are going to ride we should go get our packs and supplies now and set off, the day is waning."

"I agree," Ellchant said climbing onto the onyx colored horse. He rubbed the beasts' neck and he trotted off to the bank near the water where they had left their belongings. The others followed and they gathered again to the shimmering edge of the lake where they picked up their packs and filled their water satchels.

Aris stretched as if coming out of a long deep sleep. He donned his pale green cloak again and wiped at the hourglass design on the side of his pant leg which was stained with reddish brown dirt and streaks of green. He raised the old man's pack to him as a squire does to a knight and the old man took out a strap of leather with a bit fitting it comfortably in the horses' mouth. The horse did not even flinch but sat patiently as Ellchant secured his pack.

The others marched over to Ellchant who sat quietly on the back of the powerful onyx horse and looked up at him as they waited for his instruction. He looked regal on the creature, Aris thought, even though he sat leaning over the horses' neck. It was when Ellchant sat up that grabbed the others' attention, and Braeburn, Kallevick, and Aris looked at him for a long moment all wondering at the old man. His eyes were shining bright and the black spiraled pupils were a deep contrast to the silver iris. For that moment alone, Aris thought, for that moment alone he looked more like a king than a mere man. He knew then that he had befriended a special man, a man who knew so much about a world that seemed so strange to him. Aris wondered silently how Ellchant Pendergast knew the things he knew.

His thoughts drifted to the desert ahead of them and he could already feel the warmth of the sun on his back. He looked at Kallevick and Braeburn who stood adjusting their belts and pack straps and he admired his companions. They were strong and brave in their own ways and Aris could see that now. They each had a determination that Aris admired and was grateful for. He looked to Kallevick and his older brother smiled back at him.

Aris smiled back and turned to face their guide. Ellchant's face was stern with a sense of command that pierced through his eyes at the young hero. A flick of wind caught a few stray hairs on the old man's head and they fluttered in the breeze. Aris was waiting as if the old man was about to issue a decree and when the words came he was instantly compliant.

"We must be off to the city." Was all he said.

As if following the orders of their king the three set pace behind the man on horseback and followed in single file with Aris directly behind Ellchant. They crossed over the body of Gridel, none seeming to regard their victory or even the body's' presence but kept their steady pace onward. They had walked a good distance from the battleground and were approaching the edges of Gridel's plain when they spotted the horses in the distance. They could barely make out the faint rustling of the trees of Obadia behind them.

Aris knew that this was the jumping off point. He could turn back now and cower from what he had to do, but something inside him kept pushing his legs further. He couldn't give up yet, he wouldn't.

Kallevick didn't know if it was the fact that most of the horses left when they had fought the giant but it seemed to him that there were quite a few here. Braeburn had mentioned that the nomads usually kept packs of fifty or so and the sudden reminder of the meat in Gridel's pouch made him shudder. A nomad eating what he was made to protect. He shook the thought from his mind like a cold chill that crept in and was brushed off with a seat next to a welcome hearth.

The group came closer to the horses and Aris counted eleven. He recognized the tan one that the elf tried to mount and he nudged Braeburn.

"There's yours," he said pointing off towards the animals.

Braeburn peered under the cover of his hand, which he held to block the shining sun from his eyes. He squinted and then looked at Aris, simultaneously punching him in the arm. Aris snickered as he perceived the hint of laughter in the elf's eyes and a glimmer of a smile at the corners of his lips.

Ellchant adjusted his seating on the horse's back and he trotted over to the animals without so much as a disruptive motion to them. The others followed and each selected a horse. Ellchant reached into his pack and threw each of them a leather set of reins and a bit. Braeburn moved to the tan beast and rubbed its nose. He leaned in and whispered an apology to the animal in true Ellion tongue. The horse licked the side of his face and the elf mounted its back. Kallevick took a sturdy looking brown mare which seemed to pay him little regard but mutely followed his leg squeezes to where Ellchant sat waiting for them. Aris found a horse and regarding it for a moment recalled the spots on its hindquarters. It was shining white and the sword that he had strapped to his back was a perfect match to his steed.

He climbed up onto its back and the foursome began to drift off away from the other horses. Once they were far enough away Ellchant began to pick up some speed and before long they were at a racing gallop across the last of the plains. The brilliantly colored grassland had dimmed and small patches of pale colored dirt began to appear and rush past under the hooves of the horses. The sand began popping up in small spurts and was encroaching on the last of the vegetation.

The land stretched out before them and the sea of sand dunes where welcoming their eyes. They were a deep tan with a silver lining just as their father told them, Aris thought. Lania Desert. I'm actually here, he thought. The wind was blowing through his dark brown hair and he felt the rush of excitement as he thrust his heels into the sides of the white horse and sped past Ellchant giving a howl of excitement.

Kallevick smiled and tried catch up to the enthusiastic young man.

"Hah!" The elf shouted to the open air and burst forward to try and pass Aris.

In a sudden burst of energy Ellchant grabbed tight the makeshift reins and he gave a yell, racing after the two in the lead. Kallevick, now in dead last felt the urge to beat them in the race and bolted off as fast as the mare would take him. He too gave a yelp and kicked his heels to come in a close second with the elf.

Soon they were all riding side by side and the four companions raced across the desert, a wild and unabashed joy rushing through them all as the dunes whipped by. The heavy breathing of the horses was blast of wind and their own howls of satisfaction were a chorus shouting out to the ancient remnants of ocean. The sand was glistening as they rode and the particles of dust told them stories of how mighty waters once washed these silver shores. The sun was a blazing yellow and they stopped when they reached the crest of a long flat dune and looked out onto the land that lay before them.

On the horizon the City of Hope stood like a fortress. A great wall made of the same tan colored sand that littered the desert made the structure. An open gate with a large portcullis was placed to the left of an enormous silver turret which Aris guessed was some sort of watch tower, although he had no idea what kind of threat could come from the surrounding landscape. For all of his estimation he couldn't imagine much danger lurking out here much less any other life existing outside of the city walls. A blood red flag was erected on a pole in the midst of the turret and Aris thought with curiosity what it meant.

"Beautiful is it not?" Ellchant said from his immediate left.

"Very." Came the response, although Aris did not turn to give it. He was too busy examining the fortress like structure.

"It has been a while since I've seen this place." Braeburn commented from Aris' right. Finally the young man broke his stare and looked to the elf. His eyes were blazing blue and the color of the sands only complimented the young man's features.

Braeburn smiled and his golden eyes melded with the color of the sand. " I passed through here once before on my journey. It is a beautiful place." Braeburn smiled.

Aris smiled back slightly and he was overtaken with the look of the place once more and looked out onto the city.

"Father used to say that this place is called Hope because this was one of the few places left in the world that men still believed in the gods." Kallevick said from Ellchant's left and looked to the old man as if to ask him if his information was correct.

"Yes it is." Ellchant said, his eyes squinting in the sun. "Let's hope they still do."

"I don't recall Father ever mentioning the city before." Aris said, looking around Ellchant at his brother.

"You were probably too young to remember. I just remember being very little and Father having a conversation with Mother about this place."

Aris nodded and the image of his father's handsome face flashed in his mind and he stared out at the city walls. For the first time since they left the village he had to fight back the tears. He missed his family and his father especially and he turned to Ellchant in an attempt to change his thought process.

"Well what are we waiting for?" He asked with only half of the enthusiasm that he had originally felt upon reaching the crest of they dune their horses stood upon.

"Ellchant, are you all right?" He asked, the tone of his voice suddenly emitting concern.

"We are going to have to pass though there," he said pointing off into the distance beyond Hope.

A gathering of dark gray trees sprouted unnaturally out of the ground in a distinct line that wrapped around the edges of the sand dunes, a good mile from the outer casing of the city wall. Kallevick followed it with his eyes to the left and he watched as the line stretched out and around in a smooth curve that reached far into the south, further than his eyes were able to fathom.

"I would rather go over the Kmorath." The elf commented. "I don't want to go through there. Not if we don't have to." Braeburn peered at the area that lay behind the city through the slight heat filled haze that had gathered in front of them.

"We must pass through there." Ellchant repeated without turning to look at the elf.

Braeburn began to protest just when Aris cut him off.

"What is that place?"

"The Barren Forest." Ellchant said unflinching.

"What's in there?" Aris asked as he looked intently at the old man. Ellchant would not face him, but stared straight ahead with a severe frown and Aris didn't like the look of it one bit. A shadow crossed his face and Aris looked up into the sky but no cloud was visible above the old man's head. When he looked back at his friend the shadow was gone and Ellchant shifted to give Aris a reassuring smile.

"I don't like the sound of that place." Kallevick commented to himself.

"I don't either." Aris said quietly still staring at his old friend.

Ellchant gave the young man another reassuring smile and he wasn't altogether positive himself that it was convincing enough. He certainly knew better. The sound of howling echoed in his head and he tried once more at a weak smile to his young friend, but to no avail. Aris wasn't convinced and the look on his face was unabashed as if he could read right through Ellchant's false hope. He wasn't buying it. Not a single bit. He tugged harshly on the reins of his horse and moved forward a few paces.

"Let's go."

*　　*　　*　　*　　*　　*　　*　　*　　*　　*

They rode onto the city gate and were ordered to dismount by the four guards that were stationed there. They wore bright red robes that flared out similarly to their crimson capes, which fluttered in the wind. Their faces were unrecognizable under elaborately wrapped headdresses and Aris guessed they were some sort of masks to keep the sand out. They each carried a spear with an arrow shaped head and each of the four travelers were inspected as were their belongings.

Their weapons were examined thoroughly as were their packs.

"What is it that you are looking for?" Ellchant asked as the guards scrutinized his chain whip. They seemed pleased with the look of it and handed it back to the old man.

"We are ordered by the Judge of Hope to examine all weapons. We have been ordered to turn in any weapons, especially swords, bearing the mark of the gods." The lead guard made an expression under his headdress and Braeburn could only read it as a wordless hint at the mention of swords.

"Why is that?" Ellchant asked with false curiosity.

Aris turned to the old man as he sheathed his own blade in its white scabbard.

Ellchant looked at Aris and gave him a wink while the other guards took Kallevick's sword and passed it to their leader. The head guard hefted the well-forged blade in his scarlet glove then turned it over to examine the pommel.

"We have heard rumors of a theft in the area." The guard said to Ellchant as he handed the sword back to Kallevick. "Nice blade." He commented.

"Thank you."

Aris wondered if the guard had even noticed the feather like weight of his sword. Strange, he thought.

"Well" The guard said sizing them all up. "You are all set to enter."

The main guard saluted them and turned around. He walked over to a man that none of them had noticed and shouted an order to which the half-concealed man began

85

operating a crank. The large wooden portcullis began to rise steadily and the lead guard walked back over to the four travelers.

"Welcome to the City of Hope."

They all nodded in gratitude and as they led their horses through the gate one of the other guards that Kallevick guessed wasn't high in rank, judging from the simpleness of his robes in comparison to the others, stepped forward and followed them. They walked forward into a relatively narrow walkway with a thatched roof that looked like a back alley to a dismal town. The place was clean, but its width and lack of light didn't do much to settle Ellchant.

"My captain neglected to inform you that we are having a tournament here in a few days and you are all welcome to sign up and participate, although I don't know if your older friend there would be eligible." His face was visible and he bore no mouthpiece as his superiors did.

Kallevick, Braeburn, and Aris all laughed a bit but Ellchant was too busy looking straight ahead and he missed the young guard's invitation entirely.

Aris was almost tempted to tell the guard about the giant earlier that day.

"Ustaf!" Came a cry from the post outside the gate. "Get back here! I didn't give you permission to leave your post!"

The guard ran out of the gate to the other side to take his position. Kallevick couldn't make out the words as the portcullis was being lowered behind them but from the serious stance that the captain had it looked as though Ustaf was getting quite a scolding.

Braeburn wondered what kind of tournament they were having and he knew instantly that if food were involved that he would be the first in line to sign up. His mouth began to water.

Ellchant regarded the elf. "When are you not hungry? And besides, those tournaments that he mentioned are for fighting, not eating."

A disappointed groan came from Braeburn and Aris piped in.

"You mean fight to the death?" He asked, quite surprised.

"No, of course not. Do you think that they would allow a game like that in a place like this?" Ellchant said, pointing ahead of himself. The walkway ended and the city began to open out into wider, more welcoming surroundings.

86

"Ah, that's much better." Ellchant exhaled as he walked forward. The closeness of the walls was beginning to get to him and he tried his best to forget the forest that faced them on the other side of the city.

Aris looked up from the ground for the first time and it suddenly occurred to him that he hadn't been paying attention to where they were walking. In front of them was a beautiful garden full of colorful flowers and fruits, some of which he recognized as the ones he saw at Nari Island the day of the fair. His gaze turned left then right to see that there were stone staircases that led to the upper level of the walls. He noticed that there was a tiered walkway that ran all along the perimeter. The uppermost level looked out onto the desert he presumed.

"How do they get water out here, much less have gardens?" he asked Ellchant.

"Wells," Braeburn answered as he neared a fruit tree in a circular shaped garden. The fruit hung low on the branch and it was a deep red. Ripe and full of juice, the elf thought. He approached the vendor that Aris didn't notice was standing near the garden and Braeburn produced some coins from a pouch that he had slung on his shoulder. He paid the vendor and he picked the fruit from off the tree.

"Wells? How do they have wells here?" Kallevick asked as he watched Braeburn take a large bite out of the fruit. The elf gagged for a moment and then coughed, launching a chunk of juicy bright red fruit into the sand.

"Sour, very, very sour!" the elf said. His face puckered and his eyes were watery. Kallevick shook his head.

"When the ocean dried up and the desert took shape the only source of water came from underground reservoirs deep beneath the sand. They were discovered soon after people began to move here in the western areas. They originally inhabited the northern regions of the Kmorath but Rundagg overran most of the area and they were forced to move here. Lake Hargadon was too far away and when the first settlers arrived here they discovered the hidden reservoirs." Ellchant explained as they walked.

They led their horses through the mazes of vendors and people, and from off to the side a little boy appeared. He was probably only about six years old Aris guessed and he smiled at the kid as he approached.

"Hello friends." The boy said with an enthusiastic voice. "I am Orago. May I take your horses to the stables for you?" He said offering out his small hand. He had a bright smile and he wore clean, finely made clothes.

"What do you need our horses for?" Kallevick asked smiling at the boy.

"Well the city is too crowded to be guiding horses through the streets so it's my job to bring them to the city stable where they are cared for while you enjoy your stay."

The four companions chuckled to one another as they admired the boy.

"Do you work for yourself?" Braeburn asked.

"Nope," the boy said for the first time breaking his professional voice and pointed a few feet away to where an older man was watching them. "That's my dad. I help him, and some day I will take his job when he's too old."

The foursome waved to the boy's father.

"Well seeing as how we can't be walking through the city with horses in tow. Here." Ellchant said handing the makeshift reins to the boy.

The boy's father approached and took the reins of Aris' and Kallevick's horses. The boy took Braeburn's horse and he looked up curiously at the elf.

"Are you sure you can handle two horses there, young one?"

The boy giggled.

"Did the gods make your ears pointy?"

"Please excuse my son," the man said smiling from under a thick brown beard.

"That's fine." Braeburn said to the man and then bent down to the boy's eye level. "What do you think?" he said winking at him and rustling his hair.

The boy giggled even harder.

"How do we retrieve our horses when we need them?" Ellchant said.

"Just ask for me, Jeld, and my son and I will bring them to the inn."

"Yup." The boy chirped.

"Thank you." Ellchant said.

Jeld and Orago both nodded to them and then turned, leading the horses through the streets. Before long they were out of sight.

"This place seems friendly." Kallevick commented.

"Just be mindful of who you talk to." Ellchant replied. "Especially you." He said turning to the elf.

"What?" The elf asked, unaware of the conversation as he took another bite of fruit. The juice ran down his chin in a thin line.

"Where did the Rundagg come from, if they pushed the humans west? The Nadire Ocean is the only thing that lies beyond the northern edge of the mainland." Aris said, losing interest with the direction of the conversation.

"They came from across the sea. Most of the lands on that side of the world have been largely unexplored so whatever is over there is really nothing more than speculation."

Aris nodded.

Kallevick turned when Braeburn fell behind and from the corner of his sight he spotted the elf catching up.

They rounded about more garden vendors and moved to the right to where the inner parts of the city opened up into a central town area. Soon Braeburn was falling behind again and this time Kallevick turned fully to make sure that he didn't lose him in the crowd.

Braeburn was purchasing a piece of meat on a stick and he ran up to Kallevick holding it up excitedly.

"You want a bite?" He said through muffled mouthfuls. He chewed loudly and soon the meat was gone and he was left to lick the stick clean. "Now that was good."

"That didn't last long. Besides, I wouldn't have wanted any of that anyway."

"Why not?" the elf asked, mocking a hurt look on his face.

"It didn't look as good as that fruit did. Hey what happened to it anyway?"

"Oh," the elf said. "That thing." His face turned from sad to annoyance as if the mere mention of the fruit was bothering him. "It was awful sour."

"Yeah," Kallevick said. "I noticed. What did you do with it?"

"I ate it."

Kallevick burst into laughter to which the elf only shrugged and said.

"What? I was hungry!"

Once Kallevick's laughter died he looked around. His face became stern.

"What's wrong?" Braeburn asked.

"Oh no, I think we lost Aris and Ellchant."

A huge crowd swarmed in front of them and the two companions looked deeply into the mass of people in search of their two friends.

CHAPTER 12

Aris followed Ellchant into the thick of the crowd and as he neared
him he could hear the roar of the people ahead of them. A massive
throng was directly in front of them and Aris could pick up the scent
of sweat as he reached Ellchant when he peered over the old man's shoulder to see
what the commotion was all about.

A shallow pit had been dug into the sand but it was now so tumultuous with the
footprints of the two wrestlers that the only distinguishing border of the ring was a thin
line of black wire that was encircling them. The shouting was almost unbearable and
Aris caught another strong whiff of the sweat-covered fighters, gasping in the process.

A shorter man with green pants was circling a very large man with red pants.
The red man lunged at the green man, his bald head exposed to a stray sunbeam that
reflected off into the eyes of the crowd. The sweat that coated his head and face
glittered in the hot sunlight. The green man sprung back and crouched in a defensive
position then spun to the right and pounced like a wild cat on the red man. The red
man squirmed and swung his meaty fist to knock his opponent off from his back. He
whirled suddenly and threw the shorter man off, a cocky smile growing from beneath
his thick mustache.

Aris looked at Ellchant who stood watching with a smile on his own face. The
young man was surprised to see such an expression, as the memory of Ellchant's grave
face was stuck in his mind from earlier. There was pure fear in his eyes, Aris thought.
Something about the Barren Forest didn't take well with his old friend and Aris wanted
to know what it was about the place that troubled him. He would make it a point to
talk to Ellchant later. He promised himself. He looked back at the match to see that
the red man had the green man pinned on the ground.

But the hold did not last long as the short stocky man twisted with a flexibility
that seemed out of place for such a muscular person. He rolled to the left, unhooking
his arm from the giant man's grasp and tugged on the red man's wrist and at the same
time, kicked with his leg at the back of his opponent's knees. The red man fell knee
first into the ground with a dull thud causing a cloud of the silver tinted dust to float up
around him. The green man moved swiftly and pushed his opponent to the ground

before he could recover himself. The green man jumped on top of his fallen enemy and raised his arms in victory. The red man, his face now matching his pants, sprung from the ground before a count could be called and the short man flew from his back, his own face stuffed into the sand. The crowd roared with surprise and laughter. The green man was on his feet in an instant, wiping sand from his eyes and attempting to clean the sand that stuck to his closely cropped black hair.

He looked pale and he was fighting for air, for the impact with the ground had stolen his wind. The red man charged and raised a fist in a powerful strike, yelling in a furious war cry. The green man dodged the blow and swung his own fist hitting the man straight in the stomach. The crowd gasped in empathetic pain and Aris could feel the shift in the ground as they stepped back a moment, the sand crunching mutely under their feet. The red man hunched over for a moment then turned and backhanded the green man to the ground. He turned with his face red as much with anger as it was with pain and stomped over to the fallen man.

The green man waited, still caressing his jaw and as the giant man was straddling him he kicked him in the groin. The red man hunched over, an inhuman bellow emitted from his mouth along with some spittle and the green man ducked under the giant man's legs, taking his opponents ankles in his grasp as he did so. He tugged as hard as he could sending the red man face first into the sand.

"How'd you like that?!" The green man yelled, to which the crowd only roared furiously. The red man turned to look at his enemy and the green man rushed upon him and punched him square in the face. The crowd reeled with a sympathetic groan for the red man and the green man sat cross-legged on his fallen foe.

Aris had trouble seeing what was going on as the people in front of him were moving and exchanging coins from hand to hand. A count was called and the green man declared the victor. He did catch a glimpse of the two fighters and the man in red had not been knocked out but sat on the ground trying to gather his bearings as he was sitting upright rubbing the side of his face. The green man was being paraded around the edges of the ring, his arm held high in the air by a beautiful young woman who Aris was shocked that he had not noticed before. Once his rounds were done the woman drifted off into the crowd again and the green man helped the red man to his feet.

What a show of sportsmanship Aris thought as the two fighters shook hands and bowed low to one another in deep respect. The red man put his arm around the short man and they began to walk out of the ring, laughing as they went. The red man gave his friend a congratulatory pat on the back when out of the corner of his eye Aris spied a black robed man. His face was covered in the same style head-dress that the guards at the gate wore.

From his hand he dropped a brown satchel and Aris recognized it as a coin purse. It fell to the ground and blew away with a breeze that had gathered between the departing crowd. For a brief moment the sun seemed to cast a hazy maroon glow upon the dirt. From his other hand he grasped a wicked looking knife and even though Aris yelled to the green man in warning the audience was still too rowdy to shout over. The man in red turned to look at Aris who was frantically pointing in the direction of the man with the knife. The red man turned and as the armed assailant burst from the crowd he punched the would-be attacker out cold with one strike.

The green man and the audience shouted in shock as the red man hit the stranger with the knife and seemingly out of nowhere three red guards came and abducted the fallen attacker into their custody. The knife was confiscated and the empty change purse was nowhere to be seen.

"He must have lost a bet." Ellchant said from Aris' left. The young man turned almost forgetting the old man was there to witness the whole thing. "You did right to warn him." Ellchant said. He pointed to the man in red who watched Aris and he nodded to the young man in thanks. Aris nodded back. The two fighters regrouped and they walked off together with the cheering crowd in tow in the direction of a tavern. Aris knew it would be a long night of celebratory drinking for them and their fans.

"The winner was only a moment from death." Aris said.

"So are we." Ellchant said under his breath, his eyes still scanning the dispersing crowd.

"What did you say?" Aris asked, though his question actually demanded that Ellchant's comment merely be repeated, as opposed to being uttered again for lack of clarity.

"I can't believe someone would kill another person over money." Aris said when Ellchant did not respond.

"Well you saw what I pulled out of Gridel's pouches. That's just the way some people are. They only care about what money can buy them. It's sad."

"I just don't understand it." Aris commented.

"Neither do I." Ellchant said smiling slightly.

As Aris' words drifted off he turned to see that the dark beauty that had judged the wrestling match was approaching them. He admonished himself once again for not noticing her. She was some sight, he thought to himself. She was tall, possibly only three or four inches shorter than Aris and dark skinned with an even tan that only complimented her beauty. Her skin was smooth Aris noted as he looked at her bare arms for they were exposed from a slim fitting black top that bore no sleeves. She walked with a graceful gait and her loose-fitting pants fluttered in the breeze revealing long shapely legs.

She smiled at them as she approached her teeth a gleaming white, a bright contrast to her dark skin. Her black wavy hair was blowing in the wind curving around her heart-shaped face. She had gorgeous deep brown eyes Aris thought as the young lady stopped in front of them. Ellchant, wishing to stop his young friend's gawking elbowed him. Aris turned to look at his friend with a bit of surprise. Usually that was what Kallevick did, he thought. She must be a little older than Kalle, Aris thought. Damn she was something.

"Hello, I am Rastel Marden. Welcome to Hope." The young woman said offering her hand to Ellchant.

Ellchant took her hand and shook it gently. "I am Ellchant Pendergast and this is Aris Desarta." Ellchant smiled and then elbowed Aris again when the young man didn't move and whispered, "Quit drooling," through clenched teeth.

Aris took Rastel's hand and shook it. "A pleasure to meet you, Rastel."

She smiled and winked at him. "What brings you to the city?" She asked politely turning back to Ellchant.

"A mission of most dire importance." Ellchant said, his face becoming serious.

Rastel's smile faded and her head tilted slightly in curiosity, her eyes squinting in the afternoon sun.

94

"Can I be of any help?" She asked with genuine concern.

Aris was shocked at Ellchant's candor and he looked at his old friend as if to ask him if he was sure about telling this woman about their mission. Yes Rastel was beautiful, damn was she beautiful, but could she be trusted with such weighty information?

"We are in search of a place to stay." Ellchant said.

"That is your dire mission? A quest for nice accommodations?" Rastel asked confused.

"No, but we do need a place to stay. A place for four." Ellchant's voice trailed off as his gaze swept across the emptying area. "We seem to have lost our other two friends in the crowd."

Aris turned to look behind them and realized that they had indeed lost Kallevick and Braeburn and he hoped that they would catch up soon. Something in the old man's voice didn't sit right with him and he knew that whether or not Rastel knew of their mission they would have to enter that dark forest soon. The young woman smiled at him. It distracted him slightly but he couldn't shake the feeling of fear from creeping into his chest.

*   *   *   *   *   *   *   *   *   *   *

Braeburn and Kallevick mulled through the dense crowds and pushed their way through to a few vendors that had booths set up near a tavern. They walked silently for a while and looked through the tables set up with all kinds of wares. Kallevick couldn't help being reminded of the Nari Fair and the knife that Aris bought from Darigo's. He smiled to himself. So stubborn, he thought.

Braeburn pulled out a garment of silky material and ran his fingers over it. He put it back in the box and took a look at some tunics that lay neatly folded in a box right next to him. He lifted the first one on the top of pile that was marked with a strange currency symbol and ran the cloth against his cheek. He closed his eyes and ran the fabric along himself again to enjoy the soft material. Oh I wish I was rich, the elf silently mused.

"You need a weapon, Braeburn." Kallevick said interrupting the elf's thoughts. "What are you doing?" Kallevick's brow furrowed and he passed the Ellion a strange glance.

Braeburn promptly dropped the tunic back in the pile and placed one hand behind his back. "What did you say?" Braeburn said looking through a pile of knitted cloaks.

"I said you need a weapon." He repeated, the look of slight disbelief not moving from his features.

"Aside from my wit and extreme good looks?" The Ellion shrugged.

Kallevick's face softened and he shot the elf a mean glance.

"In fact I'd like to see you fight. I don't think you'd last very long in battle. On second thought you might. You could starve a besieged strong hold with that appetite of yours," Kallevick said laughing.

"I can hold my own you know." Braeburn said defiantly. He never turned away from his friend and continued to walk, only backwards this time so he could face the young man. "Besides, what makes you think that there will just be a weapons booth sitting around here?" Braeburn stumbled as he backed up into a booth holding several dozen knives and short swords. One of the tips of the blades jabbed him lightly in the back of the leg.

"Ah!" The Ellion yelped.

"That booth maybe?" Kallevick pointed.

"Watch yourself there, my good man." The vendor said nervously.

"Do you also sell leg armor?" Braeburn asked quietly before Kallevick reached the booth and could over hear him.

"Why you're, you're…" The man stammered in surprise. "Oh, you're not a man at all are you?"

"Yeah, I've been trying to tell him that too but he just won't listen to me." Kallevick responded as he reached them.

"Excuse me, you better watch it boy." Braeburn warned. "I've been known to be fairly lethal when necessary."

"You. You're an Ellion." The vendor remarked, his eyes widening in amazement.

The elf looked at him, his swaggering smile blossoming on his face like a well recognized hero of the day. "I am."

"Sorry to bother you." Kallevick remarked to the salesman as he pushed the elf away from the booths before his friend could regale the vendor with his overbearing charm. "Not this time."

"I can't help it if people are amazed at me when they realize what I am."

"Amazed that you're a stomach that can walk and talk?"

"Amazed that I am an elf!" Braeburn said flashing a grin.

"An elf who has a taste for food, but no taste in clothing."

"Hey that tunic was very soft!" Braeburn said defensively.

"Even though that was a man's tunic, and I am not entirely sure it was, pale pink is definitely not your color." Kallevick chuckled.

"Just because your tastes in clothes are unrefined doesn't mean that I should be teased. Besides I could think of quite a few ladies who would take quite a good long look at a good looking guy such as yourself in a fine tunic like that one."

For a brief moment Kallevick thought about himself wearing the shirt and wondered what kinds of women might like that sort of thing.

"Even if I wanted to I don't have enough money anyway." The young man said suddenly on the defensive and taken a bit off guard by the fact that the elf now had the upper hand.

"You're right though. I do need a weapon." Braeburn said.

Kallevick exhaled in relief at the change of subject. He never was good with women and he brushed away the thought.

"Axe." The elf said moving in a brisk pace towards the next vendor.

The young man shook his head.

"What do you want me to do, just use my bare hands?" Braeburn said with annoyance.

"What about your wit? If we come across any threat in the future you could use your charm." Kallevick paused and looked around. "But for those moments when it fails you could use this." Kallevick said walking over to series of staffs that leaned against the outside wall of the tavern. Each one bore it's own mark, a symbol of the maker.

"Those are thirty a piece. Good for walking, or defense." The vendor said walking over to Kallevick from behind the tabletops of merchandise. With him he carried an old staff, worn and green, the dyes used to color it faded with age. "This one I've had for about twenty years and boy let me tell you this thing has saved my life more than once."

Braeburn put an axe head that he was examining down and walked over to Kallevick, picking up a red staff almost as tall as his six-foot height.

"That one is dyed with red from the bulb fruits."

"Bulb fruits?" Kallevick asked. "You mean those big red sour fruits that are in the entrance to the city?"

"Yup, those are them. Also called akale fruit."

Braeburn's face scrunched up in disgust. "Too sour for me. Oh. What have we here?" He said lifting a bronze colored staff with a central hand wrap made of a forest green leather. "I'll take this one," Braeburn said paying the man.

"That is made of a good quality hard wood, from some of the strongest wood to be found in Obadia."

Kallevick wanted to say something, say that he was from that area, but something within him held him back. He wondered what it was as he watched the vendor thank Braeburn and the elf swung the staff with deadly precision.

Braeburn stopped when he noticed Kallevick watching.

"You are thinking about Aris again."

The statement was not entirely false and Kallevick must have had a vulnerable expression on his face, for the elf came up to him and placed his arm around his friend as they began to walk.

"First of all, thanks for helping me pick this out." He said looking at his new purchase with satisfaction. "You know Kalle, you have to let Aris go."

Kallevick looked at his companion as if to ask what he meant.

Braeburn's tone lowered and he leaned in so no one would hear him.

"When it comes down to it, if your brother is the one to bring mankind back to the gods, he is going to have to face Dinemid alone."

"I know, I just…" Kallevick began.

"Kallevick," the elf said as they stopped their pace. The elf turned to face him and looked him straight in the eye. "I know how much you love your brother and I know that you want to protect him, but you must let him go. He will be fine. Aris has the divine spark. He will succeed, I promise you and when he does the world will be right again."

Kallevick finally met Braeburn's gaze and he nodded in agreement. He silently promised himself that he would try. It would be hard letting Aris go but he knew the elf was right. As much as he wanted to help his brother he could only do so much. Ultimately Aris would have to face Dinemid alone and then even Ellchant could not help him. It was up to one, not four, to fulfill the prophecy.

Braeburn smiled at his friend and they continued to walk around the outer wall of the tavern. As they rounded the corner of the wall they saw Ellchant and Aris walking in the same direction as them and the elf trotted over. Kallevick began sinking into his thoughts again and it wasn't until he heard the shout from his brother that he snapped out of it.

"Hey Kalle, you coming?" Aris yelled from across the way.

Kallevick began to walk over and for the first time since they left home he felt calm. He knew his brother would be all right, at least he hoped and he promised himself that he would try to let Aris find his way.

CHAPTER 13

Aris adjusted in his seat as he peeled off the skin of a ripe green fruit with his knife. Ellchant was eating a bowl of soup as Braeburn and Kallevick sat with their own plates empty and talked quietly to each other.

"It sure was nice of Rastel to set us up here with a room at the Inn." Aris commented, slicing a piece of fruit and biting into it. "Though it was a bit overpriced."

"You're telling me, I was the one who paid for it. She certainly has done well with her position as Judge of the city though." Ellchant said dipping some bread into the thick broth. "She seems to be a fair Judge and she will do her namesake well. The Marden's are a good family."

"I only wish I could have met her father. It would be great to have met an actual explorer. It is a shame that he passed away." Aris said more to himself than to Ellchant. He took a long glance around the room and wondered. He was actually outside Obadia. Here he was surrounded by groups of people who had been to all those unknown regions that he could only imagine in the mysterious landscapes of his mind. Those outlying lands were their homes and the settings of their own adventures and tales. He could hardly believe it. It didn't feel real.

"Yes it is." The old man agreed, tucking his long hair behind his ear and blowing on a spoonful of soup.

Kallevick sat across from Aris, his chair turned and quietly pointed to a woman in the far corner of the room. "Now she's a beauty."

From across the room a group of finely dressed ladies sat surrounding the woman in question and chatted quietly among themselves. Kallevick sighed to himself.

"You almost wish you bought that tunic now, don't you?"

Kallevick passed Braeburn a mean glance.

"And I'm sure that you would feel comfortable just walking over and introducing yourself."

"Sure, why not?" Braeburn responded, his face light with confidence. "In fact…" The elf began to rise from his seat.

"All right sit down. I concede."

101

Braeburn chuckled to himself and sat back down in his chair.

Kallevick rotated his chair to face the rest of the group as the elf shook his head and laughed to himself.

Braeburn followed suit and shifted his seat.

"You think she was beautiful Kalle, you should have seen Rastel. Oh, she was was so…" Aris said, searching for the right word.

"Exquisite." Ellchant finished. "Well I was beginning to become concerned when Aris stopped breathing and I had to remind him to do so."

"You elbowed me."

"You were drooling like a baby."

"Could you blame me?" Aris asked, his comment dripping with truth.

"No, not really. Rastel's mother was just like her, beautiful and kind."

"How is it that you two are so inept with women? The elf chimed in. "Was your father a shy man? I mean, surely he didn't charm your mother by drooling and passing out. If that were the case it would be a wonder if your parents ever had any children."

"Well Aris is the man born of faith. Perhaps there is another meaning to that phrase." The old man smiled. He looked at the young man and noted the slight impression of a frown momentarily cross Aris' face.

"Can I get you anything else gentlemen?" Came a deep warm voice from above their heads.

A dark skinned man, much darker in tone than Rastel's skin stood above them with a tray full of dishes in his hand. He wore a simple but finely pressed apron and a gray tunic with a few deep food stains on the breast pockets. Apparently the food he served had spilled on his shirt one too many times and would not wash clean. He had a bright smile and a gray beard with white tones sprinkled throughout. His hair was trimmed short and neat.

"I think that will be all, thank you." Ellchant said smiling up at the man.

Aris had never seen too many people of such dark skin and he silently wondered to himself at how many colors the gods had to choose from when they made the world. Certainly the palate of nature was exquisite enough, but to even stretch it into the skin tones of men and women was a very beautiful, artistic gesture.

"Please forgive me if I am being slightly bold here, but may I join you all for a moment. This tray is getting very heavy and I need to rest my feet." He stood for another minute waiting as Ellchant looked at his companions silently as if to ask if they minded. The old man eyed each of his companions and Aris silently wondered again about whether or not Ellchant should have said anything to Rastel in the first place.

Braeburn stood and pulled up an extra chair, taking the tray from the man's hands and setting it down on the empty table from which he stole the seat.

"Thank you." The man said sitting with a heavy thud into the chair. "These hardwood floors can hurt your feet after a while."

"Tell us about it." Kallevick said. "We used to have hardwood floors in our house."

The man didn't seem to respond but Aris suddenly had visions of the house and his father flashed through his mind.

"What is your name, my good friend?" Ellchant asked, pushing his half-empty bowl to the side and biting a piece of bread.

"Oh, I must apologize, I never introduced myself. My name is Hildred. Melchor Hildred."

"Pleased to meet you, Melchor." Aris said shaking the man's strong hand. They all exchanged hands and Melchor sat back in his chair, stretching for a moment before beginning to talk again.

"I am a friend of Rastel's and she told me about you all and asked if I would speak with you." His face became despondent.

"Speak with us?" Ellchant said putting the bread down on the table, his eyes squinting at this change of conversation.

"Yes. I have some vital information that may help you on your journey." Melchor said leaning in. "I was told to keep quiet as Rastel mentioned that you were attempting to move relatively unnoticed along the way. I will be brief as I have a lot of work to catch up on in the kitchen." He leaned in further and the foursome leaned in with him so as to close a tight circle around the table.

"You know, some say that the world has become a void."

The four companions each exchanged glances with one another silently confirming that Melchor's cryptic speech was a bit unsettling.

"How do you mean?" Braeburn asked.

"A void where doubt reigns in the hearts of men." Melchor said as if the glances had not registered. "The land is falling apart around us and most of us care not to notice. Giants succumbing to the corruption of money and even the forests are wasting away into nothing. Our world is dying and nothing seems to be slowing the process." His face made no indication of softening and his words were harsh and dark.

"You all know of something horrible coming, something that could destroy us if nothing is done. I believe that you are on a quest from the gods, although Rastel never said anything directly about it." He pointed to Aris, his deep black eyes penetrating the young man. "You are the messenger from Galebraith, come to put Dinemid's corruption to an end."

Kallevick sat back, as did his brother and he looked to Aris who sat with his eyes wide in utter shock at this revelation. How could he know of their mission? Was he a prophet?

"You are correct, my friend." Ellchant said, putting his hand on Melchor's shoulder. "We are on the trail of a band of goblin's who stole Orsidire from Nari Island."

"You are not on the trail of a band, you are on the trail of a thief."

"What did you say?" Ellchant remarked.

"You are after a single man. He has been here. He is traveling alone and he kept mumbling the word, Magbo, which is to say in the Scarth, or Rundagg tongue, Malcom. I believe he is a goblin in disguise to hide his face from the eyes of men so as to pass through unnoticed."

"A goblin traveling alone, cloaked in dark magic? There was a raiding party that passed through the island heading west through Obadia and we assumed that they must have passed through here as well. But Rundagg don't travel alone."

"They rarely come near us but after the whispers we heard from the east we put our guards on alert. When no sign of them came we lowered our defenses. The fact that he spoke with the Scarth tongue surprised me and I had a strong feeling that the gods were sending me a message. Something about this character didn't sit right with me. He signed in the Innkeeper's log as Malcolm something or other. I looked at the log with my friend in the sitting area and neither of us could read the writing of the last name." Melchor explained.

"A Rundagg traveling alone. Was he on foot?"

"Yes. He said he lost his party and was only a few days behind them. He also said that his horse died a few miles outside the city."

"He probably ate it." Braeburn said looking at Kallevick as he remembered the giant.

"When was this?"

"Maybe a day or so ago. I mentioned it to Rastel, but she didn't seem to be bothered by it, so the red guards never had a chance to search his room. When she told me about you all." The waiter indicated with his hand waving around the table. "And that you would all be here in the dining hall at dinner time I knew I had to talk with you."

"The Rundagg worship Dinemid don't they?" Kallevick asked.

Braeburn nodded yes.

"Then this Malcolm is heading right for the Halls of Altamare with Orsidire." Ellchant said leaning back in his chair, his eyes open wide, the spirals dilating as he did so.

"What makes you so certain that he is the one with the sword?" Aris asked.

"Rundagg do not travel alone and under the dark magic of Dinemid one would be able to disguise himself from the prying eyes of men. He could try and go through the western-most edge of the Kmorath but that would take too long. It would be quicker to pass through the city, stock up on supplies and then cut straight through the Barren Forest. Dinemid would help those who help him. We may be too late. The goblins have made a pact with Dinemid and they mean to free him with the sword."

"What could he offer them that they would give their loyalty to him?" Melchor asked finally piping into the conversation.

"I'm not sure but I don't think we have much time left. We must leave tomorrow as early as we can. The raiding party must be long gone by now but Malcolm must be only a day ahead of us. Hopefully we can catch up to him." Ellchant said.

"Why do you keep guards in your city?" Braeburn asked.

"Since the weakening of the gods we have held wrestling tournaments and have had guards to help protect us from the Rundagg, and…" He paused, his face turning grim. "Other things."

"What other things?" Aris asked.

"The wolf spirits." Melchor said, his face becoming taught with fear.

Aris looked at Ellchant whose eyes were now wide in terror and Aris knew he wouldn't have to fulfill the promise he made himself. His questions for the old man were answered. He began cutting another piece of fruit, not paying any attention to what he was doing and the knife slipped, slicing his hand. His hand began to bleed and it was Braeburn, not Kallevick who was the first to react by grabbing a cloth napkin and handing it to Aris.

"You all right?" Kallevick asked, concerned.

"Yeah, it's just a nick, I'll be fine." Aris said wiping the blood from his hand. He wrapped the cloth around his hand and Melchor stood.

"Let me get you a bandage for that and then I unfortunately have to get back into the kitchen, it's starting to get busy in here. I'll be right back." The tall man turned and walked across the room to a double hinged door that swung back and forth as he entered.

Aris looked at Ellchant, whose eyes were unblinking as if the old man were in shock. His face looked calm to the casual observer Aris mused, but something in his eyes made Aris' heart skip a beat. Aris' hand throbbed for a moment as Melchor returned to the table with a clean bandage made of white cloth.

"Here," he said handing the bandage to Aris, "Take this."

Aris took it and unwrapped his hand to apply the dressing.

"The gods of Galebriath."

'What is it, Aris?" Kallevick asked, leaning in to see his brother's hand.

"The man in disguise. His name is Fortune, Malcolm Fortune."

"What did you say?" Ellchant asked, finally snapping out of his stare.

"Look." Aris said raising the napkin for the four of them to see. There in blood, as if written out on a page was the word fortune.

"You are the one, Aris." Melchor said, his face awestruck.

Aris sat back in his seat feeling suddenly light-headed and his eyes rolled back into their sockets. He slumped in his chair and without warning he fell off and hit the floor.

CHAPTER 14

In the darkness of the Barren Forest a shadowy figure ran slipping through the trees like a gust of wind. The black shroud he wore fluttered in the gait of his movement and in his arms he carried a bundle of furs and animal skins which contained a most precious item. The figure slowed to catch its breath and turned to face the direction of the desert city which he had only left a day or so before. His face was hidden within the shroud as plumes of cold air emitted from under the dark hood. His clothes were shabby and worn as if they were the only ones he owned and never took the time to repair them.

The moon was high and full in the sky and he turned once more to face the direction in which he ran. Not daring to place his bundle on the ground he shook his head furiously causing the hood of his shabby cloak to fall about his shoulders. His knotted and mangled hair stuck up in all different directions and his eyes pierced through the dirt on his face to get a better look at the ground. He adjusted his footing to steady himself and whispered out in a horrible tongue. He bore the face of a man. A most common looking man and it was that face that had kept him from being discovered while in the city. He was rubbed his unshaven chin along the bundle to scratch himself. The thought of having to bathe while he was in the city made him shiver and he now reveled in the fact that he didn't have to worry about it.

He closed his black eyes and he muttered once more unintelligibly in the strange tongue. In an instant his face was distorted, the features becoming exaggerated and stretched into a hideous form. Horns sprung from his temples and from what was once his hairline. His skin turned a sickly green and a beak-like snout protruded to replace his puffy chapped lips. His true Rundagg face was revealed and he smiled a grin full of sharp twisted teeth like crudely made beads that hung on knotted strings in his mouth. He laughed at the full moon, a harsh raucous laugh that seemed to crack the frigid air about him. He closed his molten red eyes and the laugh was cut short by the sound of howling wolves. His eyes shot open and the sound was striking, even to his pointed ears.   It bore the natural chords that most wolves used but had an undertone to it that sent shivers up the creature's back. The sounds were those of wolves but also the screams of those they hunted. The creature stood for another moment closing his eyes and sending a silent prayer up to his most gracious master.

In the deepest black of an abandoned hall a rumbling and malevolent voice broke through the darkness.

"Come quickly, my most faithful servant." It said.

The creature pulled the hood over its head, the horns piercing through the fabric and he ran as fast as his pronged feet would carry him.

*   *   *   *   *   *   *   *   *   *   *   *

Aris awoke with a start and sweat was gathered in beads on his forehead. He sat upright and after a moment he looked around himself in the darkness to see that he was in a still room sitting in bed and covered up in warm blankets.

"Aris, you're up." Braeburn said from the corner of the room.

Aris looked, his eyes scanning the room for the source of the voice. Once they settled on the shadowy figure his posture relaxed and he leaned back in the bed resting his weight on his elbows. He took a few deep breaths and swallowed hard.

"I'm thirsty." He said with a cracked and hoarse voice.

Braeburn stood up from a chair that he had been sitting in and walked over to him pouring the young man a glass of fresh water from a pitcher that sat next to the bed. He handed it to Aris who drank it down eagerly as if he had been dying of thirst. Aris handed the empty glass back to the elf and he looked down to see that he was dressed in sleeping garments.

"Thank you. What happened in the dining hall? Where are we? Where is Ellchant?" The urgency in his voice was unmistakable and the elf patted him gently on the shoulder to calm him down.

"Woah, easy there hero. Your brother and Ellchant went to get you some food after you passed out on us in the dining hall. They should be back in a few minutes. Right now we're in your room. Kalle and I are staying in the room across the hall and Ellchant is staying in here with you."

Aris turned to his left and saw another bed and then laid back down and looked out of the slatted window to see the bright moon shining silver and white in a cloudless sky. The stars were like teardrops pinpointed in a backdrop of velvet blue. It was much the same as it had been the first night of their journey and Aris wanted to see Ellchant more than ever.

"When are they coming back, Braeburn?" He asked without turning to face his friend.

"Soon."

"I heard a voice, a sinister voice in the darkness of my dreams. What was it?"

"It was the voice of Dinemid." Ellchant said as he shut the door quietly behind him. Kallevick was already in the room and he came and sat on the side of the bed feeling Aris' forehead. The young man sat up.

"His fever has gone down." Kallevick said as he looked up at Ellchant.

"Good," the old man said handing Kallevick a wash cloth. "Put this on his head."

The cool water that the cloth was soaked in soothed Aris' head and for the first time he noticed that he had a mild headache.

"Lie back down now, son." Ellchant said. "Get some rest. We'll leave tomorrow morning when you're well again."

Aris did as he was told and lay back down. The sweat had now dried and he pulled the warm covers over his arms. He felt comfortable and the sound of Ellchant's voice soothed him as he drifted off. As he was swept down the river of dreams and memory, the voice soon transformed into his father's and with a sigh he sunk into a deep sleep.

*   *   *   *   *   *   *   *   *

Aris woke again periodically throughout the night. He did not stir but lay silently, his eyes opening to look around the room and he listening intently to the old man's breathing. The slow steady sound of Ellchant's breath, along with the room that was filled with a calming yet vibrant blue light kept reminding him of a river. He closed his eyes once more and found himself drifting down that river again, the river that had carried him to sleep hours before.

111

In the darkness of his mind he saw a far off place he had never been to and a mountaintop. In its center, on the highest slope he saw the gaping mouth of a roaring waterfall. The water was clear, beautifully clear as if the liquid was molten crystal. He was flying over the landscape watching as the ground rushed past him hundreds of feet below. He flew downward to where the water met the base of the mountain and it plumed with enormous gusts of water against the stiller water that flowed outward. He plunged headlong into it and as he burst out from the rushing waters he was reborn and his spirit took shape again in something other than human form. He felt alive inside. More alive than he ever had before. It was as if something within him was awakened from a long dead sleep.

He felt the rush of the wind about him as he gathered speed and soared off again into the sky. He wanted to look down at the landscape once more but could not for the air about him was so clean, crisp and warm that he could not help but close his eyes and smile. He flew forward, his eyes opening again and he raced alongside a dragon that appeared from out of the air.

They raced and raced as the dragon's form changed and morphed as they went, speeding at an intense rate, faster and more graceful than any horse. Then without warning the dragon disappeared and Aris was falling, falling faster than he was flying only seconds before. Through the winds that howled through his ears he heard the voice of his father shouting. He was calling Aris' name and screaming at the top of his lungs. Aris looked down for the first time and as the ground rushed up to meet him he saw the face of his father, bloody and bruised.

"What have you done to me?" Cabral shouted.

Aris' heart stopped beating for a moment when the call came once more. But it was not his father's voice. It was the voice of Dinemid and it was the most horrible thing he had ever heard. He wanted to scream in absolute terror but his voice failed him. Faster and faster he fell until the ground rushed up to meet him and at last he hit, his body crumbling under the weight of his own gravity. There he lay, unable to move.

Aris' eye's shot open, scanning the room and not daring to turn or move a muscle for fear that the voice would return once more if he did so. Sweat came once more from his brow and though he wished to the gods that he could scream, his voice would not come to him. He closed his eyes and took a deep breath trying desperately to get the image of his father's face from his mind. Aris sat up in his bed as Ellchant shifted and rolled over. The young man placed his feet on the cold hardwood floor.

He turned and poured himself a glass of water and gulped it down. It was cold but it would do no good to keep drinking because the water would never quench the thirst that was deep inside of him. He sat for a moment and looked out of the window to which he noticed for the first time that their room had a balcony. He looked around for a moment in the deep blue of the moonlight and found a pair of slippers placed near the bedside and he put them on. He walked noiselessly over to the glass door that opened out onto the balcony and shut it quickly, rushing back to the bed to rip the covers off. He wrapped himself in them and slipped out of the door before Ellchant turned over again in his sleep.

Once he was on the balcony he moved to the right and found that there was a narrow walkway that ran parallel to the outer wall of the city. This must be the uppermost tier of walkways that he had seen earlier that day, he thought silently. The railings sat about two to three feet high and came up to where Aris' hip would be had he not been wrapped snugly in the blanket. He walked to an open area where the wall jutted out into a lookout post and here he made himself a seat on the outer wall, letting his feet dangle off the edge.

He looked out onto the desert and saw that the silver hued sand dunes shone like ocean waves in the blue moonlight. It was a beautiful sight to behold. The moon was ripe like a silver fruit and the stars appeared to be budding as if the whole sky were a giant tree growing them on its cosmic limbs. The line of the edge of the Barren Forest was no longer gray but black in the lunar beams. He wondered what lay beyond that ominous forest and what in turn was waiting for him in the darkness of the future.

He heard the sound of breathing coming from behind him and he shifted suddenly, wishing he had his knife with him. He turned to see Ellchant walking slowly and groggily up from the walkway toward him. Aris slumped back down in relief and he looked out on to the desert landscape once more. The old man sat down next to him and allowed his sandals to dangle over the edge of the outer wall next to Aris' slippered feet.

"Couldn't sleep?" The old man asked yawning. He rubbed his eyes. The moonshine was bright causing his spiraled pupils to flare in adjustment. His irises were ablaze with intense silver. He adjusted his seating and pushed his hair out of his face. It was messed up and for this Aris smiled slightly.

"What is it?" The old man asked sleepily.

"Nothing." Aris said turning back to the view.

"What troubles you Aris?" Ellchant said quietly, his voice deep and soothing.

At these words a lump worked its way into Aris' throat.

"I miss my family. I miss Mafre, even though she could drive me crazy sometimes. I miss the way she laughed. I miss watching my mother knit and the way she gave me a hug goodnight. And I miss my father."

Ellchant nodded and looked down the edge of the wall to the desert floor below. "I miss them too. I'd known your parents for years before you, your brother and sister were born. It's hard to believe they're really gone."

"I just," Aris said, the tears running down his cheeks in thin lines. His voice broke and he began to cry harder. "I just know I'll never see them again and I don't know if I can handle that."

Ellchant placed his arm around his young friend's shoulder and Aris leaned on his shoulder and cried.

"Thank the gods that you found Kalle and I." Aris said sniffling. "I don't know what we would have done without you coming for us."

"You would have moved on. Slowly but surely you both would have moved on. Suffering is a part of life Aris, and though your family was taken from you earlier than any of us had anticipated you would have eventually had to have said goodbye, and come with me to find Dinemid."

Aris' head raised to give Ellchant a cold stare and with a harsh pull he moved himself out of his friend's grasp.

"I know I would have to leave eventually but I never wanted to leave my father that way. I didn't want to leave any of them that way! You didn't see them Ellchant. They were beaten and tortured! Tied up like criminals." His hand went to his eyes trying hard to hold back the tears. They were like the waterfall from his dream, crystal clear and pure.

"I can't believe they're gone, they can't be gone." He sobbed and hit Ellchant's shoulder with his clenched fist.

Ellchant took the blow, knowing the young man was in pain. Aris swung his legs over the other side of the wall and stood, the blanket falling to the ground forgotten.

"Why did they have to die Ellchant, Why!? I know I could have done something. I should never have left home that day. Kalle and I should have never left home and we would all be alive."

"Aris, you would have been killed with them had you and Kalle stayed behind. There was nothing you could have done. Besides, you are the one. We need you. You are the only one who can do this, the only one who can end this madness before the world is destroyed."

"I don't want your damn mission! I didn't ask to be some hero. I want my family back!" Aris said punching Ellchant hard in the side. The old man groaned with the impact. "It's all your fault! If Dad hadn't gone to see you, he could have taken Mom and Mafre and met up with me and Kalle at the camp and they wouldn't be dead right now!"

Ellchant stood, his own blanket falling to the ground as Aris punched his friend in utter frustration and crying out in pain. The old man stood like a statue accepting the strikes as he waited for Aris to calm down.

"It's all your fault! It's all your fault!" Aris screamed with all of his might. But deep down he knew it wasn't and soon his knocks at the old man began to get weaker and weaker until he fell to his knees, sobbing. "Why couldn't I save them? Why?"

Ellchant went down on his knees and held his friend, rocking him back and forth.

"Why did I say those things to him? Why?"

"You were angry and you didn't understand. You didn't mean it."

"But I did," Aris bawled. "When I said I didn't want to see him again I meant it and when I saw what happened I couldn't take it back. I couldn't take it back. Now it's too late and I can't tell him how sorry I am and how much I love him." The tears welled in his eyes and he cried softly.

Ellchant' eyes welled up as he rocked the young man back and forth in a comforting embrace. The old man wiped Aris' face and the sobs began to lessen. Aris sniffed and Ellchant held out a hanker chief to which the young man took it and wiped his eyes.

"You have a future ahead of you. A future that demands that you be independent of your father. They all loved you and they would forgive you for your shortcomings."

"I just miss him so much Ellchant." Aris croaked. "It's not that I miss Mom or Mafre any less, it's just…. I can't help but remember the way I left him. I wish I could take it back and undo what I said."

"But you can't. You don't have that power and you must live with your past. You must embrace the future. You can't blame me and you can't blame the gods for your position in life. You just have to accept it and do what you can with what you've been given. If you say no to a single part of the life you've had you will unravel what makes you who you are. You are your pain and your suffering. Remember this, Aris, when you face Dinemid."

He took the young man's face in his grasp and looked deeply into his young friend's eyes. Aris' pupils went wide and he stared right back at the old man, his gaze intense.

"You are the messenger from Galebraith. You were chosen to do this thing because the gods know what kind of man you are. The greater your pain the greater your calling will be. Do not fear the adventure. Live it."

Ellchant looked at him for another moment and then kissed Aris' forehead as a father kisses his beloved infant child goodnight. Aris' eyes closed and a single tear streamed down his cheek, as if to mark that he had found a bit of peace among the wreckage of heartache around him.

Ellchant lifted his friend up to his feet and gathered the blankets. He wrapped Aris up and then himself.

Aris looked out into the darkness of the forest and silently wondered if he was capable of fulfilling Ellchant's beliefs. He could feel the eyes of the old man at his back.

"Is there any chance we'll make it?"

"Surrender yourself and the gates of the universe will open to you."

Aris turned to look at his aged friend. Ellchant's eyes glowed with warmth and life. All Aris could do was nod in understanding. He exhaled and stepped forward.

"Let's get back inside where it's warmer." Ellchant said quietly.

They crossed the walkway and welcomed the heat of the room as they entered into it.

Aris shut the door and Ellchant settled back into his bed.

"Ellchant." Aris said as he lay back down.

"Yes?" He replied without turning to face him.

"Do you really think that I can do it, face Dinemid alone?"

"I have all faith in you my boy." He said and fell fast asleep.

Aris lay in bed quietly listening again to the steady sound of Ellchant's breathing and soon he fell into a heavy dreamless sleep.

CHAPTER 15

The sun rose much too early for Aris' liking and the wake-up call he received from Kallevick wasn't all too friendly either. His brother came into the room and started packing up their supplies at a brisk pace and gave no regard to the fact that Aris slept or felt any reason to be hushed about it.

"In a hurry are we?" Aris asked swiveling his feet off to the side of the bed and walking over toward him.

"Ellchant said we have to get moving and I think we better not get him mad."

Aris was reminded of Kallevick's comment about their father the day they went to the Nari Fair and he recalled the night before, noting that Ellchant didn't get much sleep. He decided Kallevick was probably right. He dressed quickly and strapped his sword to his back.

They walked outside where they found Braeburn taking three of their horses back from the little boy Orago and his father Jeld.

"Are we ready to go? Where is Ellchant?" Aris asked looking around the crowded streets.

"I am here." Came the reply as Ellchant strode up to them on his horse. He looked mighty and he now adorned the leather chest-plate armor that their father had made for him. "Put these on, you'll need them." He said throwing them each a set of thick leather arm guards. "If you require anything else I suggest you find a vendor quickly and get it. We're already running later than I had planned."

"Sorry for sleeping so late." Aris called up to him sarcastically, pulling the hood of his cloak over his head.

"Gather your things. We have to leave," was his only response.

They grabbed what supplies they had, stocking up on rations with what money they had left and made for the outer wall of the city that faced the edge of the Barren Forest. They all were looked at strangely for they all bore weapons out in the open and each wore some form of armor or another. Aris also considered that no one was to ride on horseback through the densely populated city. The onlookers gazed as if the riders

119

were part of a procession of performers and they watched in curiosity as they neared the outer wall.

"Why are we heading for this side of the city?" Kallevick asked. "I thought that the gate on the other side was the only way in and out of Hope."

"These people have barricaded themselves in to protect against threats from the north. When we leave here they will be able to move freely in and out of their beloved home from this side of the city as well." Ellchant answered. "Once we enter the dark forest they will have no need to fear the lands above them."

Then in a sudden burst of magic Ellchant turned and thrust his hand forward sending a lightning bolt shooting through his palm. The bolt hit the wall and exploded with a blinding flash. The light dissipated and revealed a newly formed gate in the outer wall of the city. The crowd gasped in amazement and wonder at the spectacle. Aris felt strong and as his companions strode ahead of him he felt the words of the previous night sink into his heart. Ellchant's voice reverberated in his mind.

"Do not fear the adventure. Live it."

The portcullis was raised and the four riders bolted across the last of the distance between them and the open desert. Aris was the last to exit and before he crossed the threshold he turned his white horse aside to face the awestruck crowd. He lowered his hood to reveal his face.

"This city," he called out in a powerful voice "Is called the City of Hope. For it is the last place in Andellius where men believe in the gods. When we return this place will be called Victory. For Dinemid will fall by my hand and the world will be right again!"

The audience roared in elation and cheered as Aris galloped at top speed out of the gate, white sword drawn and held high in the air. They knew now who had come to stay in their beloved city and he was a messenger of the gods. He would deliver a message to Dinemid and the wolf spirits, and that message would be death.

*   *   *   *   *   *   *   *   *   *   *   *

They rode for some time before they reached the edge of the forest. It was early afternoon and the sun was hidden behind some clouds, an unusual sight to be witness to in Lania Desert. Before them the stark gray trees stood like ancient citadels of an abandoned castle, ominous and bleak.

"I don't like the look of it one bit." Braeburn commented.

"Neither do I." Kallevick agreed.

"We must keep moving." Ellchant said interrupting them, moving his mighty steed toward the nearest set of trees. He strode forward only another few paces and in a flash he was in the air as his horse reared up and neighed in a loud noise. Ellchant lost his balance and fell hard to the ground. When his companions moved to help him they too were thrown from their horses. The beasts cried out in terrified calls to one another as if they agreed amongst themselves that they were not going to enter the forest. Their voices scratched the ears of the foursome like metal grinding on a stone wall.

Once Aris regained his composure he stood and helped Ellchant to his feet. Braeburn moved to grab the reins of their steeds and whisper calming noises but nothing could soothe them. Kallevick tried his best but this own horse bucked wildly and snorted out in great fear. A loud screech emanated from Ellchant's horse and the others followed suit and shot off abruptly without their riders, screaming in terror as they fled. Ellchant managed to grab his pack just as his horse reared up again, bolting off to the east and towards the Kmorath with the others. Braeburn and Kallevick uncovered their ears, as the horse's calls grew fainter.

"Damn it!" Kallevick shouted as the four of them watched their rations and sleeping gear disappear with the horses into the far distance. "What do we do now?"

"We have to keep moving." Aris said adjusting the straps on his sword baldric.

"What sent them screaming off like that?" Kallevick said, his face full of concern. "I've never heard a horse make a noise like that before."

"Neither have I and I don't take it as a good sign." His brother commented.

"They hear the howls of the wolf spirits." Ellchant said wiping sand off of his blue robe. He turned and walked away from the group, heading into the forest alone.

"Ellchant, wait!" Aris shouted to his friend as he ran to catch up with the old man. Ellchant quickened his pace and Aris fell behind with the others.

"What's wrong? He's been acting strange all morning. He's barely said a word and when he does he's always curt?" Aris asked Kallevick as his brother and the elf neared.

"What exactly are the wolf spirits anyway?" Kallevick said turning to Braeburn.

The group had entered into the woods and the trees seemed to loom over them. In Obadia it was different and when the trees loomed over you it was like a protective canopy to keep the rain off of you when it was wet out and it gave some shade when the sun was hot, Kallevick thought. These trees leaned over with a bleak intensity as if they each meant to collapse on them as they walked. Their posture almost suggested that there were many eyes watching silently from above as they trekked on into the depths of the unknown region. To say the place looked unwelcome would be an understatement, he thought. Ellchant was far ahead of them and though the three of them wished to catch up, Aris and Kallevick wished to get any hint of information from their elven friend about the old man's strange behavior.

The light became more and more sparse as they walked further into the woods and Aris turned back to see that the desert floor was no longer visible. The last shades of silver dust had disappeared as they walked deeper into the unfriendly wood and Aris noted with discomfort that the shadows began to deepen. It was almost as if the trees were closing in around them. The forest seemed to be alive and it was swallowing them into its faithless, ominous bowels. Aris was momentarily distracted by the elf.

"The wolf spirits were once powerful soldiers of the gods." Braeburn expounded. "Mighty warriors who were made to protect the realm of Galebraith from any attack, should one arise. But they fell to the corruption of Dinemid and they too sought the power of the throne and wished to follow under his leadership once he had secured it. When Dinemid was cast out of Galebraith they were banished as well, transformed into horrendous wolves with the power of the evil god. For their treachery they were trapped here in these woods by the gods where they could not harm anyone." Braeburn explained.

"So we should have no worries then, right?" Aris said. "They cannot harm anyone you said." The young man hoped his words would be met with some form of consolation but the look in the Ellion's eyes only compounded the eerie foreboding.

"With the power of the gods waning the boundaries that keep them from escaping this forest have become weak and they have been known to leave here. Why do you think that the Desert City has regular guard posts? It's not just from roaming bands of Rundagg that they mean to protect themselves."

"We are going to have to face them. Aren't we?" Kallevick said, his face grim.

"Yes and that is why Ellchant is acting so strange. He knows as I do. They are merciless hunters and should one of us be killed by them, I…" Braeburn cut himself off.

"What is it?" Aris said pulling on the elf's arm to keep him from getting too far ahead of them. "What happens if we are killed by them?"

"We have to catch up to Ellchant. We don't want to get lost." The elf said, trying to break free of Aris' grasp and walk on.

"Braeburn, what happens if we are killed by them?" Aris said, pulling once again on the elf's arm, not allowing him to walk a single step further.

Braeburn turned and looked deep into Aris' eyes and then looked to Kallevick. His face more grave than the two young men had ever seen it before.

"If they hunt us down and kill us." He swallowed hard. "If they kill you, your soul will be hunted for eternity. No rest will come to you. No food. No comfort. They will never stop tracking you and just when you think that they are about to catch you and devour your flesh they fall behind again. They will forever be on your heels, their jaws snapping and biting with insatiable hunger. The moon will always be at her peak and the air will freeze like ice around you. The sound of their calls will drive you to madness."

"But it would end at some point would it not? Or you could fight back, right?" The elf shook his head.

"No. Your mind will become a slave to your fears. When they hunt, they hunt not for your flesh. They do not crave to taste you, but to break your mind. Because once you are dead they do not feed on your flesh. They feast on your soul."

CHAPTER 16

Ellchant pressed himself harder as he walked and with a final step he halted to catch his breath. The others had not quite caught up to him yet but he could hear their voices from a short distance away as he turned around and watched the grayed trees behind him. They must think I'm acting cold, he thought to himself. But he had to keep realistic about these things. He knew all too well what lay at the other edge of the forest and that they would all have to fight for their lives to get out.

He pushed the thought from his mind as Aris' face popped from one side of a tree. The others followed and he looked at the young man in the lead. He smiled at him and Aris' face puckered slightly in an expression of puzzlement. Ellchant knew that he couldn't fool the young man. Aris knew that something was amiss and he knew it bothered him. Ellchant's smile faded and he waved his hand to urge them on.

They walked for a long distance until the sun had set, at which point the old man slowed his pace and they all stopped for the evening. Braeburn gathered wood and lit a modest fire with Kallevick's set of Igris sticks. Aris sat, his back against a tree and he looked about.

"Just gray, gray and more gray." He mumbled to himself. He moved his hand to run it along the ground, hoping to grab a stray blade or two of grass and pulled it back when he found none. He looked down and realized that the forest floor was quite barren as if grazing animals had wiped it clean with their unsatisfied hunger. He looked up and could not find the stars for the canopy above him was so dense and knotted that he was surprised that Ellchant could tell the sun was setting when he called them all to a halt a moment before. He looked at the roots of a nearby tree and he noticed how they were twisted and mangled together like a beautiful clay sculpture that had been crushed under the frustrated hands of a potter.

"This place used to be beautiful once." Ellchant said, mirroring Aris' thoughts.

He looked at his old friend and he wondered how much of the world he had seen and how many stories he must have to tell. Kallevick sat down next to Aris and pulled his cloak about him.

"Aren't you cold over here?" He asked his brother, his brown eyes glowing with an orange hue from the fire.

"Not really. I'm actually comfortable here."

"I wouldn't sleep there if I were you." Braeburn's voice said from behind them. Aris jumped slightly as the elf walked around them, his arms full of branches.

"You scared me. What are you doing? The fire is good, it should stay lit for a few hours."

"We need to keep it going all night and it needs to be big." The elf responded.

"They hate fire and the bigger and hotter we keep it the further away they'll stay. We will also need to keep a watch tonight and every night until we get out of here. The fire must stay lit and we must be on the alert." Ellchant said from across the flames where he sat perched on a rock. The elf threw a few more branches onto the fire and it blazed red and gold in answer, the flames licking the cool air above.

"You better get closer." Braeburn said, piling the wood next to Ellchant. "Kalle, come with me to get more wood. We shouldn't stay too far away from the fire this time of night and I want to make sure that we have enough fuel to last us."

Kallevick stood and followed the elf off behind Aris. It was just the two of them now and Aris looked long and hard at the old man trying to silently guess at what he was thinking about. Ellchant sat and stared at the flames before him, meditating.

"Ellchant, are you alright?"

The old man raised his eyebrows and the look in his eyes made Aris wish that Kallevick and Braeburn would hurry back soon.

"I'm just tired." He yawned. "Perhaps you should take the first watch." He lay down and in an instant he was out.

Aris took off his cloak and walked around the fire to lay it over Ellchant. He sat back down closer to the fire and drew his white sword from its scabbard to examine it. It was beautifully crafted and he wondered what kind of metal was used to forge it. It wasn't of any type that he was familiar with. It weighed next to nothing and no metal that he knew of was white. I'm going to have to use this to get out of here aren't I, he thought to himself.

Braeburn and Kallevick returned each with an armload of wood and they piled it along with the other branches the elf had gathered previously.

"We should be all right as long as the fire burns all night." The elf commented to Aris.

"I never took the time to get a good look at this sword." Aris said running his fingers along the flat of the blade.

"Light, isn't it?" Braeburn said.

"Yes it is." Aris said looking hard at the elf. How could he know that? He hadn't held it as far as he knew.

"It's made of Khadian, a rare and precious metal."

"How do you know?" Aris said, his suspicion raising.

"Ellchant told me about it when we left Obadia."

Aris felt uneasy and he didn't believe the elf. He meant to take the sword, he thought. He pulled it close to him in a protective manner.

"Why don't you get some sleep Aris." Braeburn said. "You look tired."

"No, I'm fine." Aris said. He knew what the elf wanted. He wanted him to fall asleep so that he could take the sword and kill him. He stopped himself short, shocked at his own horrible thought. He looked to Kallevick who sat looking at him with eager eyes.

"Get some sleep brother, you must be tired." He said, his voice distant.

His own brother meant to take it from him too and he with the elf meant to stab him in his sleep. Aris stood quickly and held his weapon out in a defensive position.

Kallevick looked to Braeburn in a worried glance. The elf returned the gaze and they both stood, drawing their own weapons. Looking about them for any sign of danger they saw and heard nothing but watched as Aris stepped away from them. Aris' expression was full of terror and he would not break his stare. Kallevick had never seen Aris make a face like it before and he didn't like the look of it.

Aris stood stiff and tense, ready for his two so called friends to attack him. They had their weapons drawn and he looked hard at his brother. His own brother meant to kill him and as much as it scared him he wouldn't let that happen. He would kill Kallevick before he even laid a hand on him. His mind reeled from the thought and he shook his head trying to convince himself that his thinking was not straight. Perhaps he was having a nightmare, he thought? But when he opened his eyes Kallevick was nearing him and he had his own sword drawn and raised to strike. Or did he? Kallevick stepped even closer to him.

"No!" Aris yelled in a desperate cry and swung his white sword at Kallevick's head.

Kallevick ducked just in time and fell to the ground in shock, though it was more from the sudden and unexplained attack than from the actual impact with the ground.

"Aris! What are you doing?" Braeburn shouted.

"You can't have it! It's mine! You won't take it from me! I'll kill you both before you even lay a hand on me!"

Kallevick stood, his eyes full of fear. He looked to Braeburn who turned to the old man who lay asleep through the whole commotion. Without warning Aris swung at the elf and he too ducked to miss the blow.

Kallevick wished he could somehow reach his brother to let him know that he was safe. The flame of the fire seemed to intensify and it reflected red off of the blade. The next few moments blurred and time crept with a slow gait just as one's steps slow while running in waist high water. The white sword flashed from his right and Kallevick could hear the sluggish and distorted call of Braeburn's voice shouting the old man's name to wake him up.

Kallevick tried to duck again to miss the strike but the blade was sliding closer and closer to his neck as Aris' eyes glowed vibrant in the firelight, dancing with an evil brilliance. The white blade cut the air, inching it's way toward him and Kallevick was entranced, unable to move. He felt the cold metal touch just below his jaw line and at that instant he saw the old man stand up from the corner of his vision. Aris' cloak fell down about him and he raised his hand. Kallevick closed his eyes as he felt the cold steel bite ever so slightly into his neck and the old man shouted in a burst of audible power.

Then in a flash everything went white and Aris' sword was knocked from his grasp with an invisible hand. The cold biting of the steel into Kallevick's neck was no longer there and he reached for his throat to find that the side of his neck had a small scratch as if a tiny thorn had grazed him. Time regained its natural pace and Kallevick turned to see Ellchant breathing heavily. The young man fell to the ground and gasped inward swallowing huge gulps of air. His head swam for a moment and he mentally gathered himself.

Aris lay on the ground in a ball crying horribly as much from fear as he was from shock.

"I'm so sorry, Kalle. So sorry." He kept reiterating over and over, his words becoming unintelligible in between his sobs.

Braeburn put his hand on Kallevick's shoulder and silently looked at his friend to make certain he wasn't hurt.

"It's a scratch. I'll be fine." He said once he had gathered his breath.

Ellchant had walked to Aris and was holding him as he sobbed.

Braeburn comfortingly rubbed Kallevick's shoulder for a second then walked over to where the white sword lay discarded on the barren forest floor. He picked it up and tried to hand it to Aris, but the young man' face was buried deep in the old man's robe. He held it for a moment and then stuck it blade first into the ground next to the fire.

"I'm sorry, Kallevick. Are you okay?" Ellchant said looking to him.

Kallevick nodded an affirmative.

"I was trapped in my dreams and I couldn't wake up. The wolf spirits have already visited us this night. Aris was affected by their spells. He should be fine now. He thought you and Braeburn were trying to kill him. I know that sounds crazy but the wolf spirits can bend your thoughts and make you think things that aren't true." Ellchant explained.

"Is he going to be alright?" Kallevick asked.

"He will be. I have counteracted the spell and with some rest he'll be fine. Let's get that scratch mended and then get some sleep." Ellchant laid his hand over Aris who still lay curled up into a ball, crying and placed his other hand behind the young man's neck. He rubbed Aris' forehead and the young man's posture relaxed and he stretched out to lay in a deep sleep. Ellchant let the young man's head rest upon the ground and he covered him with the pale green cloak. He approached Kallevick. He looked at the wound and then placed his hand over it chanting a few words quietly into the air, his eyes closed.

Kallevick felt the scratch heal itself and he looked at Ellchant who had opened his eyes once more. "Get some sleep now, Kallevick." He heard Ellchant say and he felt the warmth of the old man's hand on his forehead and was instantly asleep. Braeburn caught him and he and the old man laid Kallevick down next to his sleeping brother. The elf looked around for a moment and then threw some more dried brush onto the fire. Without a word Ellchant did the same. They regarded one another for a moment and agreed that Ellchant should be the one to keep the first watch.

Braeburn lay down and tried to get as comfortable as he could, but the ground was hard and had no give. He looked at the two sleeping forms of Kallevick and Aris and wished to himself that he could sleep as soundly as they did. Just as he closed his eyes, he felt the warm hand of Ellchant on his forehead and in an instant he was in the land of sleep with his two young friends.

Ellchant sat, and tending to the fire he thought quietly to himself. *Well, we survived the first night. I only hope we can survive the next few as well,* he thought. He hoped to the gods that they were ready for what lay before them. Fighting Gridel seemed to be like a walk in the woods compared to what they were up against. He looked at the sleeping form of Aris and wondered at how the young man would handle himself when he reached Dinemid. Ultimately he would have to face the wicked god alone and though he wanted to help it would eventually come down to the two of them. He looked up at the knotted canopy of the forest. One thing was for sure though. It was going to be a long night.

CHAPTER 17

Ellchant's head shot from the ground and he inhaled sharply as he awoke. It was dark around him and he could barely see anything a few feet in front of him. He heard the call of wild things screaming out in the darkness. Oh no, the fire has gone out, he thought, and he jumped up suddenly to see a few sputtering embers coughing their last smoky breaths into the chilly air. He ran to the fire and grabbed a few stray branches that had been piled nearby and pushed them under the dying embers. He heard the howling in the distance and he looked at his companions' sleeping forms who lay breathing deeply. The clamor grew and he shifted his attention back to the branches. They began to burn more heavily and soon he was piling wood underneath the fire. He scanned the area and as the fire continued to grow the noises in the forest faded to nothing. He had almost invited trouble for the four of them, he thought. He should be able to keep this fire going until morning.

Once he had it blazing again he looked at Aris who lay on his side, his face shining orange in the night. He closed his eyes and his mind began to wander into a relaxed state and he began to dream. He opened his eyes again trying hard to keep himself awake and yet it didn't seem to work. He blinked and then threw some more branches and dry wood into the now inferno of a campfire and laid down, closing his eyes. He would be of no use in the morning if he had no sleep, he thought to himself. He looked one more time at the sleeping form of Aris and smiled. He has no idea what he can do, Ellchant thought.

*　　*　　*　　*　　*　　*　　*　　*　　*　　*　　*　　*

Aris was the first to rise that morning and he felt the stiffness of his deep sleep in his shoulders as he sat up. He rubbed them with cold hands, running across his neck and down his upper back. He felt the muscles and began kneading a few knots that had worked themselves in throughout the night. The ground had been cold and unforgiving and he had not slept well even with the power of the old man's magic. He had dark dreams and the vivid images of the snapping jaws of voracious wolves plagued his mind

131

as he stood up. He looked up to the gray trees and noted for the first time that he did not even hear a single rustle of leaves or any sound other than the breathing of his sleeping companions. This place was unnaturally quiet and he didn't like the feeling it gave him one bit. If any animals live here they must be pretty desperate, he thought.

He swallowed a hard dry lump in his throat and reached for his water satchel. He took a long swig from it and placed it back onto his belt. I wish we still had our supplies, he thought to himself. He looked around to see that he was the first one up and that Ellchant sat with his back propped up against an old rotting tree and was snoring loudly. He hated to do it but he knew that he would have to wake him up sooner or later and decided that he ought to wake his brother first to give his old friend another few moments of rest.

Kallevick lay on his side and he came to rather quickly, much to Aris' surprise.

"Hey, you're up early." He said, his eyes instinctively squinting. "It sure is dark in here." He commented, his eyes widening and adjusting to the sparse sunshine.

"Yeah, I noticed that too. Listen, Kalle, I just wanted to say that I am so sorry for…"

"I know, Aris. I know. I knew you weren't yourself and Ellchant explained the whole thing to us after he put you to sleep. Don't worry about it." He lightly punched Aris in the side. "Just don't ever let it happen again, alright?"

"Sure."

"Damn, it's dark in here." Braeburn said yawning. "Let what happen?"

The three of them looked up to see that the trees stood tall, as if they reached in desperation to get any chance of being touched by the sun. The forest floor was a cold deep gray and the soil was matted down firmly with thick patches of black moss that was scattered around the bases of the trees. Aris was curious as to why the moss did not grow on the trees to get closer to the sunlight and it suddenly occurred to him what the moss might be doing. He looked at the thick patches and realized that they needed no sunlight as they were feeding off of the trees themselves. He looked up to the canopy above them and saw that the very top branches were not as void of color as the hulking stalks around them. He shuddered with the realization that nature was destroying itself.

"Let Aris try to take my head off." Kallevick said turning to face the elf and his words redirected Aris' attention to the group.

"Let's get moving." Ellchant said from their right.

"Ellchant, I didn't know you were awake." Aris said.

"I wasn't."

"You were asleep a minute ago. What woke you up?" Kallevick said.

"Visions."

"Visions of what?"

"What awaits us in the days ahead. We have to get moving." He stood up and stomped out what remained of their fire. He grabbed his pack from off of the ground and they all gathered their things and they began to make their way through the woods northward.

They trekked further and as the day passed Aris found himself in the lead even though he didn't know where they were headed. Ellchant didn't seem to mind and he was certain that the old man would redirect him if he led them astray.

"Ellchant, can I ask you something?"

"Sure. What is it?"

"A few days back you mentioned that we shouldn't worry about finding the dragon Cedris and that he would find us. How will he find us if he doesn't know where we are?"

"As I have said before, he will find you. When the time has come and you need him you must simply call out his name and he will appear." He paused and looked hard at Aris. "Don't look so worried, he will come."

Aris' strained look lessened and he kept his pace slow and steady as they walked. "I also noticed that the moss is eating the trees. Am I right?"

"You do not assume. As terrible as it is to say the forest is dying. If it does then the wolf spirits will roam free and destroy at will. You see the trees mark the borders of the cage in which these creatures live. It's now their territory."

Aris noted a hint of disgust in the old man's tone.

"It's a shame really. This place used to be known as the white forest and was a place of beauty that was unspoiled by the hands of men or Rundagg. But as is with everything Dinemid touches it was turned to darkness." Ellchant continued.

"Can we stop for a while? I'm hungry and we haven't had a thing to eat since we left yesterday." Braeburn said from behind them.

"Yes. Now that he mentions it, I'm pretty hungry too." Aris said.

With this being said Ellchant turned around to face the elf. "With you it's always about the food."

"It was actually my idea." Kallevick said stopping next to Braeburn.

"Don't defend him." Aris said facing them. To an onlooker it might seem as though they were about to brawl. The two pairs stood glaring each other and Aris was the first to break the false tension by laughing when the elf stared him down as if to say that he was a dead man.

Braeburn moved forward a step.

"Wait, one minute." Aris said holding up his finger as he unhooked his baldric and the elf dropped his staff. "Let's have it out, Ellion!"

Braeburn ran and jumped on top of Aris and the two began to wrestle.

Kallevick rolled his eyes but moved to join in. He took two steps before he abruptly tripped and fell to the ground. He felt the old man's leg brush past his and Ellchant smiled down at him.

"Let's go boys, I don't like waiting." Ellchant said and walked off. "Enough horse play, we have get moving."

"I don't think so old man." Kallevick said.

Kallevick got up and in a flash he tackled Ellchant to the ground. As he lightly jabbed at the old man he felt Ellchant's torso heave and exhale as he laughed. Ellchant took the advantage and rolled Kallevick over and began to jab back when they heard a scream emanate from Braeburn. Ellchant turned to look behind him and Kallevick, suddenly taken with a fit of rage, leapt from his spot on the ground and grabbed the old man by the throat.

Aris had the elf pinned on the ground and was throttling him with his fists clenched tightly around Braeburn's neck. The elf struggled and managed to smack Aris in the face with his open palm. The young man shuddered with the blow but recovered quickly and his eyes flared with hate filled light. The muscles in his arms tightened and flexed his grip even stronger on Braeburn's throat. The elf gasped for air.

"Aris." Braeburn managed to squeal. "It's me. You don't want to hurt me."

"But I do." Aris said, his eyes flaring and started to glow with an intense red. "I want to do more than hurt you." His grip tightened.

"Please, Aris." Braeburn said almost inaudibly. He clenched his fist. "Don't."

"Oh but I will."

Kallevick was exercising the same strangle hold on Ellchant's throat. But Kallevick's grip was not as strong and Ellchant struck the young man in the temple and stood gasping for air. Kallevick fell, his hand reflexively moving to where he was struck and then without hesitation he ran for Ellchant with his fists swinging wildly.

"I'm sorry, Kalle." Ellchant said as he punched the young man in the face.

Kallevick stumbled, apparently shocked with the power of the defensive motion.

Braeburn who was struggling with Aris couldn't get free from the young man's fierce grip. He punched him in the side as hard as he could. Aris did not flinch and his pupils dilated.

Having momentarily moved Kallevick aside, Ellchant moved to aid the elf and attempted to knock Aris away by running over and colliding with him. He shoved with all of his might as he made contact with him but the young man was like a stone that wouldn't budge. Ellchant went flying and toppled over Aris headfirst into the dirt.

Kallevick was on top of Ellchant again before he knew what happened and began to use the stranglehold once more. Ellchant, seeing no other alternative kneed him in the groin. But Kallevick was immobilized only momentarily and his eyes too began to glow with a red intensity. His breath was failing him and he needed to get up so he could help Braeburn. Ellchant closed his eyes and focused his energy and used his head to strike Kallevick in the face.

Braeburn used his body to squirm his way out of being pinned and gained some of his air back when he did but he could not completely free himself of Aris' throttle hungry hands. Braeburn finally had shoved him off but Aris was quick and moved to tackle him once more. Braeburn knocked him to the ground with a powerful hit to the chest. In a flash the elf was on top of him, straddling Aris' stomach and pounding the young man senselessly. Aris screamed and struck back as best he could. The elf's eyes began to glow and the two fought furiously.

Kallevick shook his head and this time instead of barely noticing the pain he held his head as if he struggled to keep his brains from shaking and oozing out. He bobbed and weaved and hit the ground with a dull thud. The dirt smeared on his face and he didn't dare move.

Ellchant moved to put an end to Braeburn and Aris' fight and as he neared he caught a taste of the elf's fist to his face. He shook his head seeing spots before his eyes and then managed to get the elf off of Aris. Once the two were split he stood between them. Braeburn stood leaning against a tree breathing heavily, his arm wrapped around his side. He looked like a wounded animal that had managed to momentarily escape from the attack of a hungry predator. But the old man knew that neither the Aris nor Braeburn were hunters. They were all prey. Braeburn's eyes glowed a deep blood red, almost black.

Ellchant knew that they were all now under the influence of a dark magic and he realized that the conjurer's of these dark spells meant to do much more than just bruise and cut them. /The wolf spirits meant for them to kill each other so that the sword could make its way to Dinemid. With no one to stand in the way the banished god would be victorious.

Ellchant turned to look at Kallevick who lay quite still on the ground and breathing more regularly now. Kallevick's eyes opened and he looked at the old man, his eye's still glowing with the same deep blood red color that Braeburn had brewing in his. Then something most unexpected happened. The old man felt the air about him was close as if the trees had stopped producing oxygen and tried to choke him. He couldn't peel his stare away from Kallevick and the young man's face seemed to morph. A wicked smile crossed his face and he slowly rose with his hair messed up and dirt covering half of his face. He didn't even regard the dirt even though some of it had gotten into his eye. He walked slowly and ominously towards Ellchant.

Ellchant turned and saw that Braeburn was walking towards him in the same manner. He turned again and saw that Aris did the same. The three of them closed in on him and the air became thinner. He swallowed hard and struck Braeburn first. The elf fell to the ground and lay watching the other two close in on the old man. Ellchant swung his fist at Kallevick and missed. The young man punched the old man in the side and Ellchant groaned and clutched his ribs.

Ellchant breathed, a sharp pain shooting through his chest and a deep wheezing sound leaked from his mouth as he inhaled. Then suddenly everything was a blur of motion. He clenched his fist and punched Kallevick in the face as hard as he could. The young man's head swung back and he turned back immediately, the wicked smile never once fading and he laughed a malicious cackle. Ellchant turned and before he could even face Aris he saw from the corner of his eye that Aris had his white sword drawn. He turned to yell at Braeburn, trying to get the elf to snap out of it and help him but the elf merely began to laugh with Kallevick.

Ellchant tried once again to hit Kallevick but the young man caught his fist and pulled it behind his back to pin him in place. The old man's shoulders were now to Kallevick's chest. Ellchant tried knocking him in the face with the back of his head but only received another evil laugh as a reward for the failed attempt. Ellchant could feel the dirt fall off of Kallevick's face and down the back of his robe. He kicked with his heel at Kallevick's shin and that seemed to get the possessed man's attention. Kallevick yelped and he turned the old man around to face him. The smile had faded and was now replaced with a grimace so horrible it made Ellchant squirm. But before he knew what was happening Kallevick had cocked his head back and struck with all of his might.

With an almost bone-crunching blow Kallevick's head whipped forward again with such force that it sent Ellchant stumbling backward. The old man yelled with all of his might from the pain and he bumped up against something. At first he barely felt it, what with the pain shooting through his cranium. He opened his eyes and saw blobs of color smeared together in indistinguishable patterns. He saw Kallevick's face, still as grim as before and he barely noted the form of the elf standing to the left, smiling a wicked smile. Aris, where is Aris? He thought. He could barely think. His mind was shaking, as were his hands. He looked down at them.

The blade of the white sword was protruding right through his stomach. He had never seen so much red in his life. That was his blood, he thought. The pure white of the sword blade was sheathed in a coat of deep crimson. He was in too much shock to scream or cry out in pain and his only thought was where is Aris? Surely he was here. Wasn't he? He looked down again as he saw and felt the blade pass through him. It pulled itself through from behind him and he felt the tug at his back, as he went with the blades' direction and fell to his knees.

He must have backed up right onto the sword, he thought. For the first time he felt the burning and searing pain of the wound and he looked up into the sky and saw Aris' face floating above him. Aris' eyes were still a deep red as Ellchant silently mouthed the words, help me.

"Yes, I will help you." Aris responded to his thoughts. He took the old man's arm and pulled him to his feet. The old man struggled and Aris took hold of the old man's robes and embraced him. Ellchant felt the blade pass through him again. This time through his heart and he had not even noticed Aris raising the blade to meet his chest when Aris helped him to his feet. Ellchant whimpered and groaned, his breath coming in short shallow gasps. His face went pale, white as a ghost as he looked deeply into Aris' eyes.

"We will not have a guide helping us any longer." Aris said, his voice now foreign to Ellchant's ears. It was deep and brooding. It was Dinemid's. "You are no longer needed Ellchant Pendergast. Aris is mine and he will be as dead as you before long. Even if he makes it out of the forest alive, he will die by my hand."

"Aris. Oh, Aris." Ellchant groaned. Tears began to stream down his face in thin rivers.

Suddenly the dark light faded out of the young man's eyes.

"Ellchant! Ellchant!" The young man screamed. "What have I done?!"

The blood red light faded from the elf's eyes and Kallevick rubbed at his dirt filled eye when the spell faded out on him as well.

"Hold on Ellchant." Aris cried. He gripped the hilt of the sword and looked into Ellchant's spiral gray eyes. The guard was resting on the old man's chest. "Hold on!"

Aris pulled with all of his might and a stream of blood flowed from the open wound. Ellchant fell to the ground and Kallevick and Braeburn rushed to hold up his weary head. Aris threw down the sword, disgusted with the look of it and ran to Ellchant's side, holding his old friend's hand as best he could though his own hands were shaking.

"Ellchant, oh old friend. I'm so sorry. I couldn't stop it. The next thing I knew, you were calling my name and I saw the sword in your chest." Aris' eyes flooded.

"Oh, don't fret." Ellchant said, his breath shallow and weak. "Just," said Ellchant as he coughed up blood. "Just pray." he managed.

Aris closed his eyes, squeezing Ellchant's hand and sent a silent prayer to the lords of Galebraith. The elf and his brother joined in and together they meditated. Slowly a white light surrounded Ellchant, lifting him a few feet into the air and circling around the company to enclose the old man in its healing embrace. The glowing pulsed and healed his wound, mending his ripped armor and robes. Gently Ellchant glided back to the forest floor and the holy light faded from his body. After a few moments of silent wonder the group helped Ellchant onto his feet and they stood looking at him.

Aris wondered at him. The gods were with him. They still needed help through the forest and Aris thanked lords from above that his friend was alright. He silently hoped that Ellchant's time to leave this world was many long years from now.

"We've no time for any exchange of regrets or apologies and I think we all understand what has happened here."

They all nodded.

"You see Aris, that is the price of faith. The way to see with your eyes closed."

"What do you mean?" He asked.

"You may be ridiculed and mocked for what you believe but you have the hope of something better. That is the price you pay for seeing the world through your own eyes. The gods are with you Aris. Let's get moving."

CHAPTER 18

Without so much as a signal the group began their trek again through the woods and it was a number of hours before they all sat to catch their breath and forage through their belt pouches for any scrap of food. Ellchant found some in his pack and they all agreed that they would have to ration it. Kallevick began searching the forest floor when the measly bit of food did not satisfy his hunger. He stood and walked away from the group, his eyes scanning for a sign of any familiar edible root or plant.

"Ah yes." He said bending down to pick up a dark green plant from the dirt. "Karog root. Not quite as good as the stuff that grows back home but it'll do."

Braeburn walked over to him and he took the plant from Kallevick's hand to examine it. "Looks very unappealing." He said, his face cringing in disgust. He turned the plant over in his hand and found that it left a blackish ooze on his palm where the roots had been. "Oh, gross." He began wiping his hand on his leather trousers.

"What did you find?" Aris asked as the two came back over to him and the old man.

"Karog root."

"Oh, that's the plant that Father said that he ate when he got caught on that hunting expedition when he was our age."

"I remember smelling it on his breath when I pulled him out of that hunting trap."

"Hunting trap?" Aris said turning his attention to Ellchant.

"Yes. He had lost his party and he had fallen into a pit that was meant for whatever it was they were hunting. I don't recall what it was that they were after but I do remember the mint like smell on his breath when I pulled him out of there."

"You rescued him?" Aris asked with surprise.

"Why that's how we met." Ellchant said with a smile.

"It does taste almost like mint." Braeburn commented after smelling his hands and experimentally touching his tongue to the center of his palm.

"You know what I could go for," Kallevick said. "Is some venison."

In a low, soft voice Kallevick began to hum.

When the bird and the beast come to the wood
When the sun hides behind the cloud
Then man will come and...

Kallevick's voice faded out as he sung and the others became quiet as they spied a beautiful doe looking keenly in their direction. None had even heard its approach and no one moved for fear of scaring it off. Kallevick was shocked for he had not even heard the sound of a single bird since they had entered the woods. The thought of a deer living in these woods was amazing to him and he guessed that if there was one there were bound to be more. Though he wondered how these wolf spirits had not killed it. Perhaps they had gotten to the others.

"What do you know." Kallevick said turning slowly to face it, his voice soft and even. "It works. The song works."

The doe stood a mere twelve feet from them and stared intently at Kallevick as if it wished to hear more. It had sturdy legs and it looked as if it was in very good health despite the lack edible vegetation. It had a rich sandy brown coat and deep penetrating eyes, big and round like blackish brown orbs. They looked, as it were, inside Kallevick and seemed to be peering at something more than just his physical form.

Kallevick tilted his head as if the animal had made some sort of verbal response to his thoughts. He opened his mouth and he began to sing again in a low tone and stood slowly.

Then man will come and take one down
Where the bird and the beast once stood

The doe snorted. Its ears twitched and flicked, signaling at Kallevick to sing more. A breeze swept by it and a few stray hairs from its coat flew off, like leaves falling from a tree with the onset of winter. Its eye's were a deep brown, almost black and they were filled with a peace that Kallevick had never seen before.

It wanted to hear more, Kallevick thought. He was entranced with the creature and it made no indication of being frightened as he moved closer to it. His voice resonated in his chest as he sung in a low even tone.

For the gods are gracious enough to give
The bird and the beast that lay down their life

142

With those words the doe turned suddenly, its white tail a flash as it ran off into the trees.

Despite the yelled warnings of his brother and Ellchant, Kallevick took off after it at top speed, unheeding their words.

He raced over raised patches of earth and nearly tripped over rocks that had roots deep beneath the dirt. He ran and ran, spotting the white tail of the doe only a few meters off. If he could only catch up to it, he thought. The trees were a blur in his peripheral vision and they looked almost like gray statues in the dim light of the forest. He needed to merely see it once more and his prior thought of desire to feast on the venison made his stomach turn. He ran, his heart pounding in his chest. He needed to see the doe's eyes and he needed to figure out what, if anything was making it look at him the way it was. He whipped past more trees and a few stray branches caught him in the face and scratched his cheek. It was almost as if they were invisible hand's trying to grab him as he ran for they feared that the young man meant to kill the doe.

He put his hand to his cheek and wiped it. He had a small cut and he now saw that he had a few drops of blood on his hand. He disregarded it as he ran and peered into the dense mass of trees looking for the white tail of the doe among the mess of gray surrounding him. He had lost her and his pace slowed when he realized it. He looked deep into the trees and saw no sign of her. He began to turn back and head back to the others when he unexpectedly felt something wrap around his midsection and lift him a few feet off of the ground. He looked down and saw that it was the thick trunk like branch of a gray tree.

He tried to scream for help but another branch snapped around and covered his mouth before he could even utter a word. He looked around, his arms flailing, trying desperately to pry out of the grasp of the wicked tree. He struggled to free himself and found it even more difficult when another set of branches wrapped around his arms to pin them to his sides. His hands were still free but without the momentum of his arms he could do little more than kick his legs.

He looked down and saw that he was no longer off of the ground but was leaning against the tree that held him frozen in place. It was as if it meant to swallow him or at least suck the air out of him. He looked up and felt his breath lessen as the vine like tendril squeezed. How did that doe get away? He thought to himself. But

143

before he could come up with an answer he saw a flicker of light and he shut his eyes momentarily. His vision blurred and he began to see spots when he opened his eyes.

He looked forward again and his head staggered back with surprise. Standing before him was a faerie. She was not a pixie though, he thought for they were children of the Ellion. This was no child. This was a grown woman. And a beautiful one at that. Her brilliant green eyes flashed in a wink of thick dark lashes. They seemed to stretch on forever as if their source lay in the very depths of her iris. Her eyes were a deep forest green and Kallevick was reminded of the trees near his home in Obadia.

She had red hair that was shorter than Kallevick had seen on any woman before. At least if he had seen it he would have remembered it. It was a deep red, almost maroon and was naturally wavy. A few strands fell softly around her face, curving out of the crown of her head and down to lay on her temples. Temples, he thought. They ought to make a place of worship for one of such…such, he couldn't think of the words.

She blinked, bringing Kallevick back to awareness. He couldn't help but stare at her even as the vine wrapped tighter around his neck. He hadn't even noticed the one around his neck, but he did now. The thick trunk like vines around his midsection constricted further, squeezing the air from his lungs and causing green veins to creep into the corners of his vision. He groaned and his voice croaked a bit with the expulsion of air. The faerie's expression darkened and yet a slight smile seemed to play at the corners of her mouth.

Kallevick wondered if she was a hallucination, a reaction to the lack of oxygen or a siren of the forest magic meant to distract him from fighting back with the deadly trees. The faerie women became a blur and his vision was beginning to fade to black. A moment later his eyes were open and the faerie was gone and he guessed that he no longer needed to see her for he was trapped and the tree was soon to feed itself. He strained with a last desperate effort but to no avail. The vines tightened further and this time black began to flood his vision and the last of his breath escaped.

From the darkness of his mind he heard a distant sound. The vine around his neck snapped in a hissing crack. The color raced back to his face and as the vines around his body similarly snapped and fell away he too dropped to the ground. His eyes were closed tight, his neck burning with the release of the pressure and his body ached.

"Breathe!" A distinct voice yelled.

Kallevick complied, gulping in large volumes of air until his breathing regained normalcy. He opened his eyes, blurry at first but sluggishly his eyes regained their sharpness to end up focusing on the beautiful face of the faerie woman who was in turn staring back at him.

CHAPTER 19

Aris and Braeburn stood looking in the direction that Kallevick had ran off in. It had been a few moments and the three of them were becoming concerned. Ellchant sat uneasily on the ground and he too watched the forest nearby hoping to catch a glimpse of the young man running back when his senses had caught up to him. Not a sound came from the nearby trees and Aris was the first to move when he couldn't shake the gnawing feeling coming from his stomach.

"We better go after him. If he stays out there much longer he's bound to get lost." Ellchant said.

"I don't hear any sound. I can't even hear footsteps. I don't like this one bit. Let's go." Aris said, stepping forward to follow after his entranced brother.

"I agree." Braeburn said, his face solemn.

Ellchant stood and moved with the others into the cover of trees and after their friend. The branches stood within ten feet of the forest floor like an organic roof above their heads. From the soil to the start of the branches the bodies of the trees themselves were bare and their bark became deeper and deeper gray as they walked. Soon black spots began to appear on the skin of the trees and Aris was reminded of the black moss that he had seen earlier.

It was as if the branches tried to stay as far away as possible from the forest floor. Evil had poisoned the ground and it was with great hesitation that they journeyed further from their resting point. He wondered if the root that they had found was good for eating but thought better of it when he realized that Ellchant would have said something to them if it weren't. They definitely didn't want to lose their way in a place like this, Aris thought. And not just for the sake of losing their quarry. Hidden things lie in wait for them here. Things that he felt should stay hidden.

*　*　*　*　*　*　*　*　*　*　*　*

Kallevick knelt on the ground clasping his hands around his throat to rub where the vines had attempted to throttle him only moments before. He looked down at the faerie's hand and spied an elegant sword in her firm grasp. It was straight bladed and narrow with a flourished hilt. It was also pointed at him and for a moment he wondered if he was actually out of danger or if he had just become someone's prisoner. His gaze scanned upward once more to look into his rescuer's eyes.

"Thank you." He managed to croak. His voice was weak and his neck burned slightly. He moved his hand across it and he felt the soft but firm touch of the faerie as she pulled his hand away from his neck. The blade of the sword was lowered before he could let his imagination run any further. If she meant to capture him she was sure to be unkind. He knew somewhere inside that she meant him no harm.

"Don't rub it, it'll make it worse." She said. Her voice was soothing and melodious like a gentle wind blowing across a still pond. "Here." She pulled a root from a pouch that was slung over her left shoulder and hung at her right hip. "Hold this, it'll make the burning go away." She held it gently to his neck and his hand touched hers as he took a hold of the root.

"It feels like it's been sitting in the shade for a while. It's nice and cool." He commented, clearing his throat.

She didn't seem to regard his words and she looked to the ground as she took his arm. She helped him to his feet and he stood taking in a deep breath. She wore a dress of sorts and it looked as though the very fibers of it were woven from the plants of the earth. It was a pale green, similar to the green of Aris' cloak and it had thicker fibers as if the material was unevenly stitched together, giving it a more natural look. She had a rolled piece of gray fabric at her lower back and it was tied with black straps to her shoulder pouch. It must be a cloak, he thought. That's how he carried his when it was too hot to wear, he thought. He looked into her eyes once more.

"Thank you." He said. He felt foolish but strong at the same time. He smiled slightly. He knew that he was being sincere but he felt as though she may not recognize it. She managed to avoid eye contact with him and he almost wished that he could stop staring but he couldn't help himself. She was beyond any beauty that he had seen before. She was beyond words and he wished that he could express this to her. She let her arm drop from his and she moved away as if his intent stare was too much for her.

"Wait, where are you going?" Kallevick said, his attention shifting from his enamored ideals of her to the reality of the situation. His smile faded. She turned to him, her eyes moving across his face, examining him. Her form stood out like a piece of art among the garbage of gray trees. She seemed like the only thing that had any color.

"I have to go."

"But..." Kallevick began.

"Find your companions and travel safely. These woods are treacherous."

He now felt as though the roles were reversed and he saw now that he was the one that craved to hear more of her voice. He thought of singing once again and was glad that he shot the idea down when he watched her turn away from him. The last thing he wanted to do was irritate her. He was confused and he felt the compulsion to say one last thing before he lost her again. He fumbled desperately.

"Wait, what is your name?" He called after her.

She turned quickly and their eyes locked on to one another. "Iadil." She said. And with a dazzling smile that seemed to light up the trees around them she pivoted and bolted off into the trees once more.

*   *   *   *   *   *   *   *   *   *   *

It was that smile that had Kallevick on a slight high as he entered the clearing and rejoined his three companions. They were exiting an area of trees that was not too far off from where he met up with them. Before any of them could notice he went to discard the root in his hand but then thought better of it and placed it in his pouch. It was his only connection to her and he decided that he better hang on to it. He finished tying his pouch up as the others approached.

"So he returns." Aris said, shaking his head with slight dissatisfaction in his voice. "Where were you? We couldn't find you."

"Don't run off like that Kallevick. This place is not safe." Ellchant said scolding him.

"Sorry." He said, a bit surprised that Ellchant was so upset.

"Sorry wouldn't have made up for it if you had gotten yourself killed." The old man said his face taut with concern. "Just don't let it happen again. We were about to go after you but we heard you coming back."

"He probably scared that doe off anyway." Braeburn commented to Aris.

"I hope not." Kallevick said, quietly to himself.

"What happened to you? We couldn't find you." Aris repeated.

"I followed the doe and then I lost sight of her. When I did I came right back."

"What is that on your neck?" Aris said stepping forward and motioned to the red spot. "And your cheek, you got scratched. Are you alright?"

"I'm fine. I just caught a few stray branches as I ran. That's all. I'm fine, really." He found that he had better keep the story of the tree and the faerie to himself as they were unlikely to see her again anyway. Besides he wanted the looks of concern on his friend's faces to go away. It was making him nervous and he was becoming uncomfortable, not to mention the fact that he wanted the image of her smile all to himself.

"Well," he said picking a root from the ground. "Karog root's for dinner I guess."

      *   *   *   *   *   *   *   *   *   *

That night the group sat around a raging campfire and Aris found that he had to turn away from it from time to time lest he singe his eyebrows. He raised the cup, a luxury found in Ellchant's pack and took a long slow sip of the hot brew that filled it. He passed it to the elf who took a smell of it and then a long swig.

His lips puckered a bit and he tasted it, licking his lips.

"Sure does taste like mint to me." He said.

"Well it'll keep that breath of yours from killing us." Kallevick said.

Braeburn smiled and then skipped the opportunity to pass the cup onto the young man, passing it to Ellchant instead. But before the old man could get a hold of it Kallevick grabbed it and took his share. He then passed it graciously to the old man, who shook his head at the two. Once he had his taste of it he set the cup next to the small cooking pot that lay beside the fire. Steam swept up from the pot with the faint scent of the minty brew. It was the only cooking item they had along with the cup. Any utensils they may need would have to be fashioned from sticks or the food would have to be eaten with their fingers. Although finding food was more of the problem than having the correct implements for eating it, Ellchant thought.

The foursome sat quietly each staring at the fire and the cup made several rounds again before any of them spoke.

"How far off are we from the forest edge do you think?" Aris asked.

"I think the more important question here is not how far are we from the edge but how far behind we are on the trail of this Rundagg." Ellchant responded, staring deeply into the fire. "I haven't seen any tracks and I doubt he has the sense or the time to cover them if he did."

"How do you think that we could have missed his prints? Wouldn't we see them if we are on his heels?" Braeburn asked.

"Possibly. But he may know of paths through these woods that we don't."

"Melchor said that he passed through only about a day before we got to the city. We shouldn't be that far off then, right?" Kallevick said optimistically.

"Hmm. I still say that we should triple our pace tomorrow to make up for lost time. Quite a bit has transpired against us this day and we can't afford to lose any more. Tomorrow we make for higher ground." Ellchant said pointing to the upward sloping hill before them.

When they all silently agreed on this matter, indicated by another round of the Karog brew and a nod from each member of the group they settled as best they could on the forest floor. The more sleep they could get the better, Ellchant thought. As long as the fire stayed at least half as intense as it was now they ought to make it through the night without much trouble. Once everyone had drifted off he made sure that the last thing he did was throw some more fuel onto their fire and then he settled himself down and drifted off with the others.

CHAPTER 20

He was in the square again looking down the path that would carry his two friends toward him. They were not in sight at the moment. There were swarms of people, the sound of their voices and footsteps were loud and humming like bees at a favored flower. Their forms' became a mix of shadow and shape, indistinguishable from their surroundings. Their voices became muddled and began to melt into one another, becoming one.

He couldn't spot his companions anywhere and he turned back to see that Orsidire was glowing white and the familiar blue haze surrounding it was moving, shifting like steam curling around the shape of the sword. It entranced him and even though it was forged to destroy evil he had never seen such a beautiful weapon in his entire life. He found some irony in this; the fact that he found some aesthetic element to a thing made to conquer someone was rather striking to him.

He finally peeled his gaze away and looked back at his original trajectory. Now he saw that light was coming from down the path and he thought of a caravan of warriors, triumphant and glorious riding on their horses with victory following in their wake. He thought then of the joy and peace that would follow, the comfort and solace of knowing that Dinemid was gone forever and could cause harm no longer. The evil god was destroyed and all would be right with Andellius and the realm of the gods. The lords of Galebraith would be restored and the universe would flourish once more.

But a caravan did not come as he had thought and yet this did not surprise him in the least. He knew that his two friends, like his own sons would come. When the light had grown to enormous proportions and had flooded the exit of the path into the edge of the square Ellchant was surprised to find three, not two, people coming his way. He spotted Kallevick, his brown eyes shining bright with love as he held hands with a woman. But she was no ordinary woman; she was a faerie and her beauty and strength shone through her like the sun. She smiled and the two lovers looked at one another. Even before they kissed Ellchant knew that they were in love.

He spotted Braeburn, eating as usual. But the look of peace and joy on his face was unmistakable. The elf was satisfied and as he took another bite of his food he looked on at the beautiful couple before him. He chewed as he looked right at the old man and smiled, waving with his free hand. Ellchant waved back as if from a far distance. He realized that even though he was not physically close to them he felt a strong force like an invisible pull reaching for them with his very spirit. He then noticed that he did not see Aris. This troubled him, for even though his love for each of them was strong, even for the faerie woman whom Kallevick was kissing, he always knew in the deepest part of his heart that Aris was the one he loved most.

He raised his voice above the dull buzzing of the crowd. Their shapes and noises were no longer in focus and his own voice rung out clear and pronounced above them. He called out, the words undefined and in a language that he had not heard or used in many years, but Braeburn and the others knew his voice and pointed down the path in response. He could see all of them watching him from his peripheral vision with bright smiles on their faces. He peered through the foggy surroundings and saw the same light coming down the path once more, only more blazing than before.

With a light brighter than any sun he had seen and whiter than any snow he watched as Aris Desarta, the messenger of Galebriath, walked with righteous footsteps toward him. The others followed and the four were walking towards him, their combined light more joyful than any Ellchant had ever felt before. This was his family. The family he had never had; they were all his children.

As they neared the old man could not stop staring at Aris. For now the handsome young man was transformed and was more precious than any metal or stone found or wrought on earth. He was still young, as young as he had known him in life and for a brief moment Ellchant wondered if he were dead and was experiencing the bliss of being outside the confines of space and time. Aris wore a tunic, well fitted and new, unspoiled by any hint of dirt or wear. It was blue and white, intricately cut and sewn with silver thread. Ellchant recognized its colors were those shared by the sword of the gods itself. He looked over his shoulder at Orsidire to confirm his assumption. Indeed, the gods made Aris' new tunic. He looked at his young friend and saw that his face was no longer that of a boy but of a man. He was still the same age but he no longer carried the weight of guilt that had plagued his face for so long on their journey. He had a slight beard growing and his hair bore no sign of its original color, at least it only did for a moment. Within seconds blonde streaks appeared, starting at the roots of his long hair and growing down to the tips. They appeared on each side of his head like a crown and in another blink of Ellchant's eyes, the same thing was happening to the rest of Aris' hair.

The four friends walked toward him each smiling and Ellchant could not peel his eyes away from the one whom had saved the gods. Aris now stood in front of him and Ellchant knelt at his feet and bowed low. He looked up and saw that Aris now had a crown on his head, a crown in the shape of the wheel of Midgail only the arms of the wheel stood on end rather than out to the side. He also had an earring in each ear, a silver hoop pierced through each of his lobes. Ellchant looked deeply in to the eyes of his friend, the son he never had. He knew that Aris was now a new being, not quite man, not quite a god, but both.

Aris' eyes glowed with a warm fire and his smile was firm like that of a king. Yet a hint of the same young man who had cried for forgiveness in Ellchant's arms back in the City of Hope lingered in the sparkle of his eyes. Aris was a king, a king of men and would lead his race to peace and prosperity.

"Rise, wise one and come with us to where the good things lie." Aris said, his voice more powerful and filled with more strength than Ellchant had ever heard it. He complied and rose to greet his old friend, their eyes locked in an almost eternal stare. Aris looked at him and he smiled and was more than glad to see him.

Ellchant looked to his left and saw that the faerie woman was smiling along with Kallevick, who stood behind her, his arms wrapped about her. Ellchant smiled back and their expressions of joy grew wider. The old man looked to his right and saw Braeburn smiling and the two exchanged the same pleasantry and then Ellchant and Aris embraced. Ellchant looked at his family and he smiled more brightly than he had ever in his entire life.

"Come, see yourself now." Aris said, his voice rolling like thunder in the clouds. Ellchant looked about him and saw that they were no longer in the square but in a spot among the clouds and Aris, King of Andellius, led him to a silver pool that flowed from high above them.

"Look and see your true face. The face of one who knows all things." Aris said.

Ellchant looked deep into the silvery waters and saw his own reflection, a reflection so familiar and yet so strange he did not know if he saw his own face or if his mind was playing tricks on him. He spoke aloud and asked himself, "who am I?" Then he looked deeper into the silvery ripples before him and posed another question.

"Why can't I remember who I am?" He asked. He looked once more after blinking his eyes to test his vision and when he opened them he heard Aris' voice once again. But it was not the same. It was the voice that he had known in another place and in another time.

"Ellchant, wake up!" It cried.

Ellchant was awake in a moment and once his eyes cleared he saw Aris' face. It was not the face of the king that he had seen in his dream but that of a frightened young man.

"Ellchant, wake up! I think we're in trouble."

CHAPTER 21

T he old man was up in seconds and Aris pulled Kallevick's arm as the four of them gathered into a tight circle. A shrill cry pierced the night air. The ground was sloped upward before them and the sounds came down wind from the hilltop. They all stood back to back, listening for any more of the voice; when none came they settled their stance slightly, loosening the circle.

"What was that?" Braeburn asked, his face half illuminated by the firelight.

"Whatever it was it sure didn't sound like howling." Aris said. "Did you recognize it Ellchant?" The young man asked, turning to their guide.

"It sounded like a…"

The cry came out again and Braeburn's elven ears perked up in recognition.

"That's an Ellion warning call. We use it when we're trying to ward off danger. Where's it coming from?"

"That hilltop." Kallevick said, pointing. He picked up his cloak and drew his sword. "She must be in danger. We have to help her." He moved to run off again but this time Aris grabbed him by the arm.

"Oh no you don't. You running off before was bad enough and we can't afford to lose you in the dark."

"Who is she?" Ellchant asked remembering his dream.

"She? He did just say she, right?" Braeburn asked his face now struck with disbelief.

"C'mon, there isn't time, she might be hurt. We have to help her!" Kallevick said pulling free of his brother's protective grasp.

"Wait for us!" Aris yelled out to him as the three companions ran after Kallevick. Ellchant and Braeburn each grabbed flaming branches from the fire to use as torches.

The cry came once more as they ascended the hill. It grew louder and louder as they neared and without much light it was hard to place exactly where it came from. The trees around them gave no answer and they stood out like gray pillars in the darkness.

"Hello?!" Kallevick called out. "Iadil! Where are you?!"

157

Once they reached the apex of the hill their paces slowed and they scanned the area as best they could in the torch light, taking cautious steps forward.

"Who is Iadil?" Aris asked somewhat annoyed that they were getting far from the camp. His annoyance grew from lack of safety rather than his brother's quest.

"That was an Ellion call, unless my ears yearn for the sound of a Faerie voice." Braeburn said. "Am I wrong?" He asked as he turned to Ellchant.

"No. In fact you couldn't be more right. I believe our hike leader here has met this, Iadil before. Probably when he ran off earlier today."

They walked about for a few minutes, Kallevick searching desperately for the source of the call while Aris absorbed the thought of his brother's doubt in his confidence.

"Why didn't you say anything to us about the faerie before Kalle?" Aris asked somewhat coldly. "Did she hurt you?"

Kallevick turned and faced his brother.

"I didn't think it was important to mention at the time. I had already gotten you all worried and I didn't want to shock you all on top of it, that's all." he said defensively.

"Well I just wish you had told us. Maybe she could have told us how far off Malcolm's trail we are or if she even saw him." The tone in Aris' voice softened and the coldness faded as a result of Kallevick's explanation.

Suddenly there was a piercing cry that screeched high above them. The four warriors dropped their weapons and covered their ears in an attempt to block the agonizing sound from rupturing their hearing. It grew louder and the clamor was only more raucous when the foursome began screaming out in pain from the extremity of pitch. The cry stopped entirely but their own yells and curses still rung out in the night air. When Aris' hands finally fell from his ears his own voice faded and he sat breathing heavily.

"That was no Ellion call. At least it didn't sound nearly as bad when I heard it before." He rubbed at his inner ears and blinked twice. He turned to look at Braeburn, who was doing the same.

The elf made eye contact with him and then pantomimed with his hands moving to his pointed ears. He mouthed the words, 'I can't hear you' and Aris realized that even though he could hear himself speak he could not hear the voice of his friend. Then as he strained to listen to his elven friend, Braeburn's voice grew louder and louder until it was deafening.

The cry pierced the night sky again like a knife to the eye. They all collapsed to the ground screaming in pain. Aris could barely open his eyes and dark and hidden thoughts flooded his mind like a tidal wave. Thoughts that lied deep within his own heart. He saw his father before him and when his father looked upon him, Cabral drew a dagger and thrust it deep into his own throat. Then he saw his home in the village of Mulroy; it was ablaze with a purple fire steaming and coughing smoke like a great and vile dragon.

Braeburn saw the whole race of Ellion before him and when they looked into his eyes they fled from him in terror, screaming out their warning call in their wake. He ran after them faster and faster but could never catch them. No matter how hard he ran they could outrun him and soon he began to sink into the dirt. Before long it would swallow him whole. His light was extinguished and soon he would be as well.

The old man dropped his torch and fell upon the ground that appeared to swell up as he met it. Ellchant saw the silver pool before him and in the ripples of water he saw his own face, the one that looked strange and alien to him before. But now the face changed and it was the face of a mighty war god who sought to destroy the world. The image rose, no longer a reflection, and swung a powerful fist armed with a sword at his head. The god missed and cried out, his wings flaring out like wild and terrible flame. It was a dragon like the gods of Galebraith and it meant to kill the old man and his friends.

Kallevick saw the face of his beloved faerie Iadil before him and before he knew it he was bound up in the viney arms of the tree that had tried to consume him earlier that day. Iadil looked him in the eye and instead of Kallevick fearing that he may not see her face again he could not dare peel his eyes away from hers. But now her eyes were filled with a dark light like red brewing blood as she watched with pleasure as the tree strangled him slowly. Then the sound of snapping came just as it had when he was freed and the vines fell away.

He fell to the ground slower and more painfully than he had in reality and he was helped up by his love. He looked into her eyes and saw that the deadly glow had faded and was now replaced with a warm milky white kindness. But he felt the cold hard pierce of tempered steel ram itself through his chest and he needn't look down to know that she had run him through. There was no escaping death now.

Aris saw a face fading slowly into focus from the blackness of his mind and as it became more clearly defined, he knew he could not run from it. It filled him with a terror that he had never known. No man or beast he had ever seen could have prepared him for what he saw, for now the face of Dinemid stood before his very eyes. It called out his name and when Aris heard the malevolent voice again he felt the compulsion to scream. Absolute and total fear dominated his cry and he stood paralyzed by the horror within himself. His face was inhuman and mangled and it was one that would haunt his dreams.

Dreams. This was not real. It was a dream, he thought. He pushed and pushed with all of his mental energy to get the face to disappear from his mind but to no avail.

Then another cry rang out more powerful than the one that had sent the warriors on the wild chase for the faerie. It was mighty and resonated between the trees with its distinctly female tone.

In an instant the visions that the four companions struggled with vanished from their minds and they all lay on the ground, curled up into balls. Kallevick was the first to break free of his position and he opened his eyes with great hesitation, hoping this was no other dark magic. He looked as best he could at his friends and then stood to help them.

"It's safe now." He said helping Aris to his feet.

The young man opened his eyes and scanned the area about him. He could barely make out the rough shapes of his companions in the darkness. The two brothers fumbled a bit, their vision clouded by the shadows. They helped the other two to their feet and the exhausted foursome stumbled through the dark towards their camp. Soon their eyes adjusted to the blackness and in the near distance they spotted the roaring fire of their camp. It started as a warm orange glow and as they neared they saw that it was changing colors.

When they got to the clearing they saw that a figure stood in front of it with her back turned to them. She had her arms raised high in the air and she chanted in an Ellion tongue, a spell that Braeburn recalled from many ages ago. His face bore the same shocked look that it did when they ran off into the trees before. He couldn't believe his ears, or his eyes. He blinked and scratched his head. This was real.

For a moment they hesitated to move closer.

"It's alright." Kallevick said. "She won't harm us. She was the one who broke that spell."

Aris seemed to be the only one who was wary of her and he wanted an explanation but Ellchant looked on his face warm with realization. The old man knew who the young faerie woman was and he did not fear her. They made their approach and as she turned Kallevick smiled.

"Iadil."

CHAPTER 22

"Thank you." Ellchant said. "Had you not stopped them, their spell would have driven us to madness." Aris looked at his old friend. "You mean those images in our heads were one of Toirasci's spells?"

"Yes, they were the Mutterers." Iadil said quietly. "Did you not hear the spoken words creeping like an undercurrent in your hearing? Those sounds are the voices of the Wolf Spirits." She shook her head. "Toirasci and his fellow wolves were kind once. Before they fell to corruption."

"They had tried another spell on us before and I, I almost…" Aris looked apologetically at Ellchant.

The old man placed his hand on Aris' shoulder.

"We faced the Murmurs yesterday. Thankfully, we overcame it with a little faith." Ellchant said winking at Aris.

"You should be safe for now. I have done what I can to increase the power of your fire. Please, sit." The faerie said motioning with her hands around the fire like a hostess to her dinner guests.

She was a maiden of these woods and even though they had set the blaze she seemed the one more appropriate to welcome them to the warmth, Kallevick thought.

Once formal introductions were over the five companions seated themselves around the fire, Kallevick sat himself next to Iadil to recount to all, his chase of the doe. Once this had been finished they all relaxed as best they could speaking softly so as to ease the strain on their hearing. Before long they began passing the cup of Karog brew around the circle and each person sipped quietly.

"Did you happen to cross paths with a Rundagg by any chance?" Ellchant asked, his voice deep and brooding.

"I did not." The faerie woman said. "And what do you suppose I should have done if I had?"

"Killed him." Aris said. "He carries the one thing that gives us any hope."

"And what does this goblin carry that you so desperately seek? I wonder what drives four friends to such a place as this. Surely it wasn't by choice?"

"He carries the sword of the gods."

"Orsidire?" Iadil said, her face dropping in shock. "What is it doing in the possession of a Rundagg?"

"It was stolen from Nari Island and we've been on his trail. Only we didn't know that it was only one Goblin who had it until we passed through the City of Hope." Kallevick explained.

"We have to catch him or else he will bring it to Dinemid." Braeburn added.

Feeling the silence weighing in heavily Kallevick tried to break the tension.

"You know Ellchant," he began. "How hard would it be for you to conjure up some food with that magic of yours? My stomach keeps growling."

"You know I can't do that." The old man said. "I can't just make something appear out of thin air."

"Why not?" Kallevick asked, genuinely confused. "You made the gate through the wall of the city the other day. Why couldn't you just whip up some food?"

"It doesn't work that way." Braeburn said. "He took what was already in front of him and altered it."

Iadil looked at the elf, a slight smile crossing her face and a look of understanding was exchanged between the two. Kallevick shrugged his expression suggesting that he seemed content with the answer he was given.

Aris picked up on the exchange between elf and faerie and he wondered if it was an Ellion observation that he and Kallevick wouldn't necessarily place so easily. The previous look of confusion on his brother's face was enough to lighten his mood and he looked at the faerie woman and wondered why she had saved them from the mind spell that had held sway on them before. Apparently she had saved Kallevick twice today. He mused silently at what her intentions were.

"That was a protection spell you placed on our fire, wasn't it?" Braeburn asked.

"Yes it was." Iadil said, her voice even and calm. She broke eye contact with the elf and looked at the fire.

"Please forgive me Iadil." The elf said, his own gaze never once leaving the faerie's face. "I just can't believe it. I have been searching all over Andellius looking for any left of our race and now here we all are, in a horrible place, the last place I would have expected to find, well…a faerie, and here you are. I just wonder what's happened to us? Are there others hidden in the forest?"

"No. There are none left that I am aware of. And just so you are aware I did not choose to hide in these woods. When the gods sealed the borders of this place to stop Toirasci and his followers from escaping I was trapped here."

"How have you been able to keep them from catching you?" Kallevick interjected.

"I'm always on the run. I can never stay in one place for too long. The Wolf Spirits rarely come this far south as they tend to stick to the northern edge of the wood."

"How long have you been here?" Kallevick asked, leaning closer.

Aris knew without even taking the time to think about it that his brother was beginning to feel connected to Iadil. This did not surprise him because his brother was a very caring and sentimental person. He carried his father's sword with pride and that alone was a testament to Kallevick's romantic spirit. Aris looked at his brother and smiled to himself as though he were now seeing a picture of himself from only a short time ago.

Kallevick was the levelheaded one, the reasonable and cautious one and now he was more adventurous, more outwardly spirited. Aris could not stop thinking of the irony that had displayed itself as they all traveled. For the first time in his life Aris felt that he was changing, becoming more aware and more cautious than he had ever been. Ellchant must have recognized this and had warned him to guard the precious gift he had lest an enemy crush the very thing that made him who he was.

Aris looked at the old man and watched as Ellchant listened to Iadil tell of her encounters with the Wolf Spirits and the adventures that she had while trapped here in the forest. He looked at the elf and then noticed that the four of them all sat entranced by not only by her beauty, but by the strength that she carried. Aris thought she was graceful and he hoped that if they ever survived this quest and saved the world that he too could find someone that he could admire the way Kallevick admired the faerie.

This thought made him sleepy and soon he slouched in the position in which he sat and was out before Iadil had finished her storytelling. Ellchant didn't even have the chance to think before he too was sound asleep. All the excitement from that night had most assuredly tired him out, Kallevick thought.

"I've been waiting for a way out of this accursed place and when I saw that you were all here I knew the time of escape had come."

"Was this foretold?" Kallevick asked.

"No. But I could feel that something was changing when I first caught sight of you. People don't just happen to wander in these woods and when they do they're usually hunted and killed before they know what's going on. I knew that if you and your friends had made it this far that you had something the others didn't." She looked deep into his eyes.

"Forgive me." Braeburn said yawning. "I would like to learn more about what you know my dear Iadil, but I am getting very sleepy." He stood and took her hand. "It is a great gift to see a faerie alive and well in a world so full of darkness." He kissed the back of her hand gently and nodded to her.

She blushed and nodded back.

Kallevick watched and guessed that they had quite a link seeing as how they were both counterparts of the same race. But even though he understood this he hated to admit that he was slightly jealous. Not the type of jealousy that would ruin his friendship with the elf but the annoying kind that burned like a small flame and was extinguished with a moment of silent reasoning. He was being foolish. Why should he be jealous? He barely knew her. He pushed the thought from his mind. Kallevick looked to the elf who lay curled up close to the fire and was softly snoring. Kallevick chuckled to himself.

He turned back to her. She yawned and for the first time he saw that she gave some hint of being vulnerable. Her yawning in front of him seemed strange. Obviously Ellion slept as any other race did, especially true because Braeburn's snoring got louder, but something about the way she carried herself and the way she acted seemed not cold, but strong. Very strong. Those were the only words that seemed to fit and this sudden shift in her actions seemed to reveal to Kallevick the fact that she was indeed tough. But perhaps not so strong that she was beyond feeling. Perhaps his ideals of her had clouded the way he thought of her. This was the real her and he wanted to make sure that he was as genuine with her as she chose to be with him.

"I..." Kallevick hesitated. "I just wanted to thank you for saving us and...and for saving me again. I owe you."

"Well if you boys are going to help me out of here, I need you to be alive, don't I?"

Her words struck him like a block of cold ice. Did she just say what he thought she just said? He shook the thoughts from his mind. She didn't mean to use them. Or did she? He didn't know what to say to her.

"Don't look so troubled, handsome. I was just kidding. Besides, I think you need me just as much as I need you."

If Kallevick was at a loss for words before then he was in for a big surprise because he now had a million questions running through his mind. What did she mean by that? Was it that obvious that he had feelings for her? Did she just call him handsome?

"Don't think too hard. You need some sleep anyway." She said, responding to his thoughts. She leaned in and kissed him softly on the cheek. "You're welcome."

Kallevick nearly melted into his boots.

Iadil curled up near the fire and looked at him from her position on the ground.

"What?" He said, his voice cracking.

"Nothing. You're just handsome, that's all." She said smiling. And with that she fell asleep.

He knew then for sure. She did call him handsome before.

CHAPTER 23

It started in low as a muted but slurred mesh of raucous noise and slowly rose in volume to the point of ear shattering pain. The sound reverberated in Aris' ears and it was clear that this meant more than trouble because if he didn't open his eyes it could mean death, or worse.

He struggled for a moment and finally pulled his eyes open and saw that he lay on the ground, his companions surrounding the fire that had died in the night. The daylight had not broken through the trees and there was a mild cloudy mist that floated a foot above the forest floor.

The sound came again, this time louder than before and it shocked Aris that he didn't move to cover his ears. The sound was not so much loud as it was distinct. It was an animal call. It was the howl of wolves.

He stood and shook the sleeping form of Ellchant. The old man sputtered as he awoke suddenly.

"What is it?" He asked, rubbing his eyes.

The howl rung out once again and echoed off of the trees.

"Up! Everyone Up!" Aris shouted as the howls grew.

Braeburn, Kallevick, and Iadil were up in seconds, and they grabbed their gear without so much as an indication of being ordered.

"Let's go." He shouted and they all began to jog at a medium pace through the trees. Aris was in the lead and before long he caught the odor of something rotten. The howls grew louder as they ran and it was with great mental trepidation that they journeyed further north. They were running faster and the forest seemed to close in about them while the howls bounced off the lifeless gray trees. Before long the sounds died away and their gait shortened.

Ellchant followed Aris closely and soon the two of them were leading the group through the mess of trees that lay stark and cold in front of them. As they wandered they began to see that the trees were fading from a light gray to a dark gray and were becoming almost black as they journeyed further. They looked like they had been charred, set ablaze with a flame that had destroyed anything living in them. There was no sign of life about this place and even the light gray tone that they had become accustomed to in the beginning of their trek into the forest seemed more welcoming than this, Aris thought. The place was foreboding and a deep sense of urgency and worry plagued his mind. He felt heavy and his footsteps began to fall harder on the ground.

"Ellchant is there any chance we'll make it out of here alive? I mean do you think we can even catch up to Malcolm? We've lost so much time as it is. He's probably days ahead of us and we haven't even seen or heard a hint of him." The young man said to his friend.

The old man smiled. "I have no doubts, my young friend."

"How can you be so sure?"

"Well, we have you."

"What do you mean?" Aris asked, looking to the old man.

"Trust in me and have faith that the gods will see you through this." Ellchant patted Aris on the back.

Aris looked down at the ground and smiled lightly. He wasn't sure that he believed Ellchant and he was even less sure that he believed in himself. Despite the words he shouted to the people in the Desert City a few short days ago the events of recent nights had robbed him of confidence. Then something caught his eye and he stopped walking. The ground in front of him was tread up with what looked like a footpath and they were the kind of prints that could only be made with the pronged foot of a goblin.

"Ellchant, look. I think we found the trail of our quarry." Aris said pointing to the ground.

"Well, well." The old man said satisfied. "And here you are concerned that we won't catch this Rundagg."

"C'mon everyone!" Ellchant yelled to their lagging companions.

The other three who were conversing softly as they neared, stopped dead in their tracks as they spotted the footprints.

"Well what are we doing just standing here? Let's get this scum!" Aris shouted and as took off in a flash.

The others followed as best they could and Ellchant for the first time since leading the expedition was having a hard time keeping up with Aris. They ran. Their pouches and cloaks bounced and fluttered as the wind whipped around them. The trees flew by and they were now a blur becoming more and more black as they ran into the darkening wood.

Aris was far ahead of the others and soon the trail on the ground began to fade out and become sparse. He slowed his pace and looked around for any new sign of the tracks. There were more prints on the ground now and they scattered in all different directions and Aris suddenly had a vision in his mind of his companions catching up to him and then all scattering at the sight of him. He shook the vision from his mind and he looked back down the path to see Kallevick and Iadil walking toward him. He wouldn't give in to hallucinations or intense mental visions. They could be the work of some evil treachery.

"Iadil!" Aris called. "What can you make of these?"

The faerie walked up to Aris and he noticed for the first time how sweet she smelled, like wild flowers on a summer breeze.

"It looks like Malcolm got confused and spent some time deciding which way to get out of here." She said.

"The tracks go everywhere." Braeburn commented as he observed the ground. He wandered around a bit trying to discern one trail from another.

"Ellchant?" Aris said, lifting his gaze from the messy forest floor. "Where's Ellchant?" He looked down the path and saw the old man catching up with them finally. For the first time since Aris had met him Ellchant actually appeared to be old. He knew suddenly what it may have been like to know his grandparents; he had never known them because they had passed on before he was born. He might feel the same about them as he did about Ellchant and this funny old man was like them, or what he thought they would be. The thought made him smile.

"Ellchant. You've got to keep up with us, ancient one." Aris teased.

Ellchant walked up to them catching his breath and he looked at the tracks dug into the ground.

"Looks like our goblin got a bit confused." He said in short bursts. He finally gathered his breath.

"Do you think that this may be some sort of diversion that the Wolf Spirits could have conjured up to set us off our mark and delay us?" Kallevick asked.

171

"Not likely." Braeburn said. "Judging from the kinds of spells they used on us before I would be surprised if they resorted to something this elementary."

"He's right." Iadil said. "They don't bother with simple deceptions, which leads me to believe that these tracks are genuine."

"Wait." Aris said, raising his hand in the air. He looked at the ground. "Look." He pointed to the mess on the forest floor and then walked forward a few paces. He moved left, then turned sharply right and then headed straight. He walked forward a few more paces and then saw another path of tracks that led straight through the forest and weaved around the black trees.

"How did he spot that?" Iadil asked, truly impressed with Aris's tracking abilities.

"That's my brother for you. Always was a great hunter." Kallevick said smiling.

"See." Aris called to them from ahead. "The tracks go off in this direction. Those other ones turn, left and right, then stop. If Fortune was trying to set us off of his trail he did a very hasty job of it."

They all caught up to Aris and soon the light of predawn began to break around them making the tall trees around them stand out like black ghosts in the eerie blue glow. The mist began to appear again in patches and floated around them to curl around their bodies as they ran down the pronged footpath. It spun and swirled as they ran like a whirlpool of white clouds. Soon they were a great distance from their camp and though they felt the need to rest they only slowed their pace a bit for fear of losing more time. Not able to handle any more running Ellchant called for a halt. They all sat for a few moments catching their breath and Aris was the only odd one out for he was not short of air.

"I need a drink." Braeburn said reaching for his water satchel. He poured some into his mouth and swallowed hard, the cool liquid refreshing him.

Kallevick followed suit, as did Iadil, who took a long swig from the young man's water pouch.

Aris only took a small sip and Ellchant drank the last of his water, spilling some onto his beard as he tipped his water pouch back in an attempt to get as much of it into him as he could at once.

"Ellchant. I thought that we agreed that we should ration all food and water? Now you won't have any left until we get out of here."

"Don't worry about me, young Aris."

"I don't see any rivers or bodies of water around here. I just don't want us running out, that's all."

"Don't worry, we're almost out of this place. We don't have that much further to go." Ellchant said with reassurance.

"He's right." Iadil said. "We are almost on the northern most edge of the forest which means we are almost out."

Ellchant's face went white and Aris looked about him, scanning the trees for any sign of danger. He looked back at Ellchant when he saw nothing. The old man's face still bore no color and Aris saw now the same terror in his eyes that he had seen before they entered the city. Ellchant knew something and Aris was too afraid to ask.

"What is it?" Kallevick asked.

"He's here. Right now, as we speak, he watches us." Ellchant said, his voice trembling with fear.

"You don't mean..." Braeburn said.

"Yes." Iadil said, her own voice full of terror. "Toirasci. They come for us now. They could not kill us before with spells so now they hunt us."

"Hunt us?" Aris asked, his stomach beginning to turn. He recalled what Braeburn had told them as they entered into this place and the memories sent shivers crawling up his spine. There was barely a sound to be heard save for their own breathing. It was quiet. Too quiet.

Then without warning the air about them became filled with an eerie chorus of howling voices, echoing through the trees and filling in the void of silence that had only moments before permeated their surroundings. The screaming call of a howling wolf pierced the shrill air and the five companions bolted as fast as they could across the expanse that lay between them and safety.

CHAPTER 24

They ran as fast as they could, ducking under low branches and jumping over dips in the soil. Aris was still in the lead, the others were right on his tail and none dared to look behind them. Suddenly Iadil tripped over an outcropping root and when Kallevick lifted to her feet he couldn't help but see what chased them. He only caught a glimpse of it before they bolted off again but the image stuck in his mind as they ran further and further from it.

A lone wolf chased after them, larger than any wolf he had ever seen. Its eyes glowed an eerie blue, accented by the predawn light that slowly grew around them. It was the size of a small pony and stood a good four to five feet off of the ground. Its bulging muscles flexed under a coat of thick black and gray fur as it ran after them, its teeth snapping and clenching as it gave chase. Its eyes opened wide at the sight of fresh souls and it gave a barking call as it tried to pounce on the helpless duo. Kallevick and Iadil were out of reach from the beast's hungry muzzle when it landed but it sprung on its hind legs with such speed that the young man and the faerie woman could barely escape its salivating mouth and biting jaws.

"Hurry!" Aris yelled from ahead of them.

As if they needed any prodding, Kallevick and Iadil ran faster and the group sped away from their pursuers. The heroes were close together and they heard more howling coming from behind them and then to their horror more wolf calls came from their left, then their right. Off in the distance straight ahead of them they could clearly see a bright light and the cover of trees thinning out as they approached the forest edge. The light was almost blinding and no detail could be made of the land that lay beyond it.

If we could only get there, Aris thought. His chest pounded and he turned around to make sure that his companions were close behind him. He could handle the running but it was the sight of what chased them that made his heart pound in his chest. Not far behind them a pack of three wolves chased them, their legs strong and sturdy, their eyes glowing with hunger. Their claws were long and sharp and they tread up the ground as they dug into the earth for traction as they gained on the group. They barked out at them as they chased, the sound of which was like the scream of one of their victim's. It was a haunting sound. So haunting in fact that Aris was terrified to think that if they could not outrun these beasts that his voice might be the next among that chorus of screaming.

He could feel the blood rushing in his veins and when he turned back he tripped and fell. Ellchant and him were running next to one another and the two fell to the dirt hard, skidding slightly. The others tried to lift them to their feet but looking down the path they saw that it was of no use to run any longer.

Braeburn's face was distraught with horror.

"Let us turn and face them!" Ellchant shouted.

Aris, Kallevick, and Iadil drew their swords, holding them in position for battle and Ellchant tightened the straps on his chest plate, then drew out his chain whip. Braeburn looked at his staff and winced. It wasn't much he thought and for a moment he wondered if he should ask to borrow Aris' knife. The wolves came from around the bend in the trail and without stopping they launched themselves at the group, jaws open and awaiting to feed on any who were not strong enough to withstand such an attack.

Aris kneeled down and stabbed with all of his might at the first wolf as it leapt and his sword blade bent and snapped in half as the wolf's body fell on top of him.

Ellchant yelled a powerful warrior's cry and yanked his whip around, snapping with a lightning crack at the second wolf who received the blow in the left leg. It spun and flew backwards, its hind legs tearing up the dirt as it slid across the forest floor.

Braeburn rushed to Aris' side but before he could help the young man up he watched as Aris screamed and lifted the carcass of the wolf from on top of him and throw it off with all of his might.

Aris ran and pulled the broken half of his blade from the wolf's torso, reaching into the cavity it had left and pulled the bloody half out. The wolf cried out in pain and its jaws snapped and caught Aris' upper right arm and the young man cried out. He had never felt so much pain in his life but the look of glee and pure lust in the beasts' eyes gave Aris a power he didn't know he had. He lifted the broken half high in the air and stabbed it right through the wolf's face. The wolf's jaw went slack and let his arm free. He pulled away from his attacker and lifted the sword blade high in the air again and struck the dying beast once more to ensure that it would never again live to take another soul. He then took the two halves of the white sword and touched them together and without so much as a word the sword healed itself and was completely whole again.

What was not covered in blood shone whiter than anything the elf had ever seen and the image of Aris holding the mighty weapon in his grasp, his hands bloody, and the young man sweating was a sight to behold. Rich red ran down Aris' arm and Braeburn could see the wound through the hole that had been torn with the wolf's bite. The blood was dark against the olive green of his tunic. Truly Aris was a force to reckoned with.

Ellchant was sending electrically charged cracks with his whip and just as he had with the giant Gridel, struck his opponent right between the eyes and killed it instantaneously. Another wolf lunged for him and Ellchant leapt forward and onto the animal's back, wrapping the chain around its neck and pulling so hard that its neck snapped before its jaws could close on him.

Iadil and Kallevick were back to back and they stabbed and thrust their blades at the wolves that had decided to join the fray from the east and the west. They closed in around them and Braeburn jumped in and swung his staff with all of his strength at the nearest beast. The wolf stumbled backwards with the impact and the elf shouted out to his young friend, to which Aris responded by tossing him the Darigo blade. Braeburn jumped on top of the wolf and grabbed the hide of its neck and slit its throat before the beast knew what happened.

Kallevick stepped forward, thrusting down with his sword, running it through his attacker. It screamed out in pain and scratched Kallevick's leg. Kallevick shouted, his voice harsh and sharp. He grasped the hilt in two hands and swung down, striking the wolf in the head and severing it completely from the body.

Iadil was not as fortunate as her partner and she was knocked on the ground, her wind stolen from her momentarily as she struggled to get up. But before she could pull her sword up to thrust at the beast's vulnerable underside the wolf had jumped on top of her and she tried to swat the beast away with the side of her blade.

It made no sign of any irritation and its eyes changed from the eerie blue to the deep red that she had seen all too many times before. She knew it was going to feed on her soul and she shouted out her Ellion call in a desperate attempt to distract it. The wolf seemed to regard her for a moment and it began to laugh. An almost human laugh, the sound of it malicious and evil.

But the laugh was short lived as Kallevick struck the back of the wolf with his sword, slicing off the lower half of its body. The wolf barely even made a sound as it fell and Kallevick rushed to Iadil and he pulled her up before the body fell on top of her.

They looked about and as they fought off the other wolves that had gathered and they caught sight of Ellchant rising from the ground, his whitening hair streaked with red. A gift of war from his enemy, a gash from a wolf claw, to his brow. Behind him the path lay and with the sun slowly rising they saw, as if in a dream, the leader of the pack walking with almost deadly grace toward them.

Its massive shoulders shifted beneath the skin and it stood a bit taller than the other wolves, its legs more sturdy and more powerful than his companions. His head was enormous, his eyes glowed a sickly yellow, his jaw hung loose. Drool pooled out of the corners of his mouth. His fur was a light gray, almost white and had it not been for the sickly look in his eyes and the loose jaw he would have almost looked regal. It was the only indication that he had once been the leader of the soldiers of the gods. But that light had faded from his form and he now stood in the form of a wolf, one who betrayed the gods and now sought to destroy any who followed them. His ears were perked up at attention and he looked straight through to Ellchant who stood, his chain whip ready for battle.

Aris saw this, and pulled his blade from the body of another downed wolf. With a warrior cry he ran straight for the wolf, the white sword glowing orange in the light of the rising sun. He swung with all of his might but the leader of the wolf spirits side stepped the strike and shoved the young warrior off with a counter strike from his muzzle directly at Aris' torso. Aris was sent flying and he hit a nearby tree which snapped in half like a twig in a child's hands. Aris lay for a moment and then slowly began to rise.

"So, Ellchant Pendergast." The wolf said, his voice raspy and coarse like steel dragged across a gravel pit. "You have survived our spells. But you will not leave this forest alive. Your friends will join you and they too will bow to the power of Dinemid."

"No Toirasci, we will not bow to an outcast. We only bow to the true Lords of Galebraith. The rightful heirs to the throne. My friends will leave this forest unharmed. I will see to it!" The old man shouted, his voice deeper and filled with more power than had ever been heard.

"Your friends will bow, or they will die."

"I will travel to the ends of this world and to the ends of the next to defeat you. If I die, then you will join me."

Braeburn had only caught a glimpse of the exchange as he fought off another wolf with his staff and he was hit with such force to the ribs with the muzzle of another attacker that he lost his footing and he was knocked off balance. Aris was on top of the elf's attacker and he stabbed the wolf in the side. It didn't flinch nor did it cry but spun to kill Aris. Braeburn was no longer on the ground and he took the knife and threw it as hard as he could at the wolf. It spun through the air, the sharpened steel whirling and singing and then sunk deep into the wolf's chest. It fell to the ground with a crash that sent shivers through the boots of the two heroes with the impact. Aris felt dizzy and fell to his knees.

Kallevick was circling a wolf and it dug with its front paw at the dirt like an angry bull ready to charge at him. But when it leapt Kallevick was ready and he sidestepped it and slashed the side of it as it passed. Kallevick held his stance once more and from behind him he could hear the scream of the dying animal as it fell.

Iadil watched as the innards of the beast were exposed and they fell out in a lazy pile to the ground. She twirled her own sword and grabbed it so that the elegant blade faced downward and threw it like a spear at the wolf closest to her. It sunk deep into the face of the wolf, half-sticking out of its eye socket and yet it continued its attack. She jumped high in the air and flinging off her cloak she unfolded her wings which Kallevick had never seen. Perhaps she had concealed them in some part of her clothes he thought quickly as he swung at another wolf.

Iadil floated above the eye pierced beast and grabbed the hilt of her sword. Then as she was in mid air she pulled up on it like a lever and split open the vile animal's face. The wolf groaned horrendously and skidded into nearby tree, its nose bumping into the black roots. Iadil landed gracefully and her wings folded neatly back

179

into the invisible pouches that lay hidden beneath her skin, leaving no trace or hint that they existed. She stooped down and grabbed her gray cloak.

Aris stood shaking his head, trying to gather his bearings and even before his vision steadied itself he saw that Toirasci and Ellchant were locked in mortal combat. He ran to help but his steps were unsteady and he fell again to his knees. He closed his eyes and concentrated focusing his energy to stabilize himself.

When he opened his eyes he saw that there were wolf carcasses everywhere and that his friends were holding their own against the remaining enemies. The air stunk of rotting flesh and the faint smell of animal fur was pungent on his nostrils. There were more than enough pelts here to have kept the Desarta family warm all winter. Family, he thought. Suddenly he turned to look at Kallevick.

He stood and ran to his brother's side and leapt in the air, his arms outstretched as though he meant to grab the wolf by the throat and throttle it to death. But the white sword was pointed straight ahead and it sunk right into the wolf's chest. Aris knocked the wolf onto its back when he made contact with it and he landed with rib crunching force on top of it. The wolf laughed a maniacal cackle and moved to bite Aris' hands off but the young warrior was quicker and before the wolf's jaws could get even an inch closer Aris sliced with blinding speed and severed its wicked head from the body.

Ellchant was swinging his whip around, the metal skull sizzling with white-blue electric energy. It pulsated, crackled and spasmed in short bursts like miniature lighting bolts. The two enemies circled one another and Ellchant cried out, leaping and whipping with the chain sending a deadly blow at the betrayer.

The wolf dodged the strike and stepped forward, his huge front leg pawing with great speed at the old man's exposed chest. The claws scratched the surface of the leather armor and sent Ellchant stumbling backwards. There were now deep claw marks in the leather but it held together firmly just as Cabral had meant it to.

Ellchant jumped high in the air and wrapped the chain around Toirasci's neck hoping to pull the same trick he had on the other wolf but the leader of the wolf spirits flung the spry old man from off his back before Ellchant could pull the chain taut. Ellchant landed on the ground hard, unable to move. Toirasci took advantage of his opponent's vulnerability and he struck the old man with lightning speed.

The old man cried out so loud that it resonated off of the trees and Braeburn used the distraction to break a wolf's leg with his staff when it turned to see where the sound emanated from. The wolf fell and Braeburn was on top of it and slashed with the knife before it could strike back at him.

Ellchant lay, helpless on the ground for a moment and Toirasci stood like a giant sculpture of hatred and malice towering above the wounded old man.

"Now. Now you will submit to the one true god, the one who has the right, and the power to rule the universe." Toirasci said, laughing like wild cannibal about to feast on his most recent prey. "Now I get to taste the soul of a…"

Suddenly Aris came out of nowhere and leapt for the giant wolf.

Ellchant moved and pulled his dagger from inside his robes and jammed it right through the lower jaw of the beast and it lodged between its upper teeth, clamping the vile creature's salivating mouth shut. Ellchant, completely disregarding the blood streaming down his shoulder shoved with all of his might and pushed the creature onto its back.

Toirasci struggled, but his legs stiffened and the first sign of his death tremors began to appear. His limbs trembled and Aris was on top of the beast, pushing with his weight and causing blood to flow out of the wolf's nostrils.

"Now Toirasci. Now you will taste no more souls, and neither will your companions." Aris said, his voice powerful and mighty. He raised the white sword high in the air, the blade pointed down.

There was no mistake now. There was fear in the eyes of the enemy and in that instant the wolf spirit's leader cried out in terror. His lower jaw ripped open and the knife still was lodged into the upper portion of it. Blood came from his mouth and one last howl was emitted.

"Bow to the power of Galebriath! You have failed and now you will pay the price for your betrayal. May the gods grant you the mercy that we will not." And with that Aris thrust the sword down into the heart of the beast and it sunk through to the hilt, hitting the ground below it. Aris sat for a moment, catching his breath and then pulled his weapon free from the body.

Aris helped his old friend to his feet. Ellchant's steps were unsteady and Aris had to support him.

"You're going to be all right old friend. Just hang on." Aris said.

Ellchant looked deep into Aris' eyes and ran his hand softly on the side of Aris' face.

"Oh my boy. I told you you could do it. You will survive this." He said smiling.

"You will too." Aris said, his eyes beginning to well up.

"Perhaps." Ellchant said, the look on his face becoming distant. "We must hurry."

"C'mon!" Kallevick yelled from ahead of them.

Aris looked around and saw that his other companions were now standing as the sole survivors of the battle.

"One more comes." Iadil shouted. "His rage will be unleashed when he sees what we have done."

"We've got to go." Kallevick said. "I can't fight anymore."

"Well what are we waiting for? Let's get the hell out of here!" Braeburn said.

CHAPTER 25

They all ran as best they could as the elf and Aris held Ellchant to support him while they ran. The old man groaned. Braeburn looked at him with deep concern.

"I'll be fine." Ellchant said his face pale but crossed with a smile. "Trust me. I just need you all to get out of here and to bandage up this shoulder of mine."

The light grew brighter and the sun was now steadily on the rise as they closed the distance between them and the last expanse of forest. The sounds of a lone wolf gaining on them became louder and louder and they raced as fast as they could towards the light and the edge of the forest.

They burst from the forest into the blinding light. They could not see what lay before them for the darkness of the forest had shaded their eyes far too long, like a dreamer awoken from a deep sleep to the bright light of the morning sun. They turned as they heard the lone wolf howl and bark as loud as the last dying call of Toiracsi. It leapt at them its legs and claws stretched to kill them all, its eyes a deep red.

Dropping the weight of the old man to the elf Aris focused his energy and thrust his hands forward instinctively causing a wave of magic to flow from his fingertips. It was like a heat wave shooting from his hands and it distorted the air between the wolf and his companions. The wolf stopped in mid air and was frozen there as Aris closed his eyes, focusing in deep concentration. The trees suddenly began to move to close in on the wolf.

Fear shone through the red in its eyes, the only part of its body that it could move. Suddenly the trees collapsed in on it, crushing it beneath their giant forms.

"Be gone spirits of the darkness. May you now wallow in your own nightmare and be forgotten forever by the people of this world." Aris said aloud.

The dust settled and though the whole group sat in shock at what Aris had just done Ellchant leaned on the shoulder of Braeburn smiling for he knew that the young man had just discovered his power. Aris fell to his knees in utter exhaustion and as he did he began to transform right in front of them. Aris gasped in huge mouthfuls of air as though he had been holding his breath for too long. Suddenly his brown hair

183

changed color from root to tip and left two brilliant blonde streaks with one on each side of his head. In a moment Aris had caught his breath.

Ellchant groaned heavily and collapsed.

"Damn wolves." He cursed.

Braeburn moved to cradle the old man's head in his lap. The four heroes gathered closely around their old friend. Ellchant smiled and they smiled back laughing lightly in the joy that they had made it through the Barren Forest alive.

"I told you you would make it, Aris." Ellchant said, his voice weak. He groaned again.

"What is it?" Kallevick asked, his face turning from a smile to a grimace.

Ellchant's face seemed to be bogged down with shadows and his body shuddered in pain. He winced.

"I lied." He said apologetically.

"What do you mean?" Iadil asked, confused.

Ellchant's hand moved away from his side to reveal a fatal wound. His hand was soaked in red.

"I didn't want you to slow your pace for me. I had to make sure that you all got out of there safely and now you have. Now I can let go."

Toirasci had bitten him deeply and when he had cried out in the forest it wasn't from the pain in his shoulder, Aris knew.

They all came in even closer to comfort their friend as best they could.

"Have no fear young friends, we have beaten them and they can't harm another being ever again. We've conquered their magic and though your scars may remain your wounds will heal I assure you."

Aris nodded, tears streaming down his face and the others sniffled and wiped at the corners of their eyes.

Ellchant pulled Aris' tunic so that he could talk softly to him.

"This is the place from your dream Aris. The one you had after you passed out on us that night." The old man said, his voice soft and weak.

Aris wondered at how Ellchant could have known about that dream because Aris hadn't told anyone. He also wondered where in the world he was talking about. Surely not here?

"Travel fast once you leave here. Just don't steal horses from any giants."

They all laughed and with it more tears came streaming down their faces as they watched him smile.

"Where are we?" Aris asked.

"The last vision of what the world once was, a vision that will die if you should fail. But should you succeed it will be the dream of the world to come." The old man answered.

Aris looked to his brother, then to Braeburn who both returned confused looks.

"Go now. Stay here and rest for two days but no more. You are safe here and nothing can harm you. Time goes by slower here. You are already ahead of Malcolm, at least for the moment."

"What about the dragon Cedris? How do we find him?" Aris asked. Suddenly he felt as though he were back in the Nari square asking Orsidire as many questions as he could before the light had faded.

"Don't worry about the dragon. He will find you. All you have to do is call his name and he'll aid you from above. Just get Orsidire back. If it is used to free Dinemid we are all doomed." His voice was nothing more than a whisper now and they all hovered above him to catch his last words.

"We can heal him right? We prayed before and the gods can heal him again, right?" Aris said, trying to reason against what he knew was inevitable.

"The wound is too deep." Iadil said wiping her face.

"I've taken you as far as I can." Ellchant whispered. "Aris, look." Ellchant said pointing off ahead of them. None of them bothered to follow his gesture with their eyes and they all sat around him crying.

Then the old man's focus weakened and wandered into a far off gaze as if he were looking at some graceful scene off in the distance.

"Look at all those beautiful flowers." He said. With one final smile of utter joy Ellchant Pendergast slipped silently into darkness. The light and humor that had illuminated his spiral gray eyes for so long and had given his face life sunk softly into a peaceful sleep. There was no need for words or sound for the tears of the company fell to the ground in silent songs. They did not move from their spot on the ground for some time and they each took turns squeezing and kissing the back of his hand gently.

"Goodbye, old friend. You will be sorely missed." Aris managed to say as he choked up on his own words. The others cried even harder as he spoke. Now it was just the four of them and Aris wrapped his arms around his friends, his family, and they all sat huddled in a circle to share one another's pain.

Braeburn was the first to break the circle and wipe his face. Then he looked down at the face of his lost friend and saw a reflection in his eyes. Perhaps he was not dead, perhaps the gods had heard their tears and was granting life to this humble man. But upon closer examination he saw the reflection of flowers in Ellchant's eyes. The elf reverently closed Ellchant's eyes and he looked outward to the area that lay before them.

"I can't believe it." Braeburn said, his voice sounding like it had when he first saw Iadil. "I don't believe it."

"What?" Kallevick said and looked in the same direction. "By the gods."

Aris and Iadil looked up and their faces turned from sadness to absolute shock.

"The Plains of Isadore. Where the gods forged Orsidire." Aris said. "I didn't know it still existed."

"Neither did I." Iadil said, staring at the remarkable beauty of the land before them. "Neither did I."

CHAPTER 26

Aris stared with utter amazement and he closed his eyes for moment to recall the dream. When he opened them again he saw as if in a vision the landscape flying beneath him in a blur of color and light. The Plains of Isadore were beyond any beauty that he had ever laid his mortal eyes upon and the richness of the colors that seemed to saturate it were bolder and more vibrant than the colored flags at the Nari Fair.

Its hills rolled smoothly and were covered with a white grass that was accented by hints of yellow and electric blue. He could see that some places had green patches, more green than even Gridel's plain and there were flowers everywhere, thousands of them. There were like crystals, iridescent and prismatic, reflecting all the colors of the rainbow and even some that Aris had never seen before. Stem, petal and leaf were all living crystal and they glistened like icicles in the rays of the sun.

"I've never seen flowers like that before." He said almost breathless. He felt short of air. The overwhelming beauty of the place was robbing him of oxygen.

"No one has for nearly a hundred years." Iadil said.

None of them could move and their eyes never blinked for fear that the land would disappear if they did.

"What are they called?" Kallevick asked.

"Idleans." Iadil said smiling.

Her face lit up and the look of it made Kallevick's heart explode with passion. He had never seen such a smile in all his life. It was almost as if it was not real and just a bold shadow of a blissful dream. Her face seemed to glow.

"That's my last name." She said, and turned her smile on Kallevick.

The young man almost staggered back when she turned to him. The power of that face was more than he could handle and he could barely catch his breath.

"What?" He managed to say, almost whispering.

"My last name is Idlean. My family took the name from the flower."

"Iadil Idlean. Fits nicely." Braeburn said, his own face beaming with the joy of his surroundings. "Dahlgren is the name of a type of tree that grows in a land far to the south."

"Really?" Aris responded, still looking straight ahead.

"Yup." The elf said looking at the field of endless flowers.

"If this is what the world was meant to be like then we must finish what we set out to do and see to it that the gods get to make the masterpiece that they always intended." Aris stated.

"You speak of the gods as though they were artists?" Iadil said looking at him.

"They must be." Aris said, looking at her. "No one without an artist's imagination could create something this beautiful."

"He's right." Kallevick said looking at his brother.

Iadil turned and looked at Kallevick. His face was sweaty and dirty, marked with deep bags under his eyes from lack of sleep. Yet he had a reckless refinement to him that sent her faerie heart to skip a beat or two. His hair was messed up and he looked almost silly and not in the sense that he was laughable to look upon but in a way that encouraged an almost giddy admiration. She looked deep into his brown eyes and when he pulled his gaze away from his brother she shielded her eyes from his by looking at the ground. She could feel the warmth of his eyes on her and she felt as though he was enveloping her entire body in his comforting gaze.

"Let's find a place to set up and rest." Aris said.

They all agreed and stood with Aris and the elf taking the body of Ellchant and reverently lifting it to rest upon their shoulders.

"Here, Aris. I'll take him. You lead us now." Kallevick said and moved to help carry Ellchant.

Aris' expression did not waver and he looked deep into his brother's eyes.

"You are my blood and there is life in you. I will protect that life as though it were my own." He said, his eyes moving to each of his family members and grasped Ellchant's feet. Between the three of them with Braeburn holding Ellchant's left shoulder and Kallevick holding the right shoulder they moved forward. Iadil walked on the right side of the trio and they walked forward into the land.

As they walked the ground became softer and they began to smell the sweetness of the wild Idleans and Kallevick realized that it was the same smell as the faerie. It was a light fragrance and it permeated the air with its fresh scent. The sun shone yellow and engulfed everything in its glow. The land opened out before them and they began to hear the distant rumbling of running water.

"Listen. Do you all hear that?" Aris said his ears perking up. They then realized that the land was almost nestled in a sort of valley and they heard for the first time in many days the call of wild birds flying high above them.

They walked further as a thin mist passed in front of them and they saw for the first time that a great mountain stood before them and from its top sprung an enormous natural well. It was flowing downward at a great speed and it crashed down at the base of the mountain in liquid plumes. The water was clear, clearer than any glass and shone like liquid crystal. From the base of the mountain a river flowed out towards them and bent and curved around the rolling hills, cutting a smooth line down the center of the valley. The mountain was a whitish blue and reflected the rays of the yellow sun perfectly off of its surface. It had a slightly craggy face but each of the sharply cut rocks acted like a mirror refracting and shining more light all about.

There were trees of all different colors and it wasn't so much that the leaves were different shades, but the even the trunks and bodies of them bore bold colors. They grew heartily in yellows, blues, reds, and greens. Some were even purple and many were white. Some even grew like the flowers that seemed to lay strewn about everywhere and were transparent, reflecting all luminous shades of the rainbow. The land was so full of light and color that it overwhelmed the travelers. They had seen so much gray and black that this now stood out to them as a stark contrast to the darkness of the evil forest.

Aris silently wondered as they made their way closer to the falls at the irony that the gods had forged a weapon here. The one thing that they sought to recover was made in this beautiful place. This thought sat in his mind for some time and he silently promised himself that they would not fail. For if they did the beauty of this land would never live and he realized that Orsidire was made to ensure that this land would forever flourish. He knew that the universe was the same way and that this one thing, this small artifact, was the key to the salvation of the cosmos. He shuddered to think of what Dinemid would do if he entered into the realms above once more.

Suddenly a wild musical roar came from in front of them and the traveler's halted for fear of imminent danger. But they saw none and watched as a golden mass of fur and muscle appeared in the far distance, running atop one of the hills. It's long pointed horns stretched out horizontally and curved out to the sides much like a bull's and it raised its massive head and called out again.

It was like a grazer beast, Kallevick thought and though it bore a striking resemblance to the ones he was accustomed to back in Obadia this one had lighter colored fur and was not nearly as large.

"Starion!" Braeburn said, almost breathless. "Those are the most rare and unseen of the grazer beast family. I thought that they were extinct!" His face was lit with pure excitement.

Then another musical call came and then another and soon a pack of the Starion beasts gathered on the hill and they ran free and unabashed across the hills, their golden-white wooly manes fluttering in the wind. They called out to one another in song-like mating calls and ran across and down the hills toward the crystal falls.

"They are so free. So beautiful." Aris said watching them. "You don't suppose that they are aware of us, do you?"

"If they are, they must know that we mean them no harm." Iadil said. She paused, sniffing some. "They remind me of the Unicorns." She said, her voice full of sorrow.

"Yes." Braeburn said. "The race of Unicorns." His voice was accented with sadness. "For every star in the night sky, a Unicorn is honored. The gods made sure that none would forget them."

"Our father used to say that the Unicorns were the most beautiful of all the animals that the gods created." Aris said.

"He couldn't have been more right." Braeburn said.

"They were bred to help the race of Ellion travel faster across Andellius so that they could spread the word of the god's existence to mankind. They were the fastest beasts ever to roam the earth." Kallevick said, quoting Cabral. "You know I've seen their alicorns in the sky." He said looking at Iadil.

"What do you mean?" She asked, her face full of wonder. "You mean their horns?"

"I'll show you tonight when the stars are out." He said, smiling at her.

She blushed and she hoped that he hadn't noticed it.

"I wish Ellchant could see all of this." Aris said, a lone tear silently running down his cheek.

"He did." Braeburn said, wishing he could put a free hand on his friend's shoulder.

They started up again and moved toward the edge of the crystal river and as they walked they sank deeper into the land. The hills were smaller than they first appeared and their edges met in such a way that they left small valleys of their own. It was almost as if they were cut from a mold that had long since been destroyed and they all seemed to roll into one another with fluid grace. The travelers walked for some time and the rush and roaring of the falls grew louder as they neared them.

Soon the land opened up and stretched out into two large flattened hills, each one lying on either side of the crystal mountain. It was here on the right hand hill that they set up camp and laid the body of their lost friend down to rest. The falls roared with a musical tone and they found the sound comforting. They placed Ellchant on the ground and folded his arms across his chest and they all laid down next to him and took a long and well-deserved rest themselves. They sank into a dreamless sleep, each one of them breathing more freely than they had in the air constricted forest. The sound of the falling water resounded in their ears and permeated their minds, comforting them as they slept.

$*$ $*$ $*$ $*$ $*$ $*$ $*$ $*$ $*$ $*$ $*$

Aris was the first to rise and he was surprised to see that the sun was still shining bright and yellow for he had assumed that it would be near sunset by the time he awoke. But the sun shone and he remembered that it had risen just as they were coming out of the woods. He guessed from its position that it was early afternoon and he looked down at his companions and regarded them all for a moment. He even looked at the peaceful form of Ellchant and were it not for the fact that his chest was not moving up and down he would swear that the old man was asleep just as the others were.

He then felt the pain in his arm where he had been bitten for the first time and he really gave it more consideration as to how much it was hurting him. He stood and looked down at Kallevick's leg and knew that his brother would probably be in the same type of pain as him when he woke up. He looked at the faerie and then the elf. Neither had any major wounds. Braeburn had a small cut on his cheek and Aris looked at Kallevick and noticed that the scratch on his face from the tree branches was starting to heal and was not as deep as the elf's.

It was as if the two of them were brothers in a sense and the deeper cut on Braeburn's face was a symbol of his Ellion lineage. The scratch on Kallevick's face was a hint, a fleeting grasp of the power of the young man's words and his ability to tell the message of the gods as well as any Ellion. Aris looked at Iadil and then at Kallevick and he knew that they were falling for each other. The faerie had barely a scratch on her and he knew that his brother would see to it that things would stay that way.

The pain and throbbing in his arm pulled his thoughts from his friend's and he walked down the hillside and stood for a moment at the river's edge. The river rippled and ran with tremendous speed down the center of the valley and Aris knelt down and took a long drink from the crystal waters. The drink cooled his mouth and ran down his throat like an internal river and refreshed him with a surge of its magic. He took another long drink and then another.

Soon he began to hear the sounds of the birds flying overhead and he looked up into the sky to watch as they swooped and dove about, playing on the breeze. He wished that he could feel the freedom that they felt and he remembered the joy from his vision and the way he felt with the rush of the wind about him. He closed his eyes and imagined what it would be like to soar on the wind. He felt a light breeze blow through his tunic and the sudden brush of air made him open his eyes. He felt more rested than he had in days and for the first time since leaving home he felt safe. Even though he knew that he no longer had the guidance of Ellchant he had the strange feeling that they might yet make it through this.

He heard the voice of his brother from behind him. Kallevick groaned loudly.

"Oh, my leg." Kallevick said sitting up. "Ugh." He rubbed up above where he was wounded. "The muscles are all tense."

Aris turned to look. "Tell me about it. My arm is killing me. You look terrible."

"I feel pretty terrible, but I'm glad we got some sleep." Kallevick said yawning. "You don't look so charming yourself." He said taking a look at his little brother.

"Yeah. We probably could all use baths. Let's make a point of doing that tomorrow." He said rubbing his hand over the back of his head and wiped his face. "I'm all sweaty and dirty." His face curled up in discomfort.

"Definitely." Kallevick agreed and stood with some visible fatigue.

Aris rose and helped his brother to his feet. "Careful, we don't want you falling over with that gash in your leg there."

In a moment the others were awake and rubbing sore muscles, yawning as their vision cleared.

"Glad to see you awake." Kallevick joked, helping Iadil to her feet.

"This is a bit backwards don't you think. I should be the one helping you to your feet, shouldn't I?" She said taking his outstretched hand and standing up next to him.

"No one help me, I'm fine." Braeburn said, sarcastically.

"Sorry." Aris said, moving to help the elf.

"No, it's too late now!" Braeburn said, the seriousness of his face not leaving.

For a split second Aris wondered if they were all free of the Wolf Spirit's spells.

The elf smiled. "Some friend you are!" He stood and laughed to himself. "I guess I just won't share my food with you when we find some."

"I didn't want your food anyway." Aris said, playing along.

They all shared the light moment, smiling softly and when their merry expressions had faded, they all looked at the body of their beloved friend who had not moved an inch since they placed him there. The way he was positioned he looked like a fallen king, a man of great conviction with a heart mightier than any sword. The foursome looked at one another and then they all turned their gazes upon Aris as if to silently ask what the next appropriate course of action should be. Aris held up his hand and moved away from the group. Their position was close to the river and he walked up to the hill to survey the area. He had to find the perfect place to lay his friend to rest. He walked upwards, his eyes never leaving the ground and he stopped when he had reached the crest on the hill that he'd spotted. He turned and looked down at his companions then looked at the falls that lay to the right and a short distance from where they stood.

His expression must have been drastically emotional for all three of his friend's turned and looked for what he now stood gaping at. There on the edge of the hill that met the falls a rainbow had formed where the water sprayed high into the air.

"Here. This is the place." He said without moving.

"Why there? I don't see anything but the hill's edge." Braeburn said and the others nodded in agreement.

"Come up here and look." Aris said waving his hand, beckoning them to join him.

They all walked up the hill to meet him with Kallevick being helped by Iadil and they all turned and gazed at the tremendous view that had been afforded to Aris. They all stood close to one another and the tears began to well up in their eyes.

"This way he can always watch the rainbow." Aris said.

"It's perfect." Iadil said.

Aris began the task of digging into the soil which came up very easily in his hands. It was rich underneath the surface and it was a deep brown, almost black and the young man knew that was why the plants were so full of life because the earth that they were rooted in was so full of good nutrients. Braeburn helped Aris dig while Iadil and Kallevick took Ellchant closer to the river's edge and cleaned his wounds with the cool water. The Elf had just tossed a handful of soil into the pile that him and Aris made when the call came from the river.

They then reverently all took the body of Ellchant, who looked more peaceful than ever even in death and carried him up to the grave that they had dug. Iadil had pushed the wrinkles out of his robe and Kallevick had wrapped the links of his chain whip around the handle and placed it in his right hand. The old man's silvery white hair was neatly combed and tucked behind his ears. They crossed his arms once more and the company took turns kissing his forehead and saying their last good-byes. The tears ran as smoothly and as quickly as the river that was behind them and they laid their friend into the ground, giving his body back to the earth. They covered him up with his cloak and then the four quietly pulled handfuls of the dirt pile back up and buried Ellchant Pendergast, their loved and missed friend.

The tears fell with each handful of dirt and before long the hole was filled and they all stood around his grave crying softly to one another. Aris began to hum the tune

194

of the hunting song and before long the others joined in. But this was not the time to sing the words this was beyond any words to sing. Aris felt the compulsion to say something. Anything that could comfort them all, but nothing came to his mind that seemed fitting enough to honor a man who had always been there for them. Ellchant had been like a father to him and his brother and he felt a hole in his heart where he once felt the peace of having the old man near him.

"Good-bye." Was all Aris could say before his crying overwhelmed him and his face fell into his hands. He felt the comforting grip of the elf on his shoulder as Braeburn wrapped his arm around Aris.

Iadil knelt and picked five Idleans from a small patch that sprung out of the ground in front of her. She handed the others one each and kept the extra one herself. She kissed it and tossed it onto the grave. The others tossed theirs onto the burial ground and sniffed and in their minds tried their best to let themselves say good-bye.

Aris wiped his face and looked around at any other place than the grave. He turned suddenly, when a flash of light caught his eye and with him the elf moved to see what the young man stared at. Kallevick and Iadil moved when in their peripheral vision they noticed that the others were not looking at the ground.

"What is it?" Kallevick asked.

"The rainbow. Look." Braeburn commented.

They all watched as the rainbow began to glow brighter and brighter with the rays of the sun. The colors grew more and more bold and the water seemed to be splashing down on the edge of the hillside rather than gently caressing it as it had before. It was magnificent to behold. The beams of light were more intense now and Aris could do no more than smile for he knew that this was just the right place to lay their friend to rest.

CHAPTER 27

T he four travelers spent the rest of that day binding their wounds and bathing in the bowels of the crystal river, doing their best to wash their clothes from the dirt and sweat. It was a long relaxing day and for the first time since they left on their journey they all took it as a welcome sign of rest. Aris spent most of his time reflecting on his short time knowing the old man and he was certain that the others would be doing the same. He missed his old friend more than words could say and he wished that he could have done more to help him. But deep down he knew that he did all he could. Like Ellchant had told him about his family it was more important to remember the good things rather than to live regretting this or that about the time you were with them.

Kallevick had wandered off with Iadil and Aris was surprised at himself for not taking the initiative and going out to explore this strange new land himself. But he felt the weight of the task ahead of him and he found it more important to meditate than to do what his heart burned to do. The idea of catching Malcolm Fortune was taking precedence over his thoughts. He did want to see what lay beyond the crystal mountain and what lay beyond that but his mind was burdened and he could not shake himself from the task at hand.

He was sitting on the hillcrest a few feet from Ellchant's grave and the sky had slowly faded to a brilliant blue as night fell. He looked up and saw that the stars were shining in all their luminous glory, the moon, no longer full, shone as a silver crescent, like a thumb nail accenting the sky and his gaze fell upon the crystal mountain where he spied two figures climbing. Kallevick had told him that he was going to show Iadil the alicorns when the stars came out and Aris had a feeling that his brother was planning more than just a star gazing session even though Kallevick hadn't made any verbal indication of it.

Braeburn walked up from behind Aris and sat down next to him, dropping an armload of wild fruits and vegetables down on the ground.

"I figured we ought to stock up. Besides, these things are so good." The hungry elf said taking a bite from a ripe fruit.

"I really shouldn't be surprised that you can eat anymore, especially considering that we all spent the day pretty much stuffing our faces." The young man commented.

"Well what did you expect? We hadn't eaten in days and you know me. I'm always hungry." The elf said devouring the fruit.

Aris shook his head. "You would have left all of us starving if you had lived with us. My mother would have been your best friend. She was the best cook in the world."

"Do you know how to cook?" Braeburn said finishing his food. "Who knows, maybe you'll be my best friend."

"Sort of. Kallevick was the one who picked up on that more than me."

"Some good you are. Kallevick will be my friend then."

"I said that he can kind of cook, I didn't say that he was an expert at it."

"Well we'll see about that." Braeburn said teasing. His eyes flashed for a moment in the night-light and he gazed at the mountaintop where he spied the two figures settling down at the edge of the falls.

"You're probably right. He's too busy swooning over her anyway."

"Yeah, I think so too. He's never been like this before but I know my brother, and I know that what he feels is genuine."

"Hey, do you think Iadil can cook?" Braeburn said, his mouth hanging open a bit.

Aris looked at his friend with an annoyed glance.

"Like a giant bottomless stomach." Aris shook his head.

*   *   *   *   *   *   *   *   *   *   *   *

"It's so peaceful. So beautiful." Iadil said, her voice clear over the sound of the falls.

The faerie's eyes shone bright in the light of the moon as she stared out over the falls and watched the quiet valley below. Kallevick could barely peel his gaze from her and it took him a few minutes before he could survey the valley himself.

"It is." He said once he had looked below them and then turned his attention back to her. "So are you."

She turned to him and her mouth was open a tad as if she was caught off guard.

"Thank you." She said, almost inaudible over the sound of the water. She looked off into the distance again and then into the night sky. "So where are these alicorns you promised to show me."

"Right." Kallevick said, standing up to move closer to her. He sat right next to her and he could smell her sweet scent, like a natural perfume drifting on the cool air. He inhaled softly. Once he had seated himself he took her hand and made her point her finger up at the sky.

"Pick a star."

"What?" She asked, looking into his eyes and realizing for the first time that he was sitting very close to her, almost holding her from behind. She felt nervous and hoped that he didn't notice the sweat on her palm.

He wasn't sure if he was pushing it a little too far but judging from the sweat on her palm and the fact that she didn't move at all when he sat behind her he took it as a good sign.

"You know, I never got to say thank you before." She said, her voice trembling a bit. She was really nervous now and she was certain he could feel it.

He looked at her. "Thank me for what?" He asked. His expression was natural and he gave no hint that he was just asking to be fed compliments.

"For saving my life back there in the forest." She looked deep into his brown eyes and saw a strength there that she was sure that the young man himself had never seen.

"Oh." He said, looking away almost embarrassed. "It was nothing." He pulled her arm so they would be pointing together into the sky. Her skin was smooth and soft and he could feel the warmth of it under his own arm. "Look." He said, trying to divert her attention. Now he was nervous.

She finally moved her ethereal eyes away from his to look at where he pointed. She moved her hand and indicated a star. She could feel the air move behind her as she felt his warm breath on her neck when he acknowledged the celestial orb.

His finger lay on top of hers and he fought the urge to entwine his hand around her's. He wanted to lace them between her's so that their hands embraced. But he gently pressed her finger and he pointed straight at the star and then moving right he traced an invisible line a few inches in the open air. Then after their hands had moved away, a line of light appeared for a brief instant and then flickered out, fizzling like a shooting star into the atmosphere.

"How did you do that?" She said, her face alight with wonder. She turned to him, her face beaming with her stunning smile.

"You can do it with any star. The gods wanted us all to remember the unicorn's so they thought this would be the best way to do it."

"I'll say." She commented. "Do it again."

Kallevick smiled and though he knew that she probably had far more stories to tell about her life and the world in general he was glad to know that he at least had this one thing to share with her.

She pointed into the velvet sky once more and indicated another star. She wondered what else he had to share, what other little secrets and bits of magic could he show her. She wanted to know and her curiosity was peaked.

Again he traced an invisible line in the sky and then a moment later the star's light streaked across the sky leaving a dim white trail that fizzled out in a matter of seconds.

"Like a unicorn's alicorn." Iadil said, almost breathless. "I can't believe I never knew about that before."

"I was pretty surprised that you didn't know about that when I first mentioned it." Kallevick said looking into her green eyes. "My father said that the gods gave the unicorns their horns so that they could focus energy from above and that allowed them to travel at the speeds that they did."

"He taught you well." She said, her eyes flashing in the moonlight.

He looked deeply into her face, his eyes melting into hers and he leaned forward slightly. She leaned in to the point where they were almost touching and were merely a breath away from each other's face.

He looked into the green orbs that sat right in front of him.

"Can I ask you something?" He said, his voice low and deep.

"Anything." She said, her voice almost a whisper and she stopped her thoughts from getting carried away. For a brief instant she imagined herself grabbing his face and planting her lips firmly on his, letting the moment seize her. She broke the thought with her reasoning. She better at least let him ask his question.

"How do you feel about Braeburn?" He asked even though he felt rather ridiculous seeing as how she had barely met the elf a few days before. He hated to admit it but seeing as how her and the elf were both Ellion he couldn't deny that the two of them had a connection. But then again he had only met her a few days before and yet he felt so powerfully for her. So attached and so good to be around her. He knew that even if this was the last moment that he would ever spend with her that he could die a happy man. It would be a shame to not get to know her while he had the chance. He knew then that he loved her with a passion that he had never felt before. He shook his head a bit and he smiled for this thought struck him as strange. He barely knew her. But then again she barely knew him.

She wondered as she stared into his eyes at where his thoughts were leading him and for a moment she thought of her fellow Ellion who lay in the valley below them. She smiled a bit at the thought of her kinsmen. Elves were the male counterpart to the race of Ellion and she was a faerie, the female half and though the elf was handsome and regal looking, she didn't care for him the way she did for this young man.

"I think that he is silly but has a good heart." She replied.

Kallevick had almost forgotten his question entirely. Then with her answer he backed off a bit.

"I guess the question that I should be asking you is, how do you feel about me?" He wanted to say more and thousands of thoughts raced through his head. He suddenly was reminded of Aris describing what it was like for him when Orsidire spoke to him, the racing thoughts, the countless questions, the need to say everything and yet not being able to say a thing. He now understood fully how his brother had felt, only in this instance this was with another person and not with a relic of another day. His heart skipped a few beats as she smiled and she turned her gaze to the ground. Oh no, he thought, here it comes. She is going to laugh at me and say that I am just a boy, too innocent and naïve to understand much less love someone I barely know.

"Well, Kallevick." She began.

He felt a lump gather in his throat and while holding his breath the sound of her saying his name caused his heart to jump in his chest once more.

"I feel really silly saying this because I barely know you, and you barely know me." She started tracing patterns into the dirt with a nearby twig. She wanted to look into his eyes but found that she couldn't pull them from the ground.

Kallevick took her chin in his hands and pulled her attention from the dirt.

She looked into his eyes and leaned in closer than before. Her lips almost touched his and she backed off and looked into his earthy brown orbs once more.

"I know that I don't really know you yet, but I think I love you."

Kallevick exhaled and felt a cascade of emotion crash over him just like the waterfalls that they sat next to. He leaned in, their lips barely touching and closed his eyes. He leaned back and then looked into her eyes.

"Good." He said, his face full of satisfaction.

Iadil looked at him confused, almost as if she didn't know whether to be angry or insulted.

"Good?" She asked, her voice a bit guarded with caution.

"Yeah. Good. Because I am in love with you and I would hate to be the only one that felt that way."

Then without a second thought she gave in to her urge and seized his face in her hands and kissed him passionately. Their lips made love and Kallevick could feel a set of internal fireworks going off in his chest. All he could see in his mind was a vision of himself jumping off of the falls and racing the water down to the bottom. He felt like he could fly and he felt the warmth of her skin against his as she kissed him.

She couldn't stop herself and she melted under his touch as he took her face in his strong hands. Then he moved and pulled her closer, wrapping his muscular arms around her, making her shiver a bit in excitement. She knew she was safe with him and she could feel it in his kiss.

Then, after what seemed like a glimpse of eternity they disengaged and looked at one another. Kallevick had his arms wrapped around her and he couldn't believe how good it felt to hold her. He began to laugh, his face morphing and rising in a bright smile. She joined him and together they looked out over the falls and into the valley below.

"What do you suppose we should tell them?" He asked her.

"I think they knew what was going on before we did." She said laughing.

"I suppose you're right." He let go of her and then knelt before her.

Iadil's expression changed from glee to shock.

"I know I barely know you, and that you barely know me." He said.

He had never looked more handsome to her than he did at this very moment. He looked strong and more beautiful than she had ever seen him. But she had only seen him a few times and in a few different situations. She laughed at herself. He took her hand.

"But," he continued, "I want to spend the rest of my life getting to know you. If you do me this honor, I will cherish you for as long as I live and long after we pass into the realms beyond the sky. Iadil Idlean, will you marry me?"

A lone tear streaked down her face and her smile was far brighter than any sun or star in the sky. She was more beautiful than any thing he had ever seen with his mortal eyes. If she denied him, he was sure that his heart would shatter right where he stood. He held his breath and stared deep into her bright green eyes.

"Kallevick Desarta, I barely know you, but I wouldn't want to share my life with anyone else. I will marry you."

With that they kissed once again this time with even more intensity and then embraced as if they were to be torn apart, never to see one another ever again. Then as they lay next to one another staring up at the sky above they drifted off into a dreamless sleep, for this was far better than any dream.

CHAPTER 28

The birds were chirping and singing sweet love songs to one another as the two lovers awoke. Kallevick was awake before the faerie and he sat up and looked about him. He had forgotten that they had fallen asleep next to the top of the falls and the sound of the water crashing in the valley below was an invigorating and welcome noise to rise to. He looked at his beloved and watched her, studying her features and etched them into his memory, almost as if he was afraid that she was a dream and he feared losing her by waking up. He did fear of losing her and it was this thought that pulled him back to reality and he remembered that they were on a mission, a mission that would put him and his companions in mortal danger. He had no concern for himself and he made a silent vow as he watched Iadil sleep that he would never let anything harm her and should the need arise, he would die defending her.

He stood, stretching as he did and walked over to the edge of the crystal mountain and looked down to see if he could spot any sign of his brother or the elf. He looked down and his eyes scanned the glowing green and white grass looking for anything moving across the plain. He spied the elf walking towards the crest of the hill where they had laid their old companion to rest. Kallevick's mind flashed to an image of Ellchant and his kind smile. The young man smiled back at the thought and his eyes began to water. He missed Ellchant horribly and he knew that the others felt the burden on their hearts as well.

"What do you see?" Iadil said from behind him.

"Well," Kallevick responded. "Braeburn is attempting to juggle some of those wild fruits that we were eating yesterday." He said laughing. "And he is doing a horrendous job of it. He.." His words were cut off with a sudden burst of laughter.

"What is it?" Iadil asked, her voice full of merriment.

"Come here, you've got to see this."

Iadil rose and stood next to Kallevick, her arms wrapping about his waist as the two of them watched the elf juggle below them in the valley. Braeburn had found his rhythm and was keeping his balance steady, tossing three fruits in the air with ease. But when he looked up at the mountain and saw that he had an audience he missed his mark and one of the fruits hit him on the head, splattering as it landed.

The two lovers laughed and Kallevick inhaled sharply.

"You're horrible!" He shouted.

Braeburn stood still and looked at Kallevick and Iadil from where he was. A thick green syrupy juice dripped from off his nose and he wiped it away with his right hand. Then after realizing that this was also food he licked the sweet juice from his fingers. He heard Kallevick shouting again from the mountaintop. Braeburn could barely make out the words and he moved his hands to his ears to pantomime for the young man to speak up.

"I can't hear you!" The elf shouted back.

Kallevick shouted again.

"What?!" The elf became irritated.

"You bore!" Came the shout from above.

"Oh. Thanks!" Braeburn shouted back. "I guess. What in Andellius is he talking about?" The elf commented to himself.

Kallevick knew the elf could barely hear him. He pointed to the pile of clothes that lay at Braeburn's feet.

"Where's my brother?" He shouted to the fruit covered elf.

"Huh?" Braeburn shouted as he wiped his face and then cleaned his hands with his tongue.

"Where's Aris?" Kallevick shouted.

Braeburn's face became scrunched into complete puzzlement. "What?!"

"Where is Aris?" Iadil shouted.

The elf put his hands to his ears then motioned for the two of them to come down.

"Well, this isn't working. Let's see what he wants." Kallevick said turning to Iadil.

She looked up at him, her green eyes glowing in the sunlight.

"Sure thing, handsome." She said, kissing him.

He wrapped his arms around her shoulders and kissed back firmly. He pulled back and them looked at her.

"C'mon." She said leading him by the hand down the side of the mountain.

*   *   *   *   *   *   *   *   *   *   *

"A bore, huh?" Braeburn said as Iadil and Kallevick approached him a little while later.

"What?" Kallevick asked, his face indicating blatant confusion.

"Before, when you shouted to me you said I was a bore." Braeburn repeated.

Kallevick shook his head and began to laugh.

"No. No. I said you were horrible. You're a horrible juggler."

Iadil begin to laugh and Braeburn's face became stern.

"Fine. If that's the way you see me. Then this fruit is all mine. You can't have any, you'll have to get your own." He turned his nose up in the air in mock arrogance and took a large bite of fruit.

"I wouldn't want it freshly split over the head of an elf anyway. I prefer mine clean off the trees." Kallevick said picking up two of the fruits and handing one to Iadil.

"Where's Aris?" Kallevick asked, taking a bite of his breakfast.

"Well for your information, Kallevick," Braeburn said, his voice dripping with as much sarcasm as it was with ripe fruit juice. "He's taking a bath." He pointed to the base of the falls where the three of them spotted Aris' head pop from the surface of the misting and splashing water.

Kallevick turned to the elf. "You could use a bath yourself."

"Oh really?" Braeburn said flinging some juice at his friend with his sticky fingers. "If you keep this up, you will too." He said indicating what was dripping down Kallevick's face.

"Fine. Truce?" Kallevick said extending his hand.

Braeburn looked at the young man's extended hand and then at him. He then wiped his hands on his trousers and shook Kallevick's hand, which stuck to the young man's.

"Truce or not, I will get you back for your insult." Braeburn muttered under his breath and he smiled in mock conspiracy.

Kallevick turned to watch his brother.

Aris was bathing, his upper body exposed above the surface of the water and he cupped his left hand and gathered a pool of the crystalline liquid into it. Then he poured it down his right arm letting it wash the wound that was left from their narrow escape the other day. Within a few moments the wound began to heal and close and before long the bite was covered leaving a defined scar that was the only indication that Aris had been hurt. The young man turned his gaze to the sky and closed his eyes. He mouthed a prayer heavenward and his three friends mused that he was thanking the gods. Then his eyes opened and he looked at his friends and smiled.

The three travelers looked to one another, each wondering what Aris was doing. Then Aris plunged down under the water suddenly and they could not see him. A minute passed and Kallevick began to fidget.

"He's been under too long. I'm going after him." Kallevick said, beginning to loosen his tunic so he could remove it.

"No need." Iadil said as Aris burst from the silvery waters a few feet from them. His chest was glistening with droplets of the crystalline waters and his whole visage appeared to glow with a powerful light. The water level flowed just below his breastbone and Kallevick thought of him as a rock in the middle of the river, letting the water shape him and yet not letting it carry him downstream. Aris inhaled sharply and exhaled with a slow steady pace. Opening his eyes, he looked to his friends and smiled.

"Aris, are you all right?" Braeburn asked.

"I have never felt this good in my entire life." Aris said. His face was alight with excitement and the smile faded from his face leaving only slight hints at the corners of his mouth. "I had a dream last night and in it Ellchant told me to wash in the water to prepare for the final leg of our journey. I have never felt so alive in my entire life. I am ready for this. I want that sword back more than ever."

Kallevick looked at his brother and he saw a determination there that was not fully realized in Aris when they had gone to Nari that fateful day. His brother was bent on success and he could feel the drive emanate through Aris' intense glare.

Then as if sensing that his expression was overtly blatant Aris spoke.

"I feel it in my core, the deepest part of my being. Change is coming and I'm not sure what kind of change. It doesn't seem to be of the malevolent sort but the kind that is so metamorphic and drastic that it will change the very eyes in which I see the world."

They all nodded in acknowledgement and Kallevick reached for Aris' clothes. "Well you need to get dressed. I can't have you showing up at my wedding naked."

"Wedding?" Braeburn and Aris asked simultaneously.

"That's right. Iadil and I are getting married and we need your help to perform the ceremony." Kallevick said.

"I knew it. I knew you were planning more that just a star gazing session last night!" Aris said, the boyish smile returning to his face. "Well, congratulations!" He said laughing. "I guess I'm about to gain a new sister."

Iadil smiled. "I've never had a brother before."

"If you would allow me." Braeburn began. "I would be honored to perform the ceremony."

"What do you think, Iadil?" Kallevick said to his betrothed.

"That's fine with me. Just clean yourself up first." She said laughing.

For the first time since he had come from the water Aris noticed that Braeburn was covered in juice and he began to laugh.

*   *   *   *   *   *   *   *   *   *   *   *

The company spent the rest of the day relaxing. Only the lovebirds got to relax, as Braeburn saw it. Aris insisted that they send the two off for a romantic walk while he and the elf prepare a ceremony and a secret honeymoon spot for the two. This would also allow for Iadil and Kallevick to come up with vows for one another. It had taken most of the day for Aris and Braeburn to gather all the necessary materials and they had prepared a makeshift altar of sorts near the crest of the hill so that Ellchant could be present for the proceedings.

By the time Iadil and her lover returned Aris and the elf stood waiting for them and Iadil was greeted with a flower garland that was placed like a crown on her brow. She gasped in surprise at what lay before them. Kallevick was given his sword and it was sheathed at his side. His hand was placed on its hilt and the two were ordered to march toward the altar where Braeburn was dressed in a robe made of purple leaves. On his head was headdress made of red leaves. They had erected five flags of sorts, fashioned from limbs of some young trees and on each was tied a string of flowers. The poles were wrapped in flowers as well and they stood behind the elf, a deep beautiful contrast to the color of his robes. The sun was shining bright and the world seemed to glow about them.

As Kallevick walked, one hand on his sword hilt, the other on his beloved's hand he looked at the elf and felt so thankful to the gods for having given him such wonderful friends and when he looked at Iadil, a wonderful woman to marry.

Aris led the procession and stopped to bow before Braeburn who bowed back. Then as Aris stepped off to the side the two lovers came forward before the altar and were instructed to kneel. The elf turned behind him and pulled out a large dried leaf full of Idlean petals and taking a handful he scattered them onto the altar.

"Let these mark all the blessings that the gods will bestow upon you and your union." Braeburn said. "I call upon the spirit of the land and the blessing of the gods to sanctify this union."

As if on cue the heavens began to rain down pure white feathers and all manner of colored lights began to shine in between the clouds, bouncing off one another and illuminating the feathers as they fell. Kallevick and Iadil laughed and smiled with wonder and happiness. Aris smiled with his brother, and Kallevick looked at his younger brother and winked at him. Aris winked back. The attention of the couple was drawn back to Braeburn as the feathers ceased to fall.

"Let the waters of the world sing to this couple, for their love is as pure as the source of these falls."

Suddenly music erupted from the falls and the mouths of all of the company, save for the elf were all dropped wide open as they listened to the sweet and exhilarating music.

"Braeburn. How did you do all of this?" Aris said, leaning in to ask the elf.

Braeburn turned and leaned in to speak quietly to Aris as the music streamed out into the air. "The power of faith my friend."

Braeburn turned his attention back to his duties as master of the wedding. Tracing a pattern into the ground he pointed for the two lovers to look at it.

"This ring is the world and each spoke represents the five dragons. On this ring you shall confess your love and express your vows for this is the only ring you shall need to show your commitment."

Aris looked down and recognized the symbol immediately for it was the design on the pommel of Orsidire. The Wheel of Midgail.

"On this ring I do commit my love and all that I have and am to this one woman, Iadil Idlean. I promise to love no other and to be faithful and just to none other. She is my heart and my home and I will do her all the service that the gods will allow me." Kallevick said and as he did Iadil's eyes began to water. Kallevick leaned in so that only Iadil could hear him.

"Of all the fair things of Isadore, Iadil is the fairest." He whispered.

A few stray tears slipped down her beautiful face and she smiled brightly. "On this ring I do commit my love and all that I have and am to this one man, Kallevick Desarta. I promise to love no other and to be faithful and just to none other. He is my heart and my home and I will do him all the service that the gods will allow me." She leaned in so that only Kallevick could hear him.

"Of all men I've seen, you are the bravest and the most handsome."

Kallevick's smile only grew.

Aris and Braeburn looked to one another wondering what secret vows the two had made and they smiled.

"Then with these vows and with the blessing of the gods, the rightful heirs of the throne of the universe, I grant you the title and privilege of being husband and wife." Braeburn continued.

The two looked up to him and smiled, their faces alight with joy and utter happiness.

"With this union the race of Ellion will once again flourish. Do not let your love die nor let it linger on dark things for in this union flows the light of creation. You may seal this bond with an embrace of the lips." Braeburn finished and the two lovers, looking into one another's eyes kissed more passionately than they ever had and with that the two were wed.

Aris and Braeburn clapped and smiled and though the shining lights from the sky had faded, the music from the falls continued. The two betrothed began to laugh and dance and sing with the music and they all celebrated the blessed union.

*   *   *   *   *   *   *   *   *   *

That night the moon shined bright and the stars were out in all their glory as Aris and Braeburn led the two newlyweds to a secret grove that they had found and prepared for the two young lovers. It was on a small hill and at its top was a smooth concave nest that was naturally cut into the land. In it was a layer of soft Idleans and the prismatic flowers were lined in a circle surrounded by all manner of colored flowers. It had a thatched roof made from branches of the small trees that lined the dimple in the land that the Idleans were lain. It was a makeshift bed and after the elf and Aris had taken turns embracing Iadil and Kallevick in congratulatory expressions the couple lay down and watched as their two friends walked away and out of sight.

"Well." Iadil said. "How does it feel to be married?" She asked, smiling.

"Exhilarating." Kallevick said, his smile brighter than it had ever been.

"Good." Iadil said.

"Good?" Kallevick asked, wondering if she was getting back at him for his use of the word the night before. He smiled.

"Yeah. Good." She said. "Because you are stuck with me now until we die."

They laughed heartily, more from one another's company than from the joke and soon they were kissing again. Before long they began to undress and as the night moved on they began to express their love for each other with their bodies. They made love and to their right the falls still rung out their magical music. Above them the heavens were full of light as shooting stars streaked across the sky.

CHAPTER 29

Morning came soon, Kallevick thought, much too soon. He had gotten plenty of rest but he wished that he could have slept for just a little longer. He sat up as he heard his brother approach from below him and his sleeping wife. He heard the smooth sound of the water falls cascading over the edge of the crystal mountain but no more did the notes of music ring out over the sound of the running water. The music had faded out in the night and for the first time Kallevick realized this, preferring to remember the music that him and his wife had made.

"Kallevick. Psst. Kalle. You awake?" Came Aris' voice from slightly below him.

Kallevick crept toward the edge of the dip in the ground and looked out to see his brother fully dressed and armed.

"Hey." Kallevick said quietly, rubbing his bare arms and scratching his exposed chest.

"I know you two probably want to sleep, but we have to get going. Remember Ellchant said that we could stay here for two days, no longer. I didn't want to wake Iadil, and I figured I'd give you two a few minutes to get ready." Aris whispered.

"I want to sleep more, it is our honeymoon you know." Kallevick said, hoping he could coax Aris into letting him sleep another hour.

"Honeymoon or no, we have to leave. I'll give you and Iadil a few extra minutes, but we've got to get moving."

Kallevick knew he was right and he nodded an affirmative to Aris.

"We'll meet you at Ellchant's grave."

"Alright. And don't go back to sleep." Aris said, pointing his finger at him.

Kallevick yawned and his hand went to cover his mouth. He watched Aris creep away and he guessed that he did that so he wouldn't see him naked. But Aris was below him and couldn't see that he wore his pants. Kallevick turned to his sleeping beauty and curled up next to her. She groaned a little and nestled into his arms.

"Beautiful, it's time to wake up." He whispered into her ear, his voice low and smooth.

Her eyes opened and she blinked a few times, regaining her vision. Her pupils adjusted to the light and she sat up and looked at her husband. He watched as she smiled at him and her pupils dilated, then shrunk back down to where they had been before. He knew that it was like saying I love you without words and this thought made him glad.

Before Kallevick could open his mouth to speak Iadil's lips were locked with his and they shared a tender kiss. Iadil broke away leaving Kallevick stunned with excitement, as she moved to put on her dress. Kallevick kissed her back and she giggled.

"We've got to get moving." Iadil said, before Kallevick could speak again.

But before she could get her clothes back on, Kallevick was all over her and they began to embrace.

*   *   *   *   *   *   *   *   *   *   *   *

Braeburn and Aris stood at Ellchant's grave and watched as the two newly weds approached.

"I said just a few extra minutes, not another half hour!" Aris said, slightly annoyed. He understood what the two needed but there were more important things at hand.

"Sorry. But if it's any consolation to you, we didn't go back to sleep." Kallevick said his grin a little too happy for Aris' taste.

"I can see that." Aris said, his tone lightening.

"Me too. I mean, I'm sorry too." Iadil said smiling along, her head hung in mock shame.

Braeburn chuckled to himself. "What did you expect Aris? They can barely keep their hands off each other."

Aris rolled his eyes, gave in and smiled. "I know, they are very good together." He conceded. "C'mon." He said waving his hand.

After all taking brief turns kissing the ground where Ellchant lay they moved east and began to round the edge of the mountain, heading north. The sounds of the falling water and the music of the birds overhead began to fade as they trekked around the shimmering rock formation. The trees where not as colorful on this side of the crystal falls and they all noticed with some disappointment that the landscape began to lose some of its liveliness as they traveled further. They all turned and looked one last time at the place where Orsidire was born.

They all said their good-byes and each of them wished that they could stay there forever. Then as Aris looked to each of his companions to say some moving words, he found that they seemed void of any real value and he decided it best to keep his mouth shut. They all greeted him with their eyes and he knew that they all shared the same sentiments as he did. They did not need words to express what they all felt and the locking of each pair of eyes on one another was indication enough that they would all miss this place dearly. Aris turned and the others followed his lead as they trekked on into the gathering of trees before them.

A light mist had culminated in their path as they walked and soon it was a thick impenetrable fog, not allowing them any sight beyond arm's reach. The light was dusky and gray as if it was being swallowed by the misty white of the earth bound clouds. They walked closer together in the hopes that they would not lose one another and they quickened their pace as they followed Aris into the mist. The young leader felt a burden on his heart and he felt afraid, full well knowing that he was leading his friends into danger, much less into the heart of darkness. But his resolve was cemented in his mind and they would finish what they set out to do, even if that meant death.

They barely spoke and there was nothing to see although if there was it would have been impossible to spot in the fog. Not a sound came from around them and Aris felt as though they were in a void. Just as Melchor had described. It was the exact opposite of what they had just left and the young man wondered how a perfect place such as Isadore could be surrounded by places like the Barren forest and these mists. Speaking of which, he didn't even know what they were called much less how far they had traveled north.

"Braeburn." Aris called to the elf behind him. "Where are we?"

"The mists of Uldoon." Iadil answered. "They surround the Hall of Altamare where Dinemid is bound. We're probably not too far off from there now."

Aris nodded and he looked at his brother who returned a grave expression. The elf looked at them all and caught up to them. Suddenly a spot in the cloud cover vanished with a gust of wind revealing a corrugated maroon stained stone pillar that stood stout and ruined a few feet from where they were.

"What in the world is this?" Kallevick said, walking over to it and running his hands along the aged and weathered surface.

"The Rundagg came into existence here." Braeburn said, his face stern. "There were two kings, Moradoff and Komoroff and they shared this kingdom. They were charged as guardians of the white forest, which we all know now as the Barren Forest. But they fell to corruption and began to worship Dinemid. Their wickedness warped them and they were transformed into goblins. The halls were destroyed by the gods when they found out that the men had turned to evil and they where driven out. But they came back after they found out that their god had been imprisoned here."

"They are cannibals, eating anything with living flesh." Iadil added, her face full of disgust. "They have even been known to eat one another if the need arose."

Kallevick shuddered with the thought and he looked at Aris who also shivered a bit.

"Why is this dark red?" Kallevick asked, although he was unsure that he wanted the answer.

"It used to be white." Braeburn said. "But many say that the Rundagg have feasts and use the blood of their victims to paint the ruins of their former kingdom."

The loud sound of breathing came from ahead of them and abruptly the wind picked up. It blew through the four travelers and with it the mist cleared allowing them a glimpse of what lay ahead. Aris was the first to see it and he peered deep into the fog to get a better look. A gleaming red eye stared back at them. It was like a razor, cutting the air between them, sending sharp slashes through their shocked stares. Then it turned suddenly, revealing a mane of knotted and nastily tangled black hair.

"Fortune!" Aris shouted and he was off before any of the others could even verbally respond. The mist curled around Aris as he ran and he bolted off after the hideous thief.

"Aris!" They all shouted to him. They ran after him, Kallevick grabbing Iadil's hand so he wouldn't lose her. More and more patches of fresh air began to creep their way into the fog as they gave chase and with it they caught sight of stones and bricks laying strewn about and scattered in all directions, stained with a dull red. They saw pillar upon pillar and they slowed as they ran low on air. Braeburn was close behind and after they ran as far as they could they stopped to gather their breath.

The elf bent over, placing his hands on his knees, gulping in air. He looked up and his eyes focused on a nearby pillar.

"Iadil, Kalle, Look!" He shouted, running over to the pillar, his eyes wide in terror.

"What is it?" Kallevick asked as the two neared.

"Look." The awestruck elf said, his voice quivering. "It's… It's an Ellion." He pointed.

The other two looked and noted the features of a young elf, his hands stretched before his eyes as if to shield them from a blinding light. His face was full of horror and he was on his knees. The young Ellion was turned to solid stone and at the sight of this Braeburn fell to his knees and whimpered. Iadil, too shocked to say anything let Kallevick's hand fall to his side and she ran off in search of any more of her and Braeburn's kind. She shouted out in her native tongue and she stumbled and ran a little ways off.

Kallevick stood and stared until Iadil let go of his hand and he ran off after her.

"Iadil!" He shouted, trying to break the mist with his voice. He found her on the ground kneeling, her hands cupping her face as she wept openly. He ran to her and helped her to her feet. She embraced him swiftly and he looked at what she was reacting to. In front of them stood an entire family of Ellion, a Faerie, an Elf, and a Unicorn. The magic horse stood on its hind legs reared up in a great expression of fear. Its alicorn was pointed like an antenna straight towards the sky as if it were trying to signal for help from above. Its eyes, though they were stone were filled with a terror that Kallevick had never seen before and he knew then that the worst was yet to come.

Braeburn stumbled over to them, his face bloated with sadness as he wiped away stray tears.

"We've got to find Aris." Kallevick said. The elf nodded and he could feel Iadil's head move in agreement.

Just then they heard the sound of branches being snapped and broken. It was impossible to tell where it came from as the fog intensified the effect of disorientation and confusion. The sound came again and their attention was racing at a high speed.

The snapping came once more and without even a signal to each other they all began to run straight ahead into the white cloud cover. They were not alone and Kallevick almost wished that they had not left Isadore that morning.

CHAPTER 30

Aris gave chase and he was determined to catch the filthy thief before Malcolm could get anywhere near Dinemid. He ran as fast as he could, the cloud cover lifting as he headed north. Soon he saw clearly the form of the hideous goblin rushing in front of him. Fortune was hunched over and from the outer edge of his arms Aris saw a fur wrapped bundle.

"Come back here!" Aris yelled out to his quarry in desperation. To this the goblin only responded by moving away from him even faster. Aris looked ahead and saw that a great cave stood before them and it was soaked with a deep red, deeper than the red that had stained the first pillar that him and his companions had seen. He thought of his friends back in the mist and he hoped that they were all right but he didn't let that fact slow him. He knew that if he didn't catch Malcolm none of them would be safe.

He could hear the grumbled breathing of the Rundagg and Aris' pace quickened, his feet pounding the ground hard with heavy footfalls. His heart thudded in his chest and he felt the air whip about him. He had never run so fast in his life. Suddenly they were at the mouth of the cave and Fortune ducked inside, his head almost hitting a sharply cut rock that jutted out from the roof of the cavern like a fang.

Aris pushed and even though he had enough breath to yell another command to halt at the fleeing thief he chose to instead duck under the tooth like rock and run into the darkness. He was temporarily slowed as the solace of the shadows surrounded him, swallowing him whole in its menacing jaws. It was as if someone had snuffed out a candle on him and he could barely make out anything in front of him. The air was thin and a cold shiver ran down his back. But when he caught the scent of unwashed flesh not too far ahead of him he ran once more. This was the heart of evil, he thought.

A raucous cackle came from a mere ten feet ahead from what Aris could estimate in the dark. I'll make you swallow that laugh Rundagg, Aris thought. As he ran forward he saw a flash of bright light that blinded him for a split second but he kept his pace. In a moment he realized that the light had not flashed but the darkness that had surrounded him had so enveloped his vision that it appeared to flare when he stumbled upon it. His eyes adjusted to the light and when he saw what lay in his path he rushed with all of his strength.

Before him lay a cold stone slab that stood ten feet tall and was blacker than all the trees of the Barren Forest put together. It was brilliantly polished and from the tops of it were long chains made of a white glowing metal that lit up the entire cavern. Bound to those chains was the embodiment of all the world's fears; the sight of Dinemid himself struck a terror in Aris that he had never known before, leaving him breathless. At that moment he knew that the face of this one being would forever haunt his nightmares should he fail now.

His hair was a shoulder length white and from his temples to the tops of his ears his scalp was exposed, shaved right to the skin. He was like a sickly version of Ellchant and Aris wished that he had his old friend by his side at this very moment. Dinemid's face seemed frost bitten and forever dulled a gray tone. The skin of his face was stretched tightly over the bones, unnaturally taut, almost skeletal. But the eyes of Dinemid were beyond all fears, far past any vision of evil that Aris had ever conjured in his own mind when the darkness overtook him and plunged him into a nightmare. There were ghosts in his eyes, as if by some invisible cage souls were captured and tormented there, screaming in anguish.

Aris' attention was drawn back to the goblin as he unsheathed the holy sword from its wrappings and Orsidire shone like the sun. He watched in horror as Malcolm lifted the sword high into the air, both his goblin hands grasping the hilt tightly as the creature swung across with all of his might to smash the Chains of Light into oblivion. The blade made contact with the metal and as Aris leapt forward a burst of blinding white light flashed as the bonds were severed. The sound of metal striking metal rung out in the cavern, like a gigantic gong being hit with a mallet. Aris ran into Malcolm grappling with the goblin for possession of the sword but landing hard on the ground when he was kicked in the groin.

Dinemid's voice rung out in the cavern like a beast that had been starved for far too long. A hate-filled cackle filled the hall with a dark sounding menace. Shadows seemed to cling to his figure as though they thrived on the blackness of his heart. The light of the chains failed, fleeting rapidly as they lost their power. So this is what he had been planning all along, Aris thought. To use the weapon created to destroy him and free himself with it.

"Go my faithful servant. Destroy all who defy me!" Rumbled the beast.

Malcolm kneeled and held the sword up reverently to Dinemid.

Aris struggled upward and tried to snatch the sword from the Rundagg's hand but Dinemid was quicker than he and smacked the young hero to the ground with a devastating blow to the head. Aris' head hit the stone ground and bounced off slightly leaving him dazed for a moment. He watched in a haze as Dinemid raised the sword in the air, muttering in some unintelligible language. Fortune ran out of the cavern, kicking Aris in the side as he left.

The young man groaned and whimpered with the impact and he gasped for breath while his mind spun with dizziness. When Aris' vision finally steadied he watched Dinemid carve the wheel of Midgail into the stone floor of the cave and then raise Orsidire high in the air, piercing the center circle of the wheel with the tip of the blade. Aris felt a warm trickle down the side of his face and his head throbbed in pain. He felt the warmth run down his cheekbone and drip onto the cold stone ground.

The young man watched in amazement as the wheel began to glow. First the pronged tips lit then the light traced the arms of the wheel and onto the wheel itself, drawing its own outline in a clockwise turn. He tried to move but his head swam in a wave of confusion. He closed his eyes and tried to regain control.

Still lying on the ground and trying to regain his breath he saw the light from the floor of the cavern begin to rise upward five feet into the air and swirl about the room creating a rippling effect. It reflected off of the roof of the hall like the reflection of sunlight off glistening water. Then a burst came from the wheel and a globe shape appeared, whiter than any cloud he had ever seen, swirled around it were all the colors that the gods had ever made. There were some he had never even seen before.

Dinemid's face was alight with deadly excitement and he looked at the young warrior one last time before grabbing Orsidire out of the ground and jumping into the Wheel of Midgail, disappearing from sight. The light of the globe expanded to twice its size and then in a flash it shot straight up and burst through the roof, leaving a column of burning white light shooting in a line to the heavens. The cave shuddered and rumbled from the force and rocks began to fall into the cavern as dust swept across

Aris' face. The colors swirled around the column and Aris stood and ran into the light, disappearing into the unknown.

CHAPTER 31

Kallevick looked up into the sky as he heard the blast come from the cave ahead of them. The wind rushed past him and his friends clearing most of the mist in front of them away, revealing the entrance to the Hall of Altamare. Then Braeburn pointed as the column of light sped up towards the heavens at super speed. Their danger momentarily forgotten, Kallevick suddenly felt his heart sink. Aris was somewhere in that thing, he thought to himself. And there was no way to help him now. He was on his own.

"We've got our own problems," Iadil said, somehow responding to his unspoken fear.

Kallevick turned and saw that an army of Rundagg that slowly marched out of the mists was surrounding them. Some were on horseback and many were on foot.

"I think we're in trouble," Braeburn said, his voice almost queasy.

Kallevick's attention was abruptly drawn to the statues that filled in the gaps where there were no Rundagg soldiers.

"Iadil, Braeburn, look!" Kallevick said to them drawing his sword. His companions armed themselves as they watched the statues slowly fade into color and then into life. The Elves, Faeries and Unicorns blinked and rubbed their eyes adjusting to the light and they looked to one another, then to the three whom they surrounded. They then looked into the sky and they knew that their hero had come. The Race of Ellion had been revived and now they stood surrounded by the ones who had betrayed them. Some of the army recoiled in surprise, while others stood unflinching and staring with great blood lust at the three who stood at the center of the circle that had been formed.

A large Goblin that rode on horseback strode forward on his steed a few paces ahead of his troops. A second horseman came forward only a step or two behind the first.

"Now, Ellion, now is your time. Now will be your end. Dinemid is free and you all will die once and for all." His voice was raspy and coarse like a choking cat.

223

"Moradoff, and Komoroff." Braeburn said quietly to Iadil and Kallevick. "The two brothers that rule the goblin army." He said inhaling sharply as the Rundagg army began to slowly enclose the Ellion in an attempt to stranglehold them.

Just behind them Iadil heard the sound of heavy breathing and hoping that it was Aris she turned around to see Malcolm Fortune running out of the mouth of the Hall. The goblin did not slow and his lack of hesitation seemed to be an unspoken indication of attack for his fellow Rundagg. He raised his arm high in the air and in his grasp was double headed axe.

This was it, Kallevick thought. This is where we all die.

The army raised their voices in unison and calling a horrible battle cry they charged at the Ellion. The Ellion braced themselves and rushed to meet their enemy like a tidal wave crashing into the side of a cliff. Goblin riders were thrown from their horses and a group of elves had mounted some of the unicorns to take down the other horsemen. Some of the Ellion were trampled underfoot from the stampeding horses while others were cut down in a swift fashion by the cavalry of the goblin army. They fell like marionettes whose strings had been cut, flying back in the air to land hard in the dirt.

Malcolm had broken through the unarmed line of Ellion that stood between the cave and the companions at the center of the defensive circle. Braeburn spun around to face the charging Malcolm but was thrown to the side as the goblin rushed for Kallevick. Iadil stepped in his path and thrust with her faerie blade but her opponent side stepped her defensive move and she too was knocked aside. He raised the axe high into the air to swing at the young man's head.

Kallevick spun and slashed across with his father's blade slicing off some of the goblin's dirt stained clothing and leaving a nasty gash in the creature's left arm. He cried out in pain and turned suddenly on the young warrior, tackling the baffled Kallevick to the ground.

Iadil stood and ran to the goblin pushing with all of her strength to tackle him. Just as Malcolm raised his axe again to behead Kallevick, Iadil's body made contact with the goblin sending him skidding into the dirt.

At that moment Braeburn rushed to their aid and slowly the defensive circle was broken and the entire area turned into a sea of churning madness. Steel moved in blurred motion biting off the limbs of Ellion and Goblin alike, leaving gaping wounds in their wake. Some of the Ellion were able to wrestle the weapons away from their attackers and they fought with the stoutness of those who faithfully served the Lords of Galebraith. The screams of the wounded only added to the unfolding chaos. They rung out in ear shattering choruses of pain. The air was full of noise and glinting steel, slashing through flesh and armor.

Kallevick ran out with Iadil and Braeburn in tow to meet the oncoming forces. The goblins rushed forward, a bloodthirsty look of hatred in their gleaming red eyes. Kallevick's grip loosened on the hilt of his sword as he swung a crushing blow to the nearest opponent, who deflected it with his shield. The shield disintegrated under the impact and with another blinding stroke the creature fell next to it.

Iadil was right behind him and side stepped a goblin warrior who rushed to topple over her and trample her underfoot. The goblin turned on her to meet a sword blade in the face and the faerie spun to stab at another oncoming villain who fell to her side as her blade sunk into a small pocket where his armor had failed to cover him.

The air was ablaze with Ellion and Rundagg battle cries and Braeburn shouted a call of his own to join the fray. He moved swiftly and using Aris' knife cut his enemy down with a clean swipe leaving a trail of black blood running down the length of the blade. The greenish hulk of lean muscle crumbled to the ground and moved no more.

But when the elf looked up to see that him and his companions were split up he began to panic and ran into the mass of fighting bodies searching for his comrades, hoping to the gods that they had not fallen victim to the steel of the Rundagg.

*   *   *   *   *   *   *   *   *   *   *   *

Aris was flying. Inside the Wheel of Midgail the young warrior flew after the black god. Surrounding him was a circular wall like a tunnel that was made of prismatic colors and flashes of electricity. Its breadth could not be measured and Aris could only guess at how long the ride would last. The portal was filled with light and sound and it was as if the two opponents were in a sort of vacuum as they were sucked upwards at a velocity that was so rapid that the colors of light began to blend into one another. The colors swirled around like a kaleidoscope, hazy and beautiful and music seemed to be blasting at the edges of the tunnel as Aris raced after his enemy.

Aris' mind was suddenly turned from his chase and his thoughts moved inward. What would happen if he stopped now? What if he let Dinemid go? He shook his head, which still throbbed in pain, the frightening ideas dropping from his mind. He wouldn't let Dinemid's power of doubt affect him. The enemy was not far off and Aris, whose head was now clearer than before sped after him, the ribbons of colored lights falling below him as he flew.

The beast looked down from where he was and spotted the young man gaining on him. He quickened his pace and Aris' hair fluttered about him, the wind whipping past as he chased to catch up. The beast suddenly stopped his ascent and turned on Aris, swinging the godly sword. Aris dodged the blade but caught its tip on the outer edge of his tunic and it tore through so that it hung open, flapping in the whirlwind. Aris reached again for the sword and Dinemid answered with another attack, this time catching the young man and slicing a gash in his chest, ripping his tunic even more.

Aris screamed in pain as Dinemid tried to escape after delivering the wound. But Aris' hand was swift and he caught hold of the banished one's ankle and pulled him down to face him. Dinemid fell to meet Aris face to face and for a moment the young warrior saw the sense of surprise in his opponent's eyes. Aris seized the moment of opportunity, gritted his teeth and cocked his head back, grabbing the collar of the black god's robes tight with his fist.

A gigantic crack shuddered through the Wheel echoing off of the walls of the light tunnel. Dinemid whirled with the impact and his hands went immediately for his head to keep it from spinning off of his shoulders. He was thrown a good fifty feet from the young man's strike and he saw through shaky vision the approach of his foe.

Aris lunged at Dinemid with his hands a blur of fingers and fists as the two fought over the sword. Aris clenched his fist with all of his might and punched the god straight across the face. But Dinemid only turned back smiling at him as blood poured down his nostrils and into his mouth. The evil one smiled and laughed as the young warrior pulled his arm back to unleash another round of his fury. The creature lunged at Aris' throat and grabbed it with his free hand.

Dinemid smiled and laughed only harder as Aris struggled for breath. His hands were wrapped around the sickly thin wrist of the god and he could only kick with his free legs. The tip of Orsidire was lifted to his face and the man kicked at the beast's groin causing the release of his throat. Dinemid yelled out and Aris inhaled deeply as his hands immediately shot out, taking the sword by the exposed bottom half of the hilt. Dinemid turned, grasping the top half of the hilt and his eyes became a boiling sea of churning anger, the ghoulish souls swirling in a whirlpool of malevolence.

But Aris would not budge and he pulled with all of his strength, this time as both hands tried desperately to rip the sword from Dinemid's grasp. The enemy's grip was steadfast and Aris tried to land a kick into the god's side. But he misjudged and the banished one grabbed his leg with the underside of his arm, pinning him. Aris could feel the leather wrapped grip begin to slip in his sweaty palms.

Dinemid's hold loosened a bit as Aris struggled to regain possession of his leg. Aris felt the sudden change in pressure on his shin and kicked with the bottom of his unpinned boot into the exposed stomach of his nemesis, causing Dinemid to gasp with the sudden lack of oxygen. Aris pulled as if freeing the mighty sword Orsidire from the depths of the earth itself and he flew across the wheel as the lights swirled about the two fighters.

Dinemid, knowing he was about to lose control of his prize reached at the critical moment and as the man fell away he stretched out to grab tight the hilt of Aris' white sword and rip it free from the baldric. The baldric vanished into the rainbows of light, their crystalline colors spinning about the fighters in a hazy maelstrom.

Dinemid looked at the young man, his eyes still ablaze with hatred but also smoldering with fear, he flew upward. Aris gave chase with the god sword in hand and the two soared like flashes of energy up towards the heavens.

"Aris." The young man heard. He turned to look for the source of the voice and realized that it came from his opponent which flew across from him on the other side of the light tunnel. They faced one another and when the voice called out his name again he knew that Dinemid was speaking to him. But it was not the terrible voice that had haunted him in his sleep that night in the Desert City, nor was it the horrid rumble of the awakened beast that had unleashed its cackle in the Hall of Altamare. This was the voice of a friend. The voice of Ellchant.

227

Kallevick raised his sword high in the air and it's blade came crashing down on the head of a goblin warrior. Just to his right he heard the voice of his wife, her Ellion call singing out over the raucous of battle like a wind carrying the power of a hurricane. She fought stoutly next to him.

"Help!" Came the call from behind them.

"Braeburn!" Kallevick yelled as he ran to help his elven friend who had lay on his back attempting to evade the blows of a goblin war hammer. The elf dodged another strike and Kallevick was on top of Braeburn's assailant in an instant, ramming the first half of his sword blade into the lower back of the Rundagg. The beast did not scream but fell quietly to the ground. Kallevick helped the elf to his feet and the three ran off into the fray.

"Those horsemen!" The faerie yelled to her companions. "We need to stop them!" She said pointing towards the mists from which the Goblin Army had entered. There the ghoulish brothers Moradoff and Komoroff fought from high upon their steeds, slicing down any Ellion who lay in their path with long wicked looking swords. Komoroff then sheathed his sword and drew out of the leather pouch at his side an enormous blackened spearhead. Then grabbing a long polearm that had been run through the body of a fallen Ellion he fastened the spearhead to the end that had not splintered as he had pulled it from the corpse.

"Quick!" Kallevick yelled to her in response. "Find a Unicorn!"

The young man ran to a Unicorn that had just trampled a Rundagg soldier in fear and as Kallevick whispered a calming message into its ear he mounted the bare back of the beautiful creature. Iadil looked around, chopping with her sword at a goblin who ran in her path and then spotting a Unicorn mounted it and the two rode off to take care of the two brothers. Braeburn was not as fortunate and he scrambled around for a ride.

He turned and was confronted by a large goblin. The elf had decided that he was tired of being thrown to the ground and he jabbed with the Darigo knife sinking it into the foot of the unsuspecting Rundagg. It bellowed in pain and Braeburn let go of the dagger's hilt, gripping his staff with both hands. He swung it upward into the creature's vulnerable groin and then as it fell he spun the staff down, cracking the soldier's weak helmet in two to leave a dent in the animal's skull. He retrieved his knife and ran after his friends.

Kallevick could feel the power within him blaze. It was like a wild fire burning and charring anything in his path and he swung his sword as he rode, slicing the head off of an enemy fighter. He sounded out a warrior's cry as the unicorn's hooves boomed like thunder in the dirt. He could feel the creature's muscles flex under him as if the unicorn was bracing itself for the impact. Kallevick called out again and he raced at Moradoff, bringing his sword back to take the goblin's head.

But the goblin lord was well prepared and as his horse stepped out of range of the sword blade Moradoff pulled a small club from the side pouch mounted to his saddle. As Kallevick completed his swing the goblin smiled, beating the young man in the side so hard that he was thrown from the unicorn's back and hit the ground.

"Kallevick!" Iadil yelled and steered her horse in the direction of her fallen husband. Even though she'd only been a few horse strides away from attacking Komoroff, her lover needed her and she rode, her weapon clasped in a tight fist and the other hand griping the mane of the Unicorn's neck like reins. Moradoff was caught off guard and received the faerie's blade in his shoulder as she rode. The fat goblin lord fell from his horse and landed a few feet from the still stunned Kallevick.

Braeburn had finally caught up to them and seeing that his friends were busy he headed to Komoroff who had moved to help his brother. Hoping he could cut off the goblin before the creature could get to his friends, he ran. But he was knocked aside by the force of a goblin mass and the elf stumbled to the side. He could smell the rancid smell of unwashed Rundagg flesh and before he regained control of his steps he was struck in the face by a goblin fist. The elf reeled, recoiling backwards and landed so that he sat on the ground.

He heard the cry of Iadil who had turned her unicorn to face off with Komoroff. But the goblin lord had raised his spear to run Kallevick through and the faerie was too far away yet to knock him from the horse on which he rode. In an instant Braeburn let out an Ellion call which sent Komoroff's horse to stand up on its hind legs, whinnying in anger, throwing the goblin from its back.

"I told you I was good with horses!" The elf shouted out to his friends.

But Braeburn did not have a chance to see the Rundagg's surprised face as he hit the ground. Another burst of goblin fist struck him in the stomach and when the elf gasped for air he looked up to see Malcolm Fortune swinging his double headed axe at his chest.

Komoroff and Moradoff were still dazed as Iadil leapt from her horse and grabbed Kallevick, pulling him to his feet. Kallevick kissed her and then ran off to help the elf. But the elf had himself covered and rolled out of the way of Malcolm's swinging axe. The weapon's head sunk into a rotten log and Braeburn squirmed out from under the hulking mass of the Rundagg, smiting Malcolm in the face with the butt of his staff, causing the beast to let go of his weapon and grab at his broken nose.

Iadil ran and as Malcolm turned and pulled his fist back to punch the life out of her, she caught his blow with her delicate hands and her faerie wings came out from under the invisible folds in her back. She pulled his arm up above him and pulled it backwards so that he landed on his back. The creature was momentarily paralyzed.

"Now Kallevick!" She yelled.

Kallevick took hold of his sword so that the tip of the blade faced the earth and just as he was about to thrust it through the belly of the beast Braeburn shouted out to him. He turned in time to see Komoroff riding toward him, spear in hand. The goblin meant to run him through like a knight in a jousting tournament. But Kallevick moved out of the way just as the horse got within a few feet of him and the spear ran through Malcolm instead. The thief groaned with a deep gurgling sound and lay motionless.

Braeburn whistled to a nearby unicorn. It came galloping over and Kallevick mounted it, racing off to take out Moradoff once and for all. Meanwhile Komoroff had turned his horse around and was charging at Iadil who stood in his way. The faerie flew up above him and grabbed the loops that held his armor in place, pulling them as she flew past. The goblin's heavy wrought iron chest plate fell from him, hitting his horse in the head, knocking it out cold. The goblin lord flew over the suddenly inundated horse and skidded into the dirt.

Kallevick galloped at Moradoff and the goblin braced himself knowing that he could not outrun a unicorn, he stood holding his deadly goblin blade out in preparation. Kallevick shouted at the top of his lungs and jumped from the animal's back tackling the goblin to the ground before Moradoff could slice at the unicorn's legs. Then as he stood up he knocked furiously with the pommel of his sword into the Rundagg's face. But his weapon was dislodged from his grasp when Moradoff flailed in pain. Kallevick threw a punch into the chest of his enemy so hard that the goblin dropped his own sword and the two began to wrestle.

Komoroff stood and wiped the dirt from his face and before Braeburn could react he was sent flying from a blow to the side. Iadil moved to help Kallevick and she flew over to where her love and the goblin lay in the dirt wrestling, pounding each other. Braeburn stood and gasped for air and again Komoroff attacked, this time breaking off a piece of wooden shaft from the spear that now lay on the ground. Oh no, the elf thought as he looked to see that the merely injured, and not dead Malcolm, was working his way over to the faerie.

Braeburn tried to shout a warning to her but he was hit across the face with the staff and he fell to the ground in shock. He rolled over, his head swimming in pain to see Komoroff standing above him smiling with bloodlust. The elf, even in all his pain, grabbed again the knife and jammed it into the hand of the Goblin lord, who screeched and dropped his weapon. He pulled the blade from his wrist and that momentary hesitation in his attack was all Braeburn needed to puncture the tip of his unsharpened staff through the vulnerable chest of the goblin lord, ripping a hole in his lung.

Braeburn stood as a hideous last gasp came from the creature and Komoroff fell to the ground dead. The elf tried to move or call out to warn Iadil one more time but his head throbbed so bad that he fell like a leaf to the earth and he slumped into unconsciousness.

Kallevick had Moradoff pinned to ground but the goblin grabbed his face and scratched in an attempt to claw out his brown eyes as the young man choked him. Kallevick shouted and fell away from the goblin lord as he was jabbed in his already wounded side. He opened his eyes for a moment and he watched as Malcolm Fortune raised the enormous head of the spear to run it through Iadil who stood a few feet from where Kallevick kneeled. But a look of fear came into Iadil's eyes and she flew up and over him instantly and Kallevick felt a surge of awareness fill him. He stepped forward, ducking under the faerie's sandaled feet and swung his sword with all of his might slicing the spearhead from the remainder of the pole and then thrust his sword into Malcolm's face, killing him instantly.

Kallevick turned just in time to see that Iadil had flown above him and sliced with her sword taking the head of the last Goblin lord with her stroke. Moradoff's body slumped to the ground, his head rolling off it as the body landed. They had instantly saved each other's lives and at the exact same time, Kallevick thought. Iadil landed in front of him.

"Well." Kallevick said smiling tiredly at her. "I guess we can call it even now."

"I guess so." She responded, her own face alight. "You need a bath."

"So do you, but let's get out of here alive first and then we'll take a bath together."

Her expression widened in excitement and her smile grew.

Kallevick turned and grabbed her hand.

"We've got to find Braeburn." He said, his attention suddenly shifting back to the battle. Iadil's face curdled in momentary disappointment at the change of subject.

They ran over to find that Braeburn was on the ground.

"Is he okay?" Iadil asked, kneeling down to look at their friend.

Kallevick stooped down and placed his head on the elf's chest listening for a heartbeat.

"He'll be fine, he's asleep, although I don't envy the headache he'll have when he gets up."

The two lovers looked around them to assess their surroundings and found that they were out of the major field of fighting bodies left. From what they could tell most of the battle was over and they could barely make out a few last remaining Ellion and Rundagg fighting off in the distance. Bodies lay strewn about like tattered ragdolls that had been left in the rain. There were downed horses and battle flags ripped and scattered across the ground. Snapped weapons and dropped ones lay half-buried in the turf from those who had been thrown from their horses. The mist had come in again and the two lay down next to each other taking in a moment of air while the elf slept.

"How many more do you think are left?" Iadil asked.

"Ellion or Rundagg?" Kallevick replied, placing his arm around her shoulder. "Either."

"Oh I don't know. But I'm certain that without the brothers of Altamare leading them it won't take long for the remaining Ellion to make a clean sweep of it. My only concern is Aris and I don't think it looks good." Kallevick said motioning with his finger up towards the sky.

It had clouded over so deep that the fog appeared to be a bright sunny day when in comparison to the darkened sky overhead. Then flashes of spearlike lightning pierced the clouds. Thunder rolled through them and unleashed its menacing boom. But no rain came. The heavens were a churning sea of black and Kallevick silently feared the worst. If Aris failed then all this struggle would be in vain. He wondered, as he fell off into much deserved rest with his wife and friend, why he couldn't have gone with his brother. That was the one thing that lingered on his mind before utter exhaustion took over and he fell into a deep dreamless sleep.

CHAPTER 32

A ris looked straight through his enemy and he could see that Dinemid's lips did not move nor did he appear to breathe, but he was smiling. Aris opened his mind to the voice.

"I know you are not Ellchant and you cannot fool me."

"There is no hope Aris. The world crumbles all around you leaving ashes and flames in their wake. The minds of those you love cave in and crush your dreams and you are alone, so utterly alone."

Aris tried to not listen and now he admonished himself for opening up to the voice. He tried desperately to ignore what it said, tried with all of his mental energy to block the feelings from surfacing but his will weakened to them and suddenly thoughts of his family flooded into his mind. He saw his sister, his brother, his mother, and there in his own mind, he saw the face of his father. The one whom he had let down. The guilt welled up inside of Aris and tears began to stream down his face.

"Yes Aris, I know what your father meant to you. I know how you parted ways with him and yes I know what Ellchant told you about how much your father loved you. But Aris, what is done is done and you cannot go back. You cannot change what has been, only what will be."

Aris closed his eyes, trying to stifle the tears and sobs that robbed him of strength. He wanted to crumple right there and give in to the sadness.

"Aris, look to me now as I can give you all that you desire and more. I can give you all that you ask for. I will give you what you want more than anything in this world. I can give you your family back. You can even make amends with your father, the one who loved you so. I can give you the chance to take back the words that you spoke to him. Give me the sword and I will give you redemption."

Aris' eyes shot open and he cried aloud in anguish, falling to his knees, his grip on the sword tightening in frustration. He took a clear deep breath and stood up. He closed his eyes and breathed in again, this time responding to the words that lingered in his ears.

"No. The sword stays. You cannot redeem me. You were right about one thing though. I cannot change what was, but I can change what will be."

"You are more right than you know." The voice said, changing into a deeper, far darker tone. Dinemid's voice had returned and the young warrior opened his eyes and looked into the face of evil. Aris peered deep into the soul-filled eyes of his enemy, spying every tortured spirit and he screamed aloud in terror as he thought of the possibility of seeing his own face among those who swirled in Dinemid's iris.

In his mind Aris could see himself reflected in those eyes and it was not an expression of pain or anguish on his face that scared him, it was the look of understanding that made his skin crawl. He knew that there was place of darkness inside of him, a place that resided somewhere deep within the heart of every man. Aris knew that if he had the power to destroy Dinemid, he also had the power to overthrow the Lords of Galebraith if he chose to give in.

Dinemid's gaze turned upon the young warrior and his smile made Aris shiver. The black god knew what lay deep within the young man's mind. Aris knew without a single word spoken aloud that Dinemid liked what he saw there, that even if he was defeated Aris could destroy the gods if he chose to.

Dinemid's smile faded and a flicker of excitement flashed in his eyes. Aris knew that his thoughts were bent on the annihilation of the gods, but to even let himself die as long as he knew the rulers of Galebriath would see their own end, this thought made Aris weak in the knees. He felt as though they could buckle at any moment and he would pass out. He inhaled and looked back at his enemy unflinching. He opened his mind once more.

"I will not give in to your lies. Your treachery. Your words are poison, full of vile and deceit. That's why the gods took your lower jaw when you were banished, so you could speak no evil to them or any other. The gods will deliver you into my hand. Who are you to defy the Lords of Galebraith?"

"Who are YOU that the gods should send a boy to defeat ME!" The god shouted aloud.

Then Aris' voice raised over his in triumph.

"I bring a message from above. I will destroy you, that all of Andellius may know that there are gods in Galebraith and that they shall endure for all eternity." The power of those words thundered and echoed within the wheel and the light pulsed and burst in response.

The light sped past as Aris stood from where he landed earlier and he could feel the power of the sword surging through him. His countenance began to glow with a holy white light as did the sword. This was the moment that he had been born for. With all of his air he shouted to the swirling sky of the Wheel of Midgail.

"I call upon the name of the only one who can complete this sacred weapon, the name of one that can strike fear into the heart of this utter darkness. I call upon Cedris and invoke his power unto this sword Orsidire!"

As his words echoed off of the rippling walls of light, a little above from where the opponents flew a spiraling light began to glow. Soon the light expanded in size, increasing evermore rapidly as it billowed out like a geyser bursting from the wall of the light tunnel. Then in a flash and explosion of energy and sound the mighty form of the earth dragon Cedris came forth from his long sleep.

The earth dragon was elegant, from his birdlike claws to the tip of his head which resembled a green swan that had been encased in emerald scales. His wings soon filled a good portion of the wheel as he flew down towards Aris, his mouth open, chanting the secret words that caused Orsidire to glow with all the colors of the Wheel. In all the years that had past, Orsidire was finally complete. Cedris then burst through the other sidewall of the light tunnel disappearing from sight but Aris, who was too busy focusing himself for combat, had failed to notice. Then as Aris lifted the sword as a final salute to his enemy, Dinemid shouted into the expanse between them.

Then to Aris' horror the banished dragon god began to transform and somewhere deep within him Aris knew that Dinemid was using the last of his powers and this was the last trick that he could pull. Either Dinemid succeeded in his task and the universe was destroyed, or Aris would stop him. This was the final battle and the young warrior braced himself as best he could.

Dinemid curled up into himself and then he stretched his arms and legs out, throwing his head back, the black robes flying from his skeletal-like form. The black god screamed in exultation as his body began to rip apart, the remaining skin falling away from his bony limbs, like wrappings falling away from an encased corpse. Then the bones themselves began to reform, bending and bulking up as new skin grew over them. Then his head, which had been thrown back in laughter with his transformation, now fell down to meet Aris' eyes dead on. The nose stretched out and from it burst a protruding upper jaw which resembled a skull that was horse like in structure.

Jagged long teeth burst from the edges of his jaw and two curved horns tore through the remaining flesh of his face to curl inward to where a sickly dripping black mass of rotting flesh lay hanging slack under his upper jaw. This had been his mouth and it now dripped with black blood. The horse-like skull was lined with rows of smaller horns and the crown of his head had four larger horns, which were shaped much like the antlers of a deer.

His ears grew outward, ripping through the sides of his face and his horrible soul filled eyes sunk into the back of his skull revealing that they were lifeless cavities filled with a void blacker than darkness. He had no soul and that was the reason he had trapped other souls inside himself, Aris thought. The body of this god was like unto that of a man and he had horns growing from his collarbone, kneecaps, and elbows. Then his wings thrust out from his back and they flexed and flapped causing a mighty wind to stir in the already windy tunnel of lights. From his hindquarters a long whiplike tail grew and it cracked, sending ripples of sound to echo across the rotating tunnel.

Aris cried aloud and without hesitation he ran for his enemy to end him once and for all. He swung Orsidire and the blade of the god sword met the blade of the indestructible white sword in a flash of power. The two combatants stared each other down for a mere second before they exchanged another set of blows. The blades ground into one another and Aris stepped back, thrusting with Orsidire at Dinemid's chest but the black god would not be bested and stepped out of the way from the attack and slashed at Aris, cutting the warrior in the side.

Aris bellowed in pain and turned on Dinemid, gouging a devastating wound in the villain's leg. But Dinemid did not cry out in pain and sent another volley of sword strikes Aris' way. Aris met him blow for blow and for a split second he wondered if he could keep his strength up. He knew that Dinemid's best chance at victory would either be to kill him or keep Aris busy until the ride in the Wheel of Midgail came to a halt, exiting them both at the gates into Galebraith.

Aris swung at Dinemid, attempting to take off the god's head but Dinemid ducked and moved in close all at the same moment, running one of his horns through Aris' tunic and slightly piercing the warrior's forearm. Aris was too focused on trying to stay alive and did not afford himself another shout of affliction. He met his own white sword again, the blades crashing against one another in a screeching chorus of magic steel. The blades became locked with power and the two rivals were held together for an instant by the mere gravity of their weapons.

Dinemid kicked his leg out at Aris, hitting him in the wounded side but Aris caught the god's leg under his arm. Instead of letting the black one kick him in the stomach as he had done, he gripped Orsidire in one hand and swung down, slicing off Dinemid's leg from halfway up the shin. Dinemid fell away shrieking and flexed his gigantic bat like wings, flying upward at a speed so fast that all Aris witnessed was a blur. Aris looked around to see that Cedris was not in sight and the young man began to panic.

"CEDRIS!" Aris shouted to the mottled sky of the Wheel. The emerald dragon flashed before him and Aris grabbed the flowing hair that grew out of the graceful dragon's neck and down his spine and climbing onto Cedris' back, he gripped tight.

"We can't lose him! Hurry Cedris!" Aris shouted to his aid.

"Hold on Aris! Don't let go!" Cedris shouted back to him. Then just when the young man didn't think that the ride in the Wheel could get any faster Aris was shocked when he began having trouble breathing. Once he braced himself he could feel the wind whipping past him so fast that he feared that he may just yet fall off the dragon's back and lose Dinemid forever. The colors of the wheel were now more than just a blur and they scattered past them like ocean waves falling behind them faster than any water flowed on any earth. The wheel pulsed and spun around them in a clockwise motion, pounding with sound and the lights and colors were so intense that Aris was momentarily blinded.

But up ahead Aris caught sight of a black form and in the not-too far distance he spotted the gates of Galebraith, the entrance to eternity. Cedris pushed with all of his might and the two flew upward catching up to Dinemid. Aris swung with Orsidire tight in hand and nicked Dinemid's ear, causing blood to spray out and fall away from him as the three raced upwards. Dinemid roared as he and Aris, who was still perched on the back of Cedris like a holy beast of burden, exchanged a volley of sword thrusts and cuts. The two resembled a pair of jousting knights, only intending to kill one another.

239

Aris leapt from Cedris's back and onto the torso of the mighty evil, smashing with Orsidire at Dinemid's chest again and again and again, causing the god to flail in pain. But Aris was knocked aside and he watched as his own blood trailed away from him as he flew to the other side of the tunnel from Dinemid's strike. Aris looked up to see that the gates were rapidly approaching and that time was running out. He saw that Cedris was at the gates awaiting him and Aris knew that this was the final moment as he looked back at Dinemid. The one who had been banished flew with all of his might to try and regain the sword and he shouted as he flew.

"You cannot win boy, for I am more powerful than you can ever hope to be. I am beyond a man, beyond death. I am the universe! I AM A GOD!" Dinemid's voice boomed out and thundered across the wheel and seemed to sink into Aris.

Aris stared at him. Then suddenly everything else fell away from his mind. In a flash of realization, his family, his friends, all his own hopes and dreams, even his duty to his own life did not matter. For in that moment he knew that *he* did not matter, and his mind was clearer than it ever had been in his entire life. He was beyond thought, beyond desire and in his heart he did not fear. Now he knew what it was to be one with the universe. All that they had fought so hard and suffered for, he had to let it go and that was his answer. If he and Dinemid kept dueling they'd reach the gates and Dinemid would surely enter in. This was it.

"Do not forget the infinite possibilities that are born of faith." Aris shouted to his foe.

He cocked his hand back, with Orsidire firmly in his grasp and flung it with all of his might. The holy sword flew from his hand, spinning end over end like a singing bird, whirling in a blinding circle at the dragon who raced towards him.

Dinemid's fury was unchecked and he flew into the blade and it sunk into his chest, piercing his black heart. The god screamed and roared in agony and the sound of it thundered across the Wheel of Midgail, throwing Aris upward even faster toward the gate. Dinemid glowed with a light brighter than any sun and then in a flash that sent Aris reeling, the evil god exploded, the sword and the god shattering into a million pieces, sending a shockwave that shot through Aris and out of the wheel. The god and the mighty dragon sword with him vanished forever out of existence with the blast, and not a trace of either one would ever be found again.

*   *   *   *   *   *   *   *   *   *

    Kallevick jumped from where he lay, and watched as the shock wave traveled down the column of light. It reached the ground and pulsed outward, sending a shock of energy through him and his companions, dragging the mist away as it swept across the battlefield. The elf was awakened in a jolt along with Iadil. Then as the energy rippled off and away from them they all breathed a sigh of relief. In an instant they all knew. Dinemid was gone, and all was right with the world.

CHAPTER 33

"**A**ris." The voice echoed softly in the young man's ears. Aris floated gently on the wind inside the Wheel, his eyes closed as if in sleep. He lay somewhere between consciousness and a dream state and his breathing was slowed to a calming pace. He heard the voice call out his name again and though Aris could have easily just ignored it and fallen asleep, he yielded to the call and focused his mind.

There before him in a series of visions he saw the faces of his friends, one after the other, Braeburn, Iadil, and then Kallevick. The call came forth once again and when Aris' ears honed in on the voice he saw his brother's lips move. Aris' brow furrowed in slight confusion. He began to remember something. There was a blast of power and he was thrown back with it. Then suddenly it all became clear and Aris remembered that he was in the Wheel. His thoughts turned back to his friends outside on the earth below and he could see them as clear as day, all lying exhausted and dirty on the ground next to one another.

Aris reached out with his mind.

"Kallevick. Are you alright?" He asked, the mental depiction of his own voice resonating in his head.

"We're all fine. Ready for a long rest and a bath or two. Other than that we're alright." His brother responded with a weak smile.

"Good." Aris said. He felt his face curl up into a satisfied smile. His chest felt warm and it was this sensation that he welcomed with open arms.

"Aris!" Kallevick's radical shift in tone made Aris' eyes open for a moment.

Aris closed his eyes once more, and focused so as not to lose the connection with his companions. "Kalle! What's wrong?"

"Aris, you're hurt." Kallevick's voice echoed.

"Aris are you alright?" The young man heard the voices of Braeburn and Iadil chime in.

"I'm fine. I just need some sleep." He smiled brightly, his eyes still closed.

The concern on Kallevick's face slowly faded and the three began to smile with their friend in the sky.

Aris' expression became somber and Kallevick's smile wore off almost as if he knew what were coming. The others did the same when they saw Kallevick.

"I must go now." Aris said, his voice fleeting in and out of hearing range as the connection between them all began to wear off.

"Come back to us Aris." Kallevick pleaded. "Please don't leave."

"I will always be with you. Take care of Braeburn, I don't think he can make it on his own yet." Aris smiled.

Braeburn shot Aris a look of mock anger that was mixed with his unmistakable elven smile.

"And love your wife as you have loved no other. She is the jewel of the universe and make sure that you cherish her as such."

"I will." Kallevick said, looking to his wife, who smiled affectionately back at him. The young man turned back to his brother, tears forming in the corners of his eyes.

"Are you certain you can't come back. Aris, please, you're the only family I have left."

"No. You have a new family now." Aris said motioning to the elf and the faerie and with that the tears began to fall.

"Well, good-bye then." Kallevick said, unable to keep from choking up. He wanted to say so many things, so many and yet good-bye was all that could escape his mouth.

"Farewell, and may the gods bless you all for your sacrifices." Aris' voice echoed off of the walls of the Wheel and then the connection severed permanently.

*   *   *   *   *   *   *   *   *   *   *   *

The darkened sky that had threatened them only moments earlier was replaced with a bright blue sky and though the bodies of the fallen lay strewn about, not a cloud was in the air above them. The sun was shining down upon the companions where they lay and its warmth was a welcome to their weary bodies. The mist had blown away with the wind of the shockwave and the sounds of battle were now only echoes of the past and the three companions could see the remaining Ellion regrouping. They were off in the near distance, making their way towards them, walking with careful footsteps around the ruins of the Hall of Altamare and those who had perished in the fray.

Kallevick sat up from his position in the dirt and his left arm was wrapped around Iadil and it lay draped across her shoulders. She looked up at him, her brilliant green eyes sparkling with love and she leaned in, never breaking visual contact with his eyes and kissed him softly on the lips. Kallevick smiled back at her and winked. He turned to Braeburn and the elf sat closer to Kallevick and then placed his arm around the young man's shoulder. Kallevick responded by placing his right arm around the elf.

Without a word they looked to one another, shedding tears and smiling for they knew that Aris had done what they each had felt at one time or another, was impossible. Not a single utterance of speech interrupted the perfect silence and though each of them individually wanted to say so much they all sat where they were, filthy and fatigued. Kallevick knew that they would eventually have to get up and begin the trek home but for now, he sat with his family and despite the tears that rolled from his great brown eyes he smiled knowing that Aris could be at peace.

*　　*　　*　　*　　*　　*　　*　　*　　*　　*　　*

"Aris Desarta of the village of Mulroy, open your eyes." Came the command loud and clear from just above Aris. He complied and he squinted in the bright lights of the Wheel of Midgail. Once they had adjusted he looked to see he was floating slowly toward Cedris who sat perched like a great bird at the gate of Galebriath. The young man landed next to the mighty dragon, as if stepping off a moving canoe onto the firm and steady shore of his homeland.

The dragon smiled at him and it seemed to the young warrior that it was familiar in a sense, though Aris did not know how.

"Come, the gods are expecting you. You have done as they have foreseen and I must present you to them."

Aris, too much at a loss for words, stepped forward to let Cedris place his enormous arm around the young man's shoulder. They began to walk forward and

Aris was reminded of the firm ground of his homeland and for a brief second his thoughts were transported to his little village in Mulroy and he smiled for a second thinking about how humble and small that little village was. He stepped forward and suddenly he felt his heart rate began to drop off and his steps began to falter. They moved forward a few more paces and Aris halted, turning to the dragon with a look of fear on his young face.

"It's all right Aris, I promise you will be quite safe. You have my word."

Aris looked back at the gate and though he trusted the dragon that didn't stop him from feeling anxious. He walked forward with longer strides and he felt the onset of something he had never been witness to before. As he walked he felt his own heart stop beating. He figured at any second that it would pick up again and that this was just some sort of temporary physical reaction to entering into a magical realm but the sensation did not leave him. He breathed quickly and though he tried to stay calm he began to panic.

"Aris," Cedris said, the power of the earth dragon's voice flowing from his lips to soothe the young man's fears. "Do not fear, for you are in a safe place. The gods are with you."

"But why can't I breathe?" Aris said, momentarily forgetting that his heart had ceased to beat and now scared as his breath commenced to fade from his lungs.

"The body of man is mortal, but his spirit is eternal. You need not fear of your heart ceasing to beat, nor of the wind emptying from your lungs. You are one with the universe. You do not need your body." The dragon pushed Aris forward gently with his mighty claw, nodding to Aris and smiling reassuringly.

Aris complied and stepped forward, quieting his mind and not letting himself think of the functions of his own body ending. He suddenly felt as light as air and his mind calmed. The dragon Cedris nodded to him once again before Aris turned around to face the gate of Galebraith. Before him was a grand ring of colorful light where the edge of the Wheel of Midgail ended and opened out onto a flat area which looked like it was made up of white clouds that stretched as far as the eye could see. Aris momentarily wanted to turn back but he knew that the dragon would only push him forward once again.

Aris stepped reverently onto the clouds and he spotted the blue skies in between them. Before him stood two grand mirrors. One stood on the right side and another faced it on the left. The two mirrors towered above him, their reflective faces aimed at one another. Their frames were intricately carved from wood and as Aris stepped forward he caught sight beyond the mirrors of a bright white light that covered the entire distance beyond where the mirrors stood.

Aris wanted to turn back but something within him told him that no one could turn away from the sight of what lay before him. Not even he, the defender of Galebraith could be pulled aside from this gate into the heavens. He advanced and now stood between the rising mirrors. He saw himself in endlessness and he heard the voice of Cedris from behind him.

"The mirror to your right is space, and the one to your left if time. You are the temporal aspect of these two truths."

Aris' reflection stretched on forever to either side of him. The space between him and each mirror was slight and if he chose he could reach out and touch them. But his reflection went off far to either side of him and he knew that he was in the midst of eternity. He tried to take a deep breath and realized that he did not need to and so he stepped forward. Walking into the light Aris was filled with an awareness that he had never known. As he vanished into the white surging and into Galebraith, he knew without a doubt that he was beyond eternity and this was his rightful place in the universe.

CHAPTER 34

It was a long day that day, Kallevick thought as he rode on horseback through the last of the sand dunes of Lania Desert and into the first signs of Gridel's plain. The Unicorn on which he rode was sturdy and it bobbed its head slightly as they trod through the land. Braeburn rode in the lead on a mighty male Unicorn which resembled a Clydesdale with an alicorn. Iadil rode silently beside him and Kallevick momentarily wondered if she was in tune with his thoughts and remembered what he was remembering.

The day after the battle they had rested for many hours and as they awoke they had found the Ellion were burying the bodies of the fallen. Rundagg and Ellion alike where laid into the ground and a giant ceremony was held on the battlefield to honor the dead. They had gathered together and gotten to know one another as they worked and soon they left the ruins of the Hall of Altamare, this time traveling in certain footsteps towards home because the Mists of Uldoon were no more. They had discovered as they left the area that they had disappeared when the shockwave had swept across the land and blew the mists off to the far west, dissipating them into nothing-ness.

The company of elves, faeries, unicorns, and the three heroes had ridden on through the woods that had once been the Barren Forest. Kallevick now wondered in silence where the land where he had married Iadil in had gone too. He remembered the day when they had reached the edge of where it had been and he could never forget the glances that he had exchanged with Braeburn and Iadil.

They had been there on the Plains of Isadore and had been witness to all of its beauty and now it was gone, completely disappeared and all that remained was just a series of trees that led into the forest. They all knew that even the race of Ellion had not seen the place, even though they had most assuredly sung about it in their songs and poems. He knew that the memory of that sacred place would be kept forever alive in his heart and the hearts of his two companions.

They had passed through what remained of the Barren Forest, the black and withered ground no longer poisoned by the evil that had once lived in there, but was now lush and green with life. The trees stood tall and healthy, as white as the clouds that could be seen above them through the holes in the canopy overhead. There was life in the woods again and Kallevick was more eager than ever to get home and trek across the familiar paths of Obadia wood once more.

Iadil sat on her Unicorn, trotting along with Kallevick silently contemplating her own situation, wondering where her and her new husband would live. She had been trapped so long in the Barren Forest that for the first time since she had met him she had a chance to daydream about their future together. She looked over at him and he smiled at her with a loving glance. She smiled back and knew that wherever he was she would be at home.

Braeburn rode in the lead of the company and he looked regal on his steed. The large Unicorn strode with heavy footfalls which lost their crunch like sound as they stepped from the last sands of Lania Desert and were muted when the hooves of the Unicorn made contact with the grass of the plain. The fertile land absorbed the sounds and as the company rode up behind him his attention was moved inward as he thought about the City of Victory from which had they just left.

They had spent a week there relaxing. He and his friends had taken a nice long baths when they reached they city. And how could he forget the crowds that had greeted them as they entered? There had been festivals, and feasts and all sorts of noise celebrating them in their victory. They must have seen the change too and even as they looked out over the walls of their desert city they could see the line of trees that had once stood like dark citadels at the edge of the desert now stood like shining towers of life and protection.

The elf smiled as he remembered the feast they all had enjoyed that very night after a long deserved bath. He closed his eyes and licked his lips as he remembered the delicious foods that he had tasted there and with that he vowed that he would return on a regular basis to sample their cuisine again and again if he had to. As the horse rode forward a thin stray branch caught him in the face and he was momentarily flustered. The elf lost his balance and fell off the rear end of his Unicorn and landed on his bottom. The company kept their pace and moved around him, like water finding its way around a rock in a stream, diverging around its smooth edges. They entire company had passed around him as Kallevick and Iadil caught up to the stunned elf.

"This is no time to be sitting down, we're almost there." Iadil said teasing him from above him, sitting steadily on her Unicorn and pointing at the trees which had apparently taken Braeburn by surprise.

"I was just..." the elf began.

'Thinking about the food in the desert, weren't you?" Kallevick said laughing. "Always hungry, bad with horses, you're hopeless."

"Well, yeah. How could I forget that food? Could you?" Braeburn said moving back to his Unicorn which had stopped walking when the elf fell off.

Kallevick nodded in conceit, his lips curling down at the corners as he considered the argument.

Braeburn climbed on it and they were off once more following the troupe of elves and faeries into the edge of Obadia wood. They made their way around Mulroy and Kallevick promised that he would make a point of stopping there with Braeburn and Iadil and relay all that had happened to him and his brother growing up there. They halted their trek into the woods once the sun had set and they camped out under the cover of the trees. Once morning came they would end their journey by going out to Nari Island where they would tell the people of that land of their journey and the final resting-place of Orsidire.

*   *   *   *   *   *   *   *   *   *   *

Morning came swiftly and the travelers and their company made their way onto the island. They were greeted with tremendous enthusiasm and a following of people led them to the great square where only a short time before Kallevick and Aris had witnessed the sword on its pedestal. Kallevick dismounted along with Braeburn and Iadil who were led by the procession to the foundation of a large castle that was under the construction of the local builders.

A large man with red robes and a golden badge sewn on his tunic stepped forward and took Kallevick by the arm before the young man could say a word. He walked him to the finished set of stairs that lay long and wide to where the entrance of the castle was to be laid.

"I present to you the savior of our world, the one whom has defeated Dinemid and his followers and comes now before us to celebrate in his victory!"

The audience roared in elation and applause as Braeburn and Iadil made their way to the steps.

"Wait!" Kallevick tried to yell over the crowd. "Wait! We all fought and battled with Dinemid's followers but it was my brother Aris who defeated Dinemid!" Kallevick managed to yell above the commotion.

The crowd ceased its celebration.

Kallevick looked to the eyes of his audience as his wife and the elf stood next to him. The man in the red robes stepped aside and looked at the trio with a sense of utter puzzlement.

"Where is this Aris? Has he fallen in his victory?" The man asked, his tone as somber as the faces in the crowd.

"No. He has taken Orsidire and fulfilled its purpose, to defeat Dinemid forever. But Aris Desarta, my brother, is gone. Passed into the realm of the gods, Galebraith and that I suspect is how you all know that we have been victorious." The image of the great burst of power and light from the wheel that had passed through him, the elf and his wife, flashed through his mind. It must have covered the globe, Kallevick thought. "With his sacrifice we are now at peace and the light of the Lords of Galebraith shines down upon us."

"But where is he? He has not died, but is still not here. I do not understand." The man said his face still frozen in confusion.

Before Kallevick could answer a sudden burst of light flashed in the sky and a column of light appeared from the heavens and landed right behind Kallevick and the others, to which the crowd gasped in shock. The column swirled and pulsed with sound and light and from it Aris Desarta stepped onto the stairs to witness the gathering inhale in amazement. Following him was the dragon Cedris himself and with the appearance of the mighty earth dragon not a single soul uttered. The emerald covered creature bowed his head to the trio on the steps.

Aris stood, taller than before, his hair the same length but now blonde and sideburns adorned the sides of his face. He had a silver hoop in each ear and the earrings themselves were polished to a mirror shine, symbolizing his passage through the mirrors of space and time. His face was beautiful and his visage glowed with a holy light. On his head he wore a crown made of polished metal and its shape was that of the Wheel of Midgail. He nodded to Kallevick and the young man began to cry in utter joy at seeing his brother again.

Aris wore a dragon scaled leather breastplate made of blue and white alternating scales. He wore a fine white tunic under this which had blue shoulder pads and he wore white dragon scaled forearm guards, along with the pale green cloak that Ellchant had given to him which sat draped gracefully on his neck and shoulders, surrounding him. His pants were blue matching the blue on the breastplate and his eyes. But he still wore the sturdy deep red leather boots that he always had and this made Kallevick smile.

Without hesitation the entire company, elves, faeries, unicorns, men, women and children alike, bowed before the holy young man in reverence. Kallevick, Iadil, and Braeburn all moved to bow with the gathering and Aris did not let them but made them turn to face the crowd.

"I am Aris Desarta, destroyer of Dinemid and the Messenger of Galebriath. I ask that you give your thanks not to me, but to my friends. My family who has suffered many things and has been through many dangers so that you may all live with the comfort of peace."

The crowd raised their heads and a loud burst of thunderous applause and cheers were sent up into the air in thanks.

The man in the red robes stepped down from where he stood to watch the holy man. Then Aris had his three companions turned to face him. He looked to each of them individually giving them all a comforting smile. Then reaching into the column of light that sat behind him Aris pulled forth an object that was wrapped in white linen. He then pulled the cloth away to reveal three white swords exactly like the one that was strapped to Aris' side. The same sword that Ellchant had presented to him.

"My family, my friends. I now give you what our good friend Ellchant Pendergast presented me with. These are the other three indestructible white swords forged to destroy Dinemid. When these swords failed Orsidire was forged. I give these to you now as a symbol of your courage and with them you will all be appointed to rule with me in this kingdom being built here where we stand."

Aris handed two of the swords to Cedris who grasped them gracefully in his claw and the trio knelt before Aris.

"Kallevick Desarta, I appoint you first knight of the kingdom." Aris laid the flat of the blade on his brother's shoulders and then drew the Wheel of Midgail in the air with the blade. "Arise, and be honored."

Kallevick stood, receiving the sword into his hand and he turned to face the crowd who cheered. The same was done for Iadil, who was appointed the peacekeeper of the kingdom. When Braeburn received his sword he was appointed the bookkeeper of the kingdom and was to record all the history that he knew with his fellow Ellion, including the story of their adventure, as a record for the kingdom.

As the three stood on the steps they looked out over the crowd who stood cheering and clapping for their honor. But something did not sit right with Kallevick and he guessed that Iadil and Braeburn felt the same way when they turned with him to face Aris. Aris placed his hands on his brother's shoulder. The four companions stood close so only they could hear each other.

"Aris. Are you dead?" Kallevick asked quietly, his voice reflecting his fear of the answer.

"No. I live, though I am not exactly how you remember me. All things change and we will all see the sunset on our lives in due time. I have seen something though Kallevick. I saw a vision of the future. Just like the gods I now have the power of foresight."

Aris smiled at Kallevick who still looked concerned.

"What happens after? After we die, where do we go?" Braeburn asked.

Iadil said nothing but her eyes indicated that she too wanted to know the answers to all these questions as much as the others did.

The crowd began to disperse and music began to play as the tumultuous gathering celebrated and cheered. The foursome stood on the steps and Cedris stood behind them, the earth dragon watching the four companions with great interest. Aris looked to each of his friends and then turned to Cedris. The dragon nodded to him and Aris faced his family reciting:

In realms unseen by human eye

There is a place beyond the sky
Created by the gods holy hand
Out past where our world began
It is a place where the dead have gone
A place of rest while we live on
One day we will leave the realm of men
And when we die we go to them
Long after that, too long to count
The gods will on their chariots mount
And will leave Galebriath far behind
And the memory of the divine
For Andellius and Galebraith both
Will be as only dreamy ghosts
The worlds that once were so grand
Will be transformed by nature's hand
And just as beautiful as they may be
We will find true harmony

Kallevick and the others stood looking at Aris, their eyes full of wonder at what all of it meant.

"I don't understand." Kallevick responded. "So you mean one day we will be able to see Mother, Father, and Mafre again?" The young man said tearing up.

"One day, a long time from now. I will have peace with father and we will all be together, beyond eternity. In wonder." Aris answered, his gaze falling to each of his companions. "But that is many ages from now and we all have long lives to live." He said reassuringly.

"But what about Ellchant? Will we see him too? I miss him so much." Braeburn said.

"I do too." Kallevick said, along with Iadil.

"I wish he was here to see all of this." The elf said, tears welling up in his copper eyes.

"I wish we didn't have to wait so long to see him again." Iadil commented.

"You don't. Cedris!" Aris called out to the dragon. Aris' voice now resembled that of the inexperienced youth that had dreamed of exploration.

"Don't keep these poor folk waiting!" Aris said laughing as he turned back to his friends.

Cedris walked over to them and suddenly it all became clear and a wave of realization swept through the young man, the elf and the faerie. They smiled at him and for a moment all Cedris could do was smile back.

EPILOGUE

Somewhere deep within the folds of a fleshy membrane, two nerve endings flashed and licked each other with electricity. As those lightning bolts lit up the sky of a clearish fluid, the resulting haze illuminated the surrounding mountains and hillsides of tissue. Beyond this cavern of hills and canyons lay the hollow pupil of an eye which blinked a spark of light and then suddenly shut. The eye opened once more, the spiral gray iris flexing and adjusting to the early afternoon sunlight. Ellchant Pendergast blinked once again and inhaled sharply. He realized that he was staring at Kallevick who began tugging on Aris' arm. The young man stared at Orsidire and stumbled as Kallevick pulled him away.

Ellchant looked at his surroundings and took another deep breath as he realized that he was standing in the square of Nari Island and he could hear the calls of the booth holders for the Annual Trade Bazaar. He could smell the scent of firewood and he sniffed it gladly. He thought back to the vision that had just flashed before him. He remembered now. He had forgotten all those years. His friends had searched for him and they couldn't find him because when he fell he had become a man. He lived because Dinemid had not taken his immortality but he was no longer in his dragon form.

Suddenly it all came back to him. He recalled wielding Orsidire which had been incomplete, at Dinemid. The evil one had ambushed him and his fellow dragons while they were preparing the sword on the Plains of Isadore. He heard Dinemid utter the curse against the man born of faith and in a blinding move he swung Orsidire and saw the lower jaw of the god being ripped off in the battle that ensued. He saw the blade of a Rundagg sword plunge into his chest and he felt the ground rush up to meet him as he dropped Orsidire.

Then he remembered being alone, utterly alone. In the woods, naked and cold, not knowing where he was or who he was. He could hear waves crashing against a shoreline and he ran and ran until he found the water. He was on Nari Island and when he found a calm pool of water he gazed into it to see his own face, the face of an old man. He remembered now as clearly as he could see the high flying banners of the Annual Trade Bazaar.

He cringed internally for a moment at all that was to transpire and although he was relieved beyond any doubt that he had recovered his power of foresight he still knew that dark days were ahead of him and his friends. But he sighed in relief that he now knew who he was again and that he could face his future with confidence. He knew that he could not change what was to transpire but that was the price of foresight and even that he could not offset.

He moved towards the boys hoping to catch up to them but deep down knowing that they would lose him in the crowd. He moved back and forth, weaving through performers and vendors but he knew that he had lost them when they were nowhere in sight. He knew that he would catch up with them eventually. I must guide them, he thought to himself. They need me. Deep within him Ellchant knew that he would be of no use to Aris or his companions if he could not remember who he truly was.

He knew, as all the gods did, that without each person involved in the grand scheme of things, even those who planned to commit atrocious acts like Dinemid were part of a larger picture. A picture that made up the structure of the future and a plan of the universe. He inhaled once more and he looked down the path that led to the Great Bridge connecting the island to the mainland.

"This is it." Ellchant quietly said to himself. "This is the sign that the Messenger of Galebriath has come." Dinemid's days were numbered, he thought.

"I am Cedris. This is my destiny."

THE END

The Nari Scrolls: The story of Aris and his quest for Orsidire has been translated from an ancient text that was found on the Island of Nari. Though most has been lost to the passage of time, this tale and the following poem fragment was recovered. In days long past, the history of the world was kept intact through the oral traditions of rhyme. This is one of the only poem fragments that remains.

(An excerpt from the Tale of Orsidire)

From forth the flames of holy forge
Upon the Plains of Isadore
The Dragons formed the sacred sword
To end for all, the Banished Lord
A power pulsed within its name
The Blade burned bright with hallowed flame
In darkness blazed this godly fire
And so they called it Orsidire

The Mythic Number and its representation in The Boon of Orsidire:

You have Five arms of the Wheel of Midgail surrounding a circle, which represents the world.

The Five Elements: Earth, Wind, Fire, Water, Spirit

The Five Dragons: Cedris, Norg, Talos, Altos, and Mistal

The Five Heroes: Ellchant, Braeburn, Kallevick, Iadil, and Aris

The Five Villains: Toirasci, Moradoff, Komoroff, Malcolm, and Dinemid

The Five Swords: The Four White Dragon Swords, and Orsidire

The Desarta Family: Cabral, Martaban, Kallevick, Mafre, and Aris

The Five Senses: Sight, Sound, Smell, Taste, Touch

The Human Body: Two Arms, Two Legs, and a Head

The Hands and the Feet: Five Fingers per Hand, and Five Toes per Foot

The Hierarchy of Races:

Good:	Evil:
The Dragon Lords of Galebraith	Dinemid
The Race of Ellion: Three Counterparts	The Wolf Spirits
Elves- Male	The Rundagg
Faeries- Female	The Race of Giants
The Race of Unicorns	The Race of Men
The Race of Men	